A TASTE OF VENGEANCE

L. A. FOLEY

This book is a work of fiction and all characters and events are fictitious. Any resemblance to actual people, living or dead, is coincidental and not intended by the author.

A Taste of Vengeance.

ISBN 978-0-9892687-1-4

ANDERSON
HOUSE

Roger, the wind beneath my wings

I would like to acknowledge my dear friend and honest, helpful critic, Dick Bizot, without whom this book would not have been possible. I would like to thank my friends and supporters: Afesa Adams, Jim and Laura Crooks, Kathleen McKenzie, David Lafitte, Joyce Bizot, Shirley Stetson, Bryant Rollins and Sandy Hansford. Thank you also to Holly Bebernitz, Kathy Combass, Topher Sanders, and Larry Bassington for their helpful comments and suggestions. Special thanks to my daughter, Reen Foley, and sisters, Betty and Judy Anderson, my son Tim and his wife Monique for their unwavering support and to Richard Hecht, my wonderful and talented son-in-law, for designing the cover.

Also by Linda A. Foley

<u>Fiction</u>

Road Rage

<u>Non-fiction</u>

A Psychological View of the Legal System

The YoCoShe Experiment: An evaluation of a Model Program for Delinquent Youth

Female offenders in Duval County (with C. Rasche and L Finely)

CHAPTER ONE

Albino vultures picking at road kill – that was what Tori Vincent called jump-suited technicians examining a homicide victim. She hated death scenes. But, Tori reminded herself, she had no choice. She was a forensic psychologist and her job was to probe the psyches of the dead and those who murdered them. She dreaded the death scene she was heading to more than most. She'd be working with Herb Morrison, *the detective with a charisma bypass,* she thought.

Tori crossed the University of Florida campus to Rolfs Hall, oblivious to live oaks draped in Spanish moss, budding azaleas and students scurrying like book-carrying worker ants. Ten o'clock and the sun was so intense her heels were sticking in the asphalt. The humidity could wilt an artificial flower. She willed her antiperspirant to keep her dry as she climbed the ancient wooden stairs three flights to the English Department. She strode down the hall past milling students and showed her ID to the uniformed officer. If she were religious she would have made the sign of the cross. Instead, she took a deep breath, counted to ten, exhaled and slipped under the yellow crime scene tape.

"Good morning, Detective Morrison," she said.

Detective Herb Morrison of the Gainesville Police Department eyed the slim strawberry blond. "Doctor," he said, his New Jersey accent swallowing the r. He turned, blocking the door and her view of the death scene with his muscular body. *Arrogant chauvinist,* Tori thought.

"Who's she?" asked a light-skinned black woman, jerking her thumb in Tori's direction.

Tori extended her hand. "Tori Vincent." Tori considered herself tall at 5' 7", but even in three inch heels she looked up to the other woman.

"*Doctor* Victoria Vincent," Morrison said. His voice could curdle milk. "Chief put her on the case."

The policewoman cocked her head. Tori felt the other woman's eyes scrutinize her Ann Taylor suit, hesitating at the skirt's short hem and traveling down her legs to her Prada heels, before shaking her hand. "Detective Dottie Epstein," she said. *Why didn't I wear slacks?* Tori thought.

Dottie glanced at Morrison before asking Tori, "How're you supposed to help?"

"I'm a forensic psychologist. I teach at the university. The chief wants me to do a psychological autopsy on the deceased."

"A what?" Dottie asked.

"A psychological autopsy. It's like profiling, but it's done on the victim. I'll evaluate his psychological state prior to death."

"How? He's dead."

"I'll talk with people who knew him."

"Cut the psychobabble," Morrison said. "Epstein, make yourself useful. Fill her in on the vic."

Tori watched a venomous look flash across Dottie's face. *Dottie has the same antipathy toward Morrison as I do,* Tori thought. She said, "I'd like to view the scene without background information. It could bias my appraisal."

Morrison moved aside and said, "Yeah, yeah, sure. Be my guest." Tori bristled at the big man's mock chivalry as he bowed and extended his arm. She knew he did not want her help. She had heard him tell the chief that psychological autopsies were as scientific as séances.

The whiff of death assaulted Tori's nostrils as she stuck her head into the cramped office teeming with albino vultures. Lights blazed on the body – a man wearing shorts slumped over a desk. She noted perspiration on his shirt, a Ralph Lauren polo, no less. A tennis racket was propped against the bookshelf. An open bottle of Pepsi rested near a laptop on the cluttered desk.

"He died alone," Tori said.

2

Morrison scoffed. "How'd you come up with that?"

"Look how he's sitting. His back is to the other chairs in the office," Tori said. "He wouldn't do that if someone was with him." She turned to Dottie. "Who is he?"

"Dr. Bradford Coleman."

So that's Brad Coleman, Tori thought. Nasty rumors about the sought-after bachelor surfaced in her memory.

"English prof," Morrison said.

"I bet she figured that out," Dottie said, "seeing as he died in the English Department."

Morrison glared at his colleague. Tori pressed her lips together to suppress a grin.

Tori said, "This is the work of someone who's never hurt anyone before; someone who doesn't want to watch her victim die. She wants to stay at arms length. She hates him and wants him dead, but doesn't stay around to see him die."

"She?" asked Dottie.

"Yes," Tori said. "The killer's a woman."

"Yeah, yeah, right," Morrison said. "You psychic? What's her name and address."

"I'm not psychic. I'm a forensic psychologist," Tori said through clenched teeth "Coleman's got a reputation for seducing and dropping coeds. He charms women and then discards them. The castoffs hate him."

"You know Coleman?" Dottie asked.

"Know of him." Tori looked at the crime scene. After a moment she said, "The murderer doesn't want to get her hands dirty. That's why she used poison. It's as if she is killing for someone else."

Dottie asked. "Who's she killing him for?"

"Someone he hurt, or maybe she's trying to protect other women from being hurt."

"An altruistic murderer, how quaint," Morrison said.

Tori thought, *I wonder if I could get the murderer to take out Morrison.*

At the sound of voices one of the techs looked out the door and winked at Dottie. Dottie's face brightened into a smile.

"Who's he?" Tori asked.

"Jason Nolan."

Morrison raised his eye brows. "Fraternizing with a tech?"

Dottie flushed. "He's a friend," she said.

"Yeah, yeah, sure." Morrison said.

Pulling off his latex gloves, Jason Nolan joined them outside the office.

"Well?" Dottie asked.

"Sorry, Dottie. I can't say 'til the ME examines the body."

"Not officially," Dottie said. "What do you think?"

"Me, I'd wager it was poison."

"Is there a suicide note?" Tori asked.

"No, ma'am, nothing like that," Nolan said.

"Why ask about a suicide note?" Morrison asked. "You just said he was murdered."

"I could be wrong," Tori said.

"Oh?" Morrison said. "Not infallible?"

Tori said, "The murderer might have left a note to make it look like suicide."

"Get your fucking hands off me," a voice commanded, directing their attention down the hall. Tori recognized her former lover arguing with a uniformed officer. *Oh, no.* She'd avoided Steve DeMaio since their break-up four years earlier. DeMaio pushed through the gauntlet of gawkers, and burst the yellow crime tape as he bolted toward them.

"Who the hell's that?" Morrison asked.

"Dr. Steven DeMaio – a chemistry professor," Tori said.

"What's going on?" DeMaio asked. "What's happened to Brad?"

Dottie blocked DeMaio's access to the office. "I'm sorry, Dr. DeMaio, Dr. Coleman is dead."

"That's crap! I talked to him yesterday – he was fine." DeMaio shoved Dottie aside and went into Coleman's office. Blood drained from DeMaio's face leaving him paler than his dead friend. He wobbled. He grabbed the doorjamb. His eyes bulged, fastened on his friend's corpse.

Tori said, "You'd better sit down."

DeMaio did not move. He opened his mouth but emitted no sound. Morrison clutched the ashen-faced professor by the upper arm and marched him out of Coleman's office. As Morrison hauled him from the scene, DeMaio's head turned for a last look at

4

his dead friend. Morrison said, "I'll get him taken home. Epstein, wait for the M. E. with the doc."

While Dottie replaced the yellow police tape, Tori asked, "How long've you been Detective Morrison's partner?"

"Two weeks."

"Pulled the short straw, huh?"

Dottie gave a one-sided grin. "You got it! My last partner said I was pushy. Ergo the chief teamed me with the other Yankee who can't get along with southern cops."

"As my grandmother used to say, 'It keeps from breaking up a better pair.'"

"Welcome to the team from hell."

"New Yorker?" Tori asked.

"Brooklyn. Don't think I've got a Florida accent?"

"Hardly. But not Brooklyn either. New York City. You went to college in the city; the other students gave you a hard time about being from Brooklyn so you changed your accent."

"You are psychic. They teased me about my Brooklyn accent. Ergo I worked at getting rid of it. You're a northerner, aren't you? Where you from?"

"Connecticut."

A white-haired man approached the newly reinstalled yellow tape. Dottie lifted it for him and said, "Dr. Dixon, this is Dr. Vincent, a forensic psychologist."

Acknowledging Tori with a barely perceptible dip of his head, the doctor said, "Thank you, miss. Where's Detective Morrison? Isn't he in charge?"

"He's arranging for someone to take a distraught professor home," Dottie said.

"I see." Dr. Dixon went into Coleman's office and set up his equipment.

Tori said, "I'd like to scrutinize the scene without Morrison watching over my shoulder."

Dottie agreed and the two women stood in the doorway. Brad Coleman's office was a photocopy of every faculty office on campus – the requisite faux wood grain desk, dog-eared books jammed into metal book cases, a file cabinet, a blue executive chair, and two side chairs. An open window looked across Buckman Drive to Pugh Plaza inviting spring breezes into the office. Pots of purple African violets peeking out the window and hanging pots of spider plants attested to Brad Coleman's green thumb. Above his desk hung a Green Peace Poster and a computer generated sign – "The UF English Department is a nuclear free zone."

The women watched Dr. Dixon conduct his examination for a few minutes before Dottie asked him, "What do you think's the cause of death?"

Dixon peered at Dottie over his half glasses. "Don't you worry, miss. I'll write up a report for Detective Morrison." He returned to his work.

Tori observed the back of Dottie's neck redden.

Dottie said, "I'm Detective Morrison's partner."

"Yes, yes, I know." Dixon kept his back to the women. "Detective Morrison will take care of it when he gets back."

"Answer her question," said an ugly voice.

Tori turned. Morrison stood behind her, his face sinister, a vein throbbing at his left temple. *Doesn't like competition for title of Chief Chauvinist?* Tori thought. Dr. Dixon adjusted his glasses on his nose. "I'm talking to you," Morrison said.

"Yes, yes, I know." Dixon sat on his haunches. "I can't tell the cause of death until I do an autopsy and get a toxicology report. It doesn't look like a natural death – he's young and appears healthy. Could be an aneurysm." He scratched his head. "My best guess is poison. His mouths contorted and I smell almonds. Cyanide poisoning would explain the smell and contortion." Dixon looked at Dottie. "Any reason he'd want to kill himself?"

"We don't know, yet," Dottie said. She slipped on a pair of latex gloves and asked Jason to hand her Coleman's laptop. She opened his calendar. "He was supposed to play tennis with Steve DeMaio this morning."

"That guy I sent home," Morrison said.

As Morrison and the two women proceeded to the main office of the English Department, Dottie said, "Thank you, Morrison."

"Yeah, sure. We're partners, aren't we?" he said.

Tori thought, *maybe he's not a chauvinist – maybe he doesn't like psychology...or me.*

CHAPTER TWO

A police officer stood by the English Department office blocking access to the crime scene. A man with a ponytail and sparkling stone in his left earlobe whispered to a middle-aged woman in stretch pants. Both bystanders straddled book bags. When Morrison and the women approached, the ponytailed student asked, "What's happening, dude?" Morrison ignored him and ushered Dottie and Tori into the office.

A gray-haired woman paced back and forth wringing a handkerchief while a trio of coeds whispered in front of the desk. Dottie evicted the protesting students before introducing Morrison and Tori to Betty Lou Hancock, the secretary for the English Department.

Morrison asked, "Who's the boss?"

"Dr. Gibson is chair of English," Betty Lou said. "He's in Tallahassee – at a meeting. I called him soon's this awful thing happened. I'm waiting on him to finish with the chancellor."

"Epstein, you got Gibson's name?" Morrison asked. Dottie nodded as she jotted it in her notebook. Morrison turned back to Betty Lou. "Get him in here."

Betty Lou crossed her arms, her eyes defiant. "He's coming soon's he can. He's in Tallahassee about the budget. He's got to see the chancellor."

Tori thought Morrison's look would cut holes through Betty Lou.

"I said get him here. NOW," Morrison said, the muscles in his throat taut.

Betty Lou Hancock stuck her chin out, ambled to her desk, settled her ample body in the chair and took a deep breath. She opened the bottom drawer and pulled out her purse – all in slow motion. She shoved her abused handkerchief into the purse and rummaged around until she found a neatly ironed replacement before phoning Dr. Gibson.

Passive aggressive, Tori thought, *Morrison brings out the worst in people – particularly women. Betty Lou is used to running the department and she's not about to let some arrogant intruder shove her around.*

When Betty Lou completed the phone call, Morrison asked, "Who found the dead guy?" Tori observed the tightness in his voice as he controlled his irritation.

Betty Lou responded with a spasm of weeping, handkerchief clutched over her mouth.

"Dr. Coleman wasn't just a professor in the department," Tori said, "You were close to Dr. Coleman, weren't you?"

Betty Lou nodded. Tori gave Betty Lou's shoulder a squeeze. When Betty Lou stopped whimpering, Tori rephrased Morrison's question. "Why did you go to Professor Coleman's office this morning?"

The secretary gulped, wiped her eyes, and said in an almost inaudible voice, "I was putting up mail. I heard screaming. I went to see what the ruckus was. Some li'l gal darted out of Brad's office."

"Where's this girl?" Morrison asked.

"She run off."

"Who is she?"

"Some student. I don't remember her name."

Morrison asked. "What happened after she ran off?'

Pushing a stray lock of gray hair behind her ear, Betty Lou looked as if she would burst into tears, but she took a breath, dabbed her eyes, and said, "I went in his office. Bless his soul, I thought he was playing a joke, you know." She looked from Morrison to Dottie to Tori. When Tori nodded, she continued. "I said, 'Stop fooling around.' He didn't answer so I shook his arm."

She swallowed hard. Her voice cracked. "His arm... It fell, like a rag doll or something. I, I knew ..."

"How well you know this Coleman guy?" Morrison asked.

"Brad was like a son to me."

"DeMaio was Coleman's friend, right?"

"Brad and Steve liked the same things," Betty Lou said.

Yeah, Tori thought. Gossip about Coleman's and DeMaio's sexual escapades with coeds spread across campus like the BP oil spill. When Coleman, notorious for switching partners, ditched a current love interest, coeds lined up outside his office feigning need for academic help. Campus wags reported coeds took numbers to hold their place in the queue like people shopping for pies.

Betty Lou said, "Steve's got that god-awful New Jersey accent. It grates on my nerves, but gals think he sounds 'cool.'"

Somehow, Betty Lou had missed Detective Morrison's Jersey accent. Tori caught his eye. He winked. *Holy Toledo, the cop has a sense of humor*, Tori thought.

Betty Lou said, "Bless my heart, I don't know why gals go gaga over him, he's not handsome or nothing."

Tori knew why. As Betty Lou said, DeMaio could not be called handsome; but he had a great physique and his gray eyes radiated sexuality. His animal magnetism attracted Tori and she had a fling with him, but she sure as hell wasn't going to tell Morrison about it.

"Did Dr. Coleman seem depressed or despondent lately?" Tori asked.

Betty Lou eyed Tori. "What're you going on about? You mean was he suicidal?"

"Yes."

"That's downright ridiculous."

"I thought as much," Tori said. "What about Dr. Coleman's love life?"

"He's madly in love with Trish Acosta. She's the sweetest li'l thing, a southern lady." Dottie wrote Trish's name in her notebook.

"Who's this Trish Acosta?" Morrison asked.

"A grad student. She's in chemistry and she..."

"Yeah, right. Anyone got reason to kill Coleman?" Morrison asked.

Betty Lou narrowed her eyes. "Everyone loved Brad. He mentored kids at the Boys Club. He was helping poor kids get into college and..."

"Yeah, yeah, sure," Morrison said. "When Gibson gets here, have him stay put 'til I get back."

Betty Lou sat up straight. Her face left no doubt as to her hostility. Tori thought Betty Lou was going to make a nasty retort, but she swallowed and mumbled, "Okay."

"Epstein, wait for Gibson. Try and find the student what found the body," Morrison said. "Check with the techs. See what they got at Coleman's house."

"I thought we were partners," Dottie said. "I want to interview people."

"We are partners. I'm the partner what's in charge and you're the partner what follows orders."

Dottie looked annoyed, but said, "Yes, sir," and gave him an exaggerated salute.

"I want to go to Coleman's house and get a feel for the man," Tori said.

"A feel for him?" Morrison asked. "Is that some kind of psycho-shit? No way you go there. The techs'll tell us what's what."

"But, the chief told me..."

"Fuck what the chief told you." Morrison said. "He told me you'd do interviews and that's what you're doing." He headed toward the door. "Come with me."

Tori was tempted to imitate Dottie's salute, but thought better of it. She looked at Dottie. The two women transmitted antipathy toward Morrison like texting cell phone messages. When Morrison opened the office door, the ponytailed man and middle-aged woman were accompanied by the three coeds Dottie had expelled from the office, a twenty-something man, an elderly gent in an out-of-date blazer, and a trim middle-aged woman in slacks and a silk blouse. The rubberneckers assaulted Morrison and Tori with a barrage of questions.

"There was an unfortunate incident. I'm not at liberty to answer questions," Morrison said.

10

"Is that useless information supposed to pacify the assemblage?" the old man asked. "What do you mean an 'unfortunate incident?'"

"Who are you?" Morrison snapped.

"I'm Dr. Winston Whitherspoon and I demand to know what's going on." His frail voice gave little substance to his demand.

"You heard me," Morrison said. "I can't give specifics."

"Can't or won't?" the old man asked.

"Both."

"Did something happen to Dr. Coleman?" asked a petite brunette in torn jeans and snug tee-shirt.

"Why's the main office locked?" demanded the woman in the silk blouse. "How am I supposed to get my exam copied?"

"Why's Betty Lou crying?" asked a female voice whose source Tori could not determine as the gathering had attracted additional members.

"I can't answer questions until we're done investigating," a stone-faced Morrison repeated. He turned to the uniformed officer and barked, "Keep them away from the scene."

CHAPTER THREE

Steve DeMaio's small rented duplex was in the dilapidated College Park section of Gainesville referred to as the "student ghetto." DeMaio's duplex was unkempt, with peeling green paint and stones missing from the porch wall. Live oaks hovered over the house and yard, obstructing sunlight, retaining dampness and encouraging moss. The yard consisted of patches of brown-tipped grass strewn with Spanish moss, twigs and leaves deposited by a recent storm. Stepping stones to the porch, barely visible beneath the debris, creaked and shifted beneath Tori's and Morrison's weight.

Morrison turned to Tori. "Think DeMaio really lives here?"

"According to Betty Lou, he does," Tori said, crinkling her nose at the moldy odor emanating from the mildewed porch floor. Tori had never been to DeMaio's house during their brief relationship.

Shrugging his shoulders, Morrison rang the bell for the duplex on the right. The name plate was blank, but the left one said "Weiss."

After the second ring, Steve DeMaio, in shorts and a gray sweatshirt, opened the door. He said, "So, beauty and the beast – what can I do for you?" Tori didn't appreciate the flippant description and Morrison's face indicated he had a similar reaction. Neither responded verbally. DeMaio wiped sweat from his forehead and the back of his neck with a towel, which probably had been white once, but now was grungy gray. DeMaio saw Morrison eyeing the towel and said, "I've been working out."

Morrison nodded.

"You coming in?" DeMaio asked in a voice which was anything but welcoming.

Tori sniffed. The duplex smelled musty. The walls were bare, as were the well-worn hardwood floors. There were two broken-slated blinds on the front windows. Even without drapes the room was dark – sunlight could not penetrate the canopy of trees. Surveying the futon, nondescript chairs, 1960s Formica coffee table, and homemade glass-brick bookcase; Tori silently classified the furniture as early Salvation Army. She thought the duplex more suitable for a poverty-stricken graduate student than a professor.

Loud rock music assaulted the visitors from the dining area that DeMaio used as an exercise room. The area was equipped with a weight bench, step machine, stationary bicycle, and rowing machine. Tori estimated the value of the exercise and stereo equipment at many times that of the other furnishings. DeMaio turned off the stereo and draped the towel around his neck.

"Sit down. Sit down. Want some Gatorade?"

Morrison feigned gagging at Tori behind DeMaio's back while she said, "No thank you."

Morrison pulled out a handkerchief and ceremoniously held it by one corner while shaking it open before brushing off a chair and sitting. Tori frowned at the detective before sitting in the other chair.

DeMaio squatted in front of Tori's chair and flipped up a lock of her hair. "I liked your hair better when you wore it longer."

Tori pushed DeMaio's hand away. "Keep your hands to yourself."

"Still the ice queen." DeMaio smirked.

Tori said, "Still a Neanderthal."

Tori cringed as she observed Morrison's brain churning as he watched her interaction with DeMaio.

STOMP!! Tori saw Morrison kick aside a huge cockroach he'd executed with his shoe.

"Need a bug sprayer in here."

"I don't want chemicals around."

"Aren't you a chemist?" Morrison asked.

"That doesn't mean I want to breathe toxic fumes."

"Rather have cockroach shit all over?"

Unperturbed, DeMaio said, "I'll cramp up if I don't stretch. I've been on the step machine." He bent his right leg and shifted his weight to it, his left leg stretched behind him. Then he switched and stretched his right leg. Tori could not refrain from looking at DeMaio's muscular legs and tight buns. She felt Morrison eyes on her watching DeMaio and looked down.

Morrison asked, "Know why we're here?"

"Conducting a survey on crime in the neighborhood?" DeMaio asked as he stood.

"Coleman's death's a joke, huh?"

DeMaio grabbed a plate of unidentifiable congealed food from the coffee table and stashed it on a bookshelf. He sat on the futon, pulled the towel from around his neck and wiped his face. He leaned toward the detective, resting his arms on his thighs while twisting the towel in his hands. "It's how I cope. I laugh so I don't cry." His voice was raw.

Morrison mumbled something sympathetic which Tori didn't catch.

Clenching his fists around the towel and wringing it tightly, DeMaio said, "Why'd anyone kill Brad?"

On their way to DeMaio's home, Morrison had suggested that Tori conduct the interview, "You know, professor to professor." So Tori began by asking DeMaio, "How well did you know Brad Coleman?"

His eyes on the towel he was twisting and untwisting, DeMaio said, "We were best friends – did everything together." DeMaio stood, still fidgeting with the towel, and paced. "Brad lives, I mean lived," his voice cracked, "a couple blocks from here." He motioned with his head. "We ran together mornings and worked out a couple nights a week." He sighed. "That is, until Brad got all lovey dovey with Trish." DeMaio stopped pacing and looked at Tori. "Lately, I only saw Brad when we mentored kids for the Boys & Girls Club and for our Tuesday tennis game."

"You played tennis with Brad this morning?" asked Tori.

After wiping his hands with the towel, DeMaio draped it around his neck again before answering. "Nah, we didn't play today. He called last night and cancelled."

"Why?"

"Didn't say." DeMaio sat, his shoulders slumped, a frown on his face.

"Where did you and Brad play tennis?"

"Flavet courts. On campus, over by Trusler Hall."

She asked, "What did you do this morning instead of tennis?"

DeMaio's eyes sent missiles into hers. "I sure as hell wasn't killing Brad because he canceled our tennis game."

"Answer the question," Morrison said.

DeMaio scowled at Morrison before looking back at Tori with a somber expression. "I didn't have time to get another tennis partner, so I ran."

"On a track? On campus?" Tori asked.

"On campus, yeah. Track – no – on an activity route. You know, the Healthy Gators. You must've seen those tacky logos on campus."

"Anyone see you?" Morrison asked.

DeMaio pulled on his beard. "I didn't notice. I was pissed at Brad for not giving me more notice. I ran early – around 7:15. Students don't get up early."

"How did Brad meet Trish?" Tori asked.

"I introduced them." DeMaio looked into the distance with unfocused eyes, his voice softer. "I dated her last fall. Trish was new on campus. A beauty – long black hair, incredible violet blue eyes and a body you could kill for."

Morrison raised his eyebrows. "Oh?"

DeMaio's eyes flung wide open. "Oh damn! I didn't mean that the way it sounded. It's just an expression."

Smiling in a way she hoped was reassuring, Tori said, "I understand. Please continue."

Looking at Morrison, DeMaio wiped his forehead again before saying, "Trish was my lab assistant – that's how we got involved."

"Involved? What's that? You screw her?" Morrison asked.

"No, we played tiddlywinks."

"Professors allowed to screw students?"

Tori could feel the two men's mutual antagonism polluting the air.

"I didn't rape her," DeMaio retorted.

15

"You were her boss," Morrison said. "That's coercion, abuse of power."

"Coeds want to have affairs with professors. They're the aggressors, not me."

"This Acosta woman threw herself at you?" Morrison asked.

"Practically. I walked her home after a movie and she invited me in. She left no doubt she expected me to stay for breakfast. I'm human. I stayed."

Tori said, "But she decided she'd rather be with Brad Coleman. Why? What ended this romance?"

"I don't know." DeMaio leaned forward, elbows on his thighs, resting his chin on his clenched fists, eyes unseeing. "I thought we were doing great. Out of the blue she says she's dumping me for Brad." DeMaio shook his head. "Who knows with chicks?"

The melody "Can You Feel the Love Tonight" rang through the room. Tori grabbed her purse and pulled out her cell phone. DeMaio started singing, "There's rhyme and reason to the wild outdoors when the heart of this star-crossed…"

Tori thought, *if looks could kill*, as she shot murderous thoughts toward DeMaio.

"Still pining for the magnificent ex? For a shrink, you're pretty screwed up," DeMaio said.

"Put a sock in it," Tori said. She flipped open the phone. "I'm in a meeting, Kiddo. See you later." She shut her phone.

"You need anger management lessons." DeMaio smirked.

Standing to look down at DeMaio, Morrison said, "Shut the fuck up." His eyes sent the same message Tori's had.

Tori looked at Morrison and said, "My son. He calls when he gets home from school."

Morrison sat down. Tori said to DeMaio. "Your best friend stole your lover, the hottest woman on campus. You must have been furious. Wanted to get even."

DeMaio sprang up, pointing a finger at Tori, his face flushed. "Don't put words in my mouth. I was surprised – that's all. Brad and I quarreled about a coed once and swore never to let a chick mess up our friendship."

Tori put a restraining hand on Morrison's arm as he started to stand. She asked, "If it was no big deal, why wasn't Brad running with you?"

DeMaio said in a lower voice, "I don't know. Brad wouldn't talk about it."

"Was Brad depressed or despondent?" she asked.

"Nah, nothing got Brad down."

"Not even angering his best friend by stealing his girlfriend?"

DeMaio glowered at Tori. "I told you I wasn't upset."

"Was Brad planning to marry Trish?" Morrison asked.

"Brad? Marry?" DeMaio laughed. "Never, he's always lusting after the new coed in his class."

"Who's the new coed?" Morrison asked.

DeMaio shrugged. "I don't know, but it's his pattern."

"What about you?" Tori asked. "You involved with anyone?"

DeMaio winked at Tori. "Interested?"

Morrison sent a dark look to DeMaio, but Tori held her hand up like a traffic cop and said, "I'm interested in knowing whether you are involved with anyone." Tori thought, *How could I have dated that self-centered egotist?*

Unabashed, DeMaio sat on the couch and spread his arms over its back. "No one in particular, but I'm not moping over Trish, if that's what you're getting at."

Morrison asked, "What do you know about the blue cooler in Brad's office?"

"After tennis Brad goes back to his office and drinks a 12 oz. bottle of Pepsi. I told him Pepsi would dehydrate him, but he insisted it gave him energy. He said he had no other vices and one bottle of Pepsi a week wouldn't kill him."

Interesting choice of words, Tori thought.

"No other vices, huh," muttered Morrison. DeMaio and Tori glanced at him, but neither responded.

"Who wanted Brad Coleman dead?" Tori asked.

"I've been thinking." DeMaio scratched his head. "Fall semester this chick fell hard for Brad and asked her husband for a divorce. The husband went berserk and threatened to blow Brad's head off."

"What'd Brad do?" Tori asked.

"He promised he'd stay way from the wife."

"Coleman liked the adrenaline rush from an adulterous affair," Tori said. "He didn't play by the rules, right? He wouldn't stay away from the wife, right?"

"Don't know. Brad was a risk-taker. Like you said he liked the adrenaline rush. A couple weeks ago, Brad told me he saw the wife. I didn't get details, I was running to class."

"What's the woman's name?" she asked.

"Janet."

"Full name?" Morrison asked.

"Christ, you're lucky I remember her first name. She was cute, but not worth getting your brains blown out for."

"Anyone else who might want to kill Brad Coleman?" Tori asked.

"Brad taunted Whitherspoon – the old coot in his department, but he's a wuss. He wouldn't have the guts to kill Brad."

"Anyone profit from his death?" Morrison asked.

"How would I know?"

Tori thanked DeMaio for his help and Morrison grunted. As they left, Morrison said, "Don't leave town without telling me."

"Yeah, right. It's mid-semester. What am I going to do? Cancel my classes and fly to Istanbul?"

"Don't leave town," the detective reiterated, his voice displaying his irritation.

DeMaio closed the door with such force Tori felt the reverberation.

"Guy's got a bad attitude," Morrison said.

Tori walked to Morrison's car parked at the curb and stood by the passenger door fumbling in her purse for her sunglasses. She felt, rather than saw, a shadow descend on her. She looked up to see Morrison towering over her. "Don't tell me you're going to open the door for me."

"No, I want to see your face."

Tori started to put on her sunglasses, but Morrison held her arm down and asked, "What the hell's with you two?"

"He's an over-sized adolescent pumped up on Viagra. His brain takes its orders from his penis."

Morrison snorted. "The description fits, but it's more than that. It's personal."

"It's none of your damn business."

Morrison looked at her for a moment before letting her arm go. Then he said, "As sure as I'm standing here, he's lying. The Acosta girl was more to him than DeMaio let on."

18

"No way," Tori said. "Remember his reaction to Coleman's death. He didn't fake that. He doesn't have strong enough feelings for women to kill over one."

"Maybe not. But how come his girlfriend falls in love with his best friend and he doesn't have a clue?"

Tori said, "Right. Not credible."

"Something else," Morrison said. "He didn't ask about the poison – Strange. A chemist doesn't ask what poisoned his best friend?"

CHAPTER FOUR

WHOOSH! Dottie jerked her head up and jumped to her feet. CRASH! THUD! She drew her revolver as the brown object slammed on the desk in front of her. Dottie stood to her full 6'2" in heels and looked down on the red-faced man in an ill-fitting jacket. He raised his hands and backed away, looking down the barrel of her gun. "Don't shoot, don't shoot."

Dottie, who had been listening to Betty Lou Hancock's agonizingly detailed description of Brad Coleman's many virtues, re-holstered her gun. "Sorry. I over-reacted. You startled me." She extended her hand. "Detective Epstein."

The man's eyes crawled from where they had tracked the gun to Dottie's holster up to her face. "Davis Gibson." He shook her hand and motioned with his head. "Come into my office."

Gibson snatched his briefcase off Betty Lou's desk and walked across the room into his office, Dottie at his heels. He slammed his brief case on his bare desk and turned to Dottie, "Do you remember the character in Peanuts – the one who walked around with a cloud of dirt over his head?"

She nodded. "Sure. Pig-Pen."

"Yes, Brad Coleman was like Pig Pen, but it wasn't dirt around his head, it was bad karma. He brought it everywhere he went."

"You didn't like Dr. Coleman."

"Nobody liked Coleman."

"What can you tell me about his murder?"

"Nothing. I was driving to Tallahassee when they got him."

"Who's 'they'?"

"Whoever murdered the bastard."

Dottie fixed her eyes on Gibson, her brows scrunched together and hands on her hips. He returned her stare – but lost the match. Gibson took a deep breath and sat. "Sorry. I was in Tallahassee trying to get an increase in our budget. I'm working against a deadline. Please have a seat and I'll try to help."

Dottie sat facing Gibson's pristine teak desk. "Did Dr. Coleman have enemies in the department?" she asked.

"Enemies is a strong word, but it'd be an understatement to say Brad Coleman was unpopular with his colleagues. Professor Whitherspoon wrote a scathing letter opposing Coleman's tenure."

"Did you oppose Coleman's tenure?"

"Yes. He was an unabashed pain in the ass who thought he knew more than anyone else. He provoked everyone."

"But he got tenure."

"Yes. The faculty didn't want to make waves. They and the dean supported his tenure and he got it, yes."

"What about Dr. Whitherspoon?" Tori asked. "Did he hate Coleman enough to kill him?"

Gibson leaned back in his chair, sticking his thumbs under his belt, "Yes, he hated him enough, but he's too smart to kill Coleman."

"Is there anyone else who wanted Dr. Coleman dead?"

"The list of who didn't want him dead is shorter."

"Give me that list."

"Betty Lou Hancock. He buttered her up, brought her flowers and candy, said she was his Florida mother. He was always going to her house for dinner – God knows what she saw in him. The others on the list would be the new faculty who thought he was clever and co-eds he hadn't screwed yet."

"You aren't on the list?"

"No. But, I told you I was driving to Tallahassee when he was killed."

"Can anyone attest to your whereabouts?"

He opened his eyes wider. "No."

CHAPTER FIVE

Tori sat in her university office, feet resting on a stool, grading a paper – the fifth in an endless stack on her desk. She was staring at the paper while thinking about Steve DeMaio. *Could he kill someone? Am I being objective about Steve? Was Steve lying about Coleman canceling their tennis game? If Coleman wasn't playing tennis with Steve, who was he playing with?*

Her thoughts jumped to Morrison and she ruminated, *He's an arrogant, chauvinist and I'm not letting him tell me...* A ring interrupted her thoughts.

"Dr. Vincent," she said into her phone.

"Hi, Sis."

"Cindy?"

"How many sisters do you have?" Tori heard the familiar husky laugh.

"What's up?"

"I'm getting married."

"You are married."

"Derrick is old news. We're getting a divorce."

"You've only been married a year."

"To be precise, we've been married 16 months," Cindy said.

"Don't you think you should give the marriage a chance?"

"Don't play shrink with me. You were married to Gerry for ten minutes and have been stuck with a kid ever since."

"I'm not *stuck* with Sean. I love my son." Tori's anger was hot enough to boil water.

"Yeah, yeah, yeah. Anyway. Do you want to hear about Curtis?"

"You don't have to marry every man you sleep with," Tori said. She picked up a large paper clip and an elastic band.

"I do if they're rich." The husky laugh.

"You've been married twice and you're 32," Tori said. She propelled the rubber band with the paper clip. It hit the bookcase, landing near the photograph of Cindy and their mother – Tori's target.

"Sweetie, I'm building my retirement fund."

"Is that all Derrick was to you?" Tori opened a drawer and pulled out a pile of rubber bands.

"When did you get self-righteous?" Cindy asked. "It doesn't become you."

"Tell me about Curtis," Tori said. She shot the next rubber band toward the photo, missing by a yard. "No let me tell you about him. He's a multimillionaire. You designed a house for him in New Canaan and you fell in love."

"The house is in Greenwich," Cindy said.

Tori enjoyed the irritation in her sister's voice.

"He's not married?"

"He's in the process of a divorce," Cindy said.

"Why am I not surprised? Did the divorce proceedings start before or after you designed the house?"

"You're so funny. Yes, I designed the house for him and his then wife…"

"But he found you more interesting – a sexy architect," Tori said, shooting another rubber band into the bookcase.

"You got it."

"Isn't that how you met Derrick?"

"You *are* perceptive. You must be a shrink." Again, the husky laugh.

"Cindy, I'm worried about you," Tori said.

"Can it, Tori. Worry about yourself. It's been 15 years since your husband walked out."

"It's been nine years since *I left* Gerry," Tori snapped. The heat in her voice could boil water.

"You need a profession that lets you meet interesting men," Cindy said.

"Like architecture?"

The laugh. "You got it, Ciao."

CHAPTER SIX

Dottie left the Police Department seething, driving her midnight blue Suzuki Sidekick far above the speed limit. She felt edgy and cantankerous. She'd spent the better part of the day interviewing Betty Lou, who prattled on and on before answering her questions. Then the English chair, Gibson, took out his annoyance with Coleman on her. Meanwhile Morrison brought Tori to interview Steve DeMaio, while she was stuck listening to Betty Lou's eulogy of Coleman.

On top of everything else, Morrison questioned her relationship with Jason. Dottie had met Jason Nolan when he did an internship at the Gainesville Police Department. Two reserved, soft-spoken liberal cops thrown into a den of loud-mouthed conservatives, they became fast friends.

She headed north on FL 24 to Waldo to meet Jason at the Beer & Billiards. The hangout was what its name suggested, a billiard hall selling beer. She and Jason had been going there since it opened his senior year at U F.

A loud siren blared. Dottie looked in the rearview mirror and saw pulsating blue lights. "Damn!" She pulled to the side of the road and slammed her fist against the steering wheel. *Why can't I drive the speed limit? I know Waldo's a speed trap. AAA even erected a billboard to warn stupid drivers – like me. Damn!* It was too late to berate herself. She'd try to get out of a ticket. *I'll own up to my lapse, chastise myself, and eat humble pie – that usually works with cops. Who should know better than me? I've got lots of experience.*

She collected her license and registration, hopped out of her Suzuki and started to walk toward the police car looking repentant. Then she saw her nemesis, Junior Nolan, Jason's older brother getting out of the squad car. She froze. She hated Junior Nolan worse than the liver her mother made her to eat as a kid. And the feeling was mutual. After mentally reciting every curse word she knew, Dottie manufactured a smile.

"Hey, Junior. What's up?" she asked in a cheery voice.

Junior swaggered to her car, chewing on his ever-present wad of Redman tobacco. He rested his foot on the bumper of her Sidekick. He supported his massive upper body with the arm holding his clipboard resting on his beefy thigh while spitting tobacco at her foot. He adjusted his firearm. "Well, well, well. If it ain't the skinny black gal with the lead foot. Didn't your important boss the detective teach you better?" He leered.

"Junior, was I going over the speed limit?" She exuded innocence while trying to ignore the tobacco oozing toward her black pump.

"Don't bullshit me, girl. You know damned well you was goin' 15 m.p.h. over the limit."

"You're right. I didn't realize it until I heard the siren." She tried to look contrite.

"That ain't no excuse. You're a sworn officer, even if you're a cop for kiddies at the college. You know better'n to break the law. I've warned you 'bout speedin' before."

"Look, Junior, if you're going to give me a ticket, go ahead, but forget the lecture. I'm late." *So much for laying on the charm,* she thought. *Why can't I keep my big mouth shut?*

"Yeah, I'm gonna give you a ticket, girl." He gloated. Putting a new wad of tobacco in his mouth, Junior snatched her license and registration and filled out the ticket.

"You think 'cause your boss is a detective you can get away with murder," he said around the tobacco bulging in his cheek.

"I can't get away with murder, but I sure as hell can get this ticket fixed." *That's it. Throw a grenade into the flames.*

"Your boss won't fix no ticket."

"We'll see about that. See you in court." She plucked the ticket from Junior's hand and stomped to her car.

"Hey. Don't you know you gotta be nice to *REAL* cops? Have a nice day, li'l girl. Ya hear?"

She cursed under her breath.

"You ain't saying nothing bad about a law enforcement officer, are you? I wouldn't want to run you into the station."

She pretended not to hear his taunt. Junior wouldn't press his luck. Morrison might not fix a speeding ticket, but he wouldn't like someone arresting his minion either.

"I'll let you go this time, but I'm watching for you, li'l girl. Drive over the speed limit and I'm gonna git you."

Dottie clenched her fists. She fantasized about pulling out her revolver and shooting Junior between the eyes – no, right in his big mouth. Jason had warned her Junior wanted to "put her in her place." Junior hated his younger brother hanging out with a black woman.

She waited until Junior drove off before continuing up FL 24. She was steaming, as ticked off with herself as with Junior. She was an incorrigible speeder. Most cops let her off, but Junior delighted in ticketing her. Junior was right about Morrison not fixing the ticket, but, maybe Jason would do it again.

CHAPTER SEVEN

Tori's heart pounded. Her sweaty palms clutched the steering wheel as she squinted, trying to locate the address on a mailbox in the dark. She crawled along, until she spotted Coleman's street number. The Victorian house was about four blocks from DeMaio's duplex, but in a nicer area – the ritzy renovated section successful professionals preferred. Coleman owning the upscale house was as improbable for a young faculty member as DeMaio's living in the student ghetto. *Coleman must've had another source of income,* she thought. *His salary wouldn't buy that house.* Tori went at a snail's pace as her eyes took in the gray house, trimmed with elaborate white gingerbread.

Tori drove around the corner at the end of the block and parked. She dried her palms on her slacks. She pulled a dark knit cap over her head, tucking in her strawberry blond hair. She checked the street and rearview mirror. Dark shadows seemed to move. *Is that someone standing by the tree?* She took a deep breath. *I'm imagining things. There's no one there.* Heart thumping, she slipped out and locked her car. She speed-walked to the front door of Coleman's house. She looked to either side, took the latex gloves from her jacket pocket and pulled them on. Using the key she'd finagled from Betty Lou, Tori unlocked the door, stepped inside and closed it behind her. Steadying herself against the door, she pulled out a flashlight. *I feel like a cat burglar,* she thought. *But, I'm not a thief. I'm a forensic psychologist trying to get inside Brad Coleman's head. I wouldn't have to sneak around if that overbearing asshole of a detective listened to me. He doesn't understand psychology and mocks me to hide his ignorance.* Flicking on the flashlight with shaky hands, Tori's eyes followed the circle of light as it crept up the wall to highlight an M. C. Escher lithograph in the foyer. *I'm no appraiser, but that Escher looks authentic.*

She skulked toward the living room where the light beam caught a spooky series of faces peering at her from an Andy Warhol print. The light leapt around the room pouncing on prints, etchings, watercolors and a couple of oil paintings. She whistled. *Wow! Expensive taste for an assistant professor. And he hired a decorator. No untrained eye selected those colors and arranged traditional furniture like that,* Tori thought. *The latest window treatments, too. Everything understated, but expensive.* Coleman's green thumb was evident everywhere: a fichus tree greening the foyer, African violets awaiting the morning sun in the kitchen greenhouse window, rubber plants in the den, and orchids of every hue in the living room.

Morrison had told her the evidence technicians had found nothing important when they searched the house. She was convinced the search was perfunctory – the techs told her they thought Coleman committed suicide. She climbed the stairs to Coleman's bedroom. Photographs on his nightstand and dresser were of him: hiking, playing tennis, white-water rafting, skiing, and water-skiing. *Narcissistic or what? The object of his adoration – himself.*

Easing open the night stand Tori found an array of sex paraphernalia: condoms, a vibrator, some raunchy DVD's and *Playboy. What did you expect, girl? A Gideon bible?* Going to the tallboy dresser, she rested the flashlight on the upper surface while she opened the small top drawers – cufflinks, watches, odds and ends in one and socks in the other. Opening the second drawer she felt like a voyeur, *how many pairs of bikini underwear can one man own?* In the third drawer were dozens of tees and running shorts. The bottom drawer held ten or twelve dress shirts still in their original wrappings. Tori was closing the drawer when something caught her eye – something tan peeked out beneath the shirts in back. She retrieved a manila envelope and opened it –

pulling out photographs – dozens of photos. She spread the pictures on the dresser and focused the light on them. Girls – naked girls in graphic poses, reclining on large cushions in front of a fireplace. "YUCK!!" Tori put her hand over her mouth to keep from gagging. She put the photos back in the envelope and replaced it in the drawer. She rubbed her hands against her slacks to remove the filth she felt from touching the photos even through latex gloves. A noise outside startled her and her heart skipped a beat. *Stop spooking yourself,* she thought. *It's only a squirrel.* She completed her search of Coleman's bedroom – a closet full of slacks, jackets, shirts – *a clothes hound – typical narcissist –* nothing else of interest. The other two bedrooms were fully furnished, but the drawers and closets were empty.

Tori went downstairs to Coleman's office – a page from the English gentleman's country home. The flashlight beam traveled, like a tourist guide indicating points of interest, across hunter green walls lined with bookcases and a roll top desk in the place of honor. Tori surveyed the room, analyzing the character of its former occupant. "AAAGGHH!" The trembling light found large cushions resting by the massive fireplace in the corner. She gasped – *how disgusting. Those are the cushions in the photos of the girls.* Images of Coleman and the girls reclining on the cushions polluted her thoughts. She shuddered. *He took those photographs. He was a worse pervert than I imagined.*

Tori took a couple of breaths and moved to the desk. Lifting the roll top, she spied some official looking documents – certificates of appreciation from the Boys & Girls Club of Alachua County. *Brad Coleman was a volunteer mentor for boys? Go figure.* She pulled out letters stuffed in a cubby hole and stood reading them by the flashlight tucked under her arm. The fourth letter turned a light on in her brain. At the same moment she felt a hard metal object against her head and a deep voice growled, "Don't move."

The flashlight clanged to the floor. She heard a scream. She didn't realize the scream was hers until a huge hand clamped over her mouth and the scream stopped.

CHAPTER EIGHT

Jason Nolan was sitting at their usual booth in the Beer & Billiards when Dottie arrived for their 6:30 p.m. meeting. Jason, as tall as his brother, but slender where Junior was husky, had grown a mustache to look older. He looked like a sixteen-year-old with a mustache, but Dottie would never tell him. Jason signaled to the barman Jimmy to pour Dottie a draft as she slid into the seat next to him.

"What's up? Why're you late? What happened? You're all but foaming at the mouth," Jason said.

"Your asshole brother. That's what's up."

"He stop you again?"

Dottie glared, fury engraved on her face. "That fucking scrote knew I was coming and waited for me."

"Dottie, you drive like a Yankee on speed. Slow down. If Junior doesn't get you, you'll kill yourself."

"Don't tell me how to drive. Tell your brother to quit terrorizing women so he can boff them."

"Did he try anything with you?"

"I wish he had. I'd bust him so fast; he'd be in the cooler before he zipped his fly," Dottie said. "I'm not sure if I'm more pissed at your brother or myself. You could show some sympathy."

"I did the first three times he caught you."

"The system sucks."

"Maybe Morrison can fix the ticket," said Jason.

31

Dottie sighed. "I don't want to think about Junior. Let's talk about the murder. What do you know?"

"Coleman was poisoned."

"No shit! Everyone knows that. Any fingerprints?"

"Yeah. Coleman's and another set."

Dottie leaned forward. "Whose?"

"If we knew that, we'd know who poisoned him."

"Any note?"

"No."

"Tori doesn't think it was suicide, but we'll have to treat his death as a homicide until we know."

"Who's Tori?"

"She's a forensic psychologist – the reddish blond with Morrison this morning," Dottie said.

"The astronaut's wife in designer clothes?"

"Aren't you observant?"

"I guess I have some of my brother's genes."

"I hope not," Dottie said.

"I'm surprised Morrison wants to work with a forensic psychologist."

"He doesn't. The chief made him."

"Bet the university's PR people are going nuts," Jason said. When Dottie wrinkled her nose at him, he added, "Don't you remember Danny Rolling?"

"No, who's he?"

"The Gainesville Ripper. He murdered and mutilated five students in Gainesville in 1990."

"What happened?"

"They caught and executed him, but not before lots of parents took their kids out of UF. Even after Rolling was caught, students didn't feel safe living in Gainesville. It was a nightmare for the university."

"To say nothing about the women," Dottie said.

CHAPTER NINE

Tori was trembling so hard she thought she would pass out. The huge hand across her mouth blocked her nose and a black fog began to engulf her. *I will not faint*, she told herself.

"Shut up and I'll move my hand," the voice growled.

Tori nodded and took a deep breath as the man removed his hand from her mouth and roughly turned her to face him. She stared into the gun, wrapping her arms around herself to keep from shaking. Perspiration dripped under her arms and down her back, a chill went up her spine. The gun barrel seemed to expand and suck her into it. She could not pull her eyes away from the gun. She had never been so terrified. Thoughts of Sean rushed into her consciousness. *What an idiot I am. I'm going to leave my son an orphan. Maybe Gerry and his floozy wife will take him. Or Cindy and one of her husbands. Anyone's better than Mom.*

Feeling her knit hat torn off, Tori looked up into the face of her captor.

"Dr. Vincent? What the fuck you doing here?" asked Morrison. "Breaking and entering's a crime."

Tori pushed the gun aside with a quivering hand. "I wasn't breaking and entering. I was trying to understand Brad Coleman." She took a couple of deep breaths. "What are you doing here? You scared the life out of me."

"Me? What am I doing here?" Morrison's voice was menacing. "I'm a cop. You broke into a house. That's a crime."

"I told you, I didn't break in. I had permission."

"From who?"

"Coleman's parents," she lied.

"If you got permission, why sneak around?"

"I didn't want you to find out. I needed to get a feel for Brad Coleman," Tori said.

"Rifle through the guy's underwear so you get a 'feel' for him? This some kind of sexual fetish or psychological bullshit?"

"Don't be absurd. It has nothing to do with sex. It has to do with understanding the person who died."

Morrison said, "The techs found nada."

She stuck her chin out. "They didn't look in the right places."

"What the fuck you mean?"

"They didn't find Coleman's stash of nude photos of girls," Tori said, "taken over there." She pointed to the fireplace.

"What photos?" Morrison turned to the officer behind him. "You find photos?"

"There weren't any photos of nude girls," the officer said.

"Not only did they miss the photographs of nude girls," Tori said, "they also missed photographs of Coleman's kid and angry and threatening letters from his ex-wife. I found those in the desk."

"Coleman wasn't married."

"That's what he wanted people to think."

"Yeah, so what if he was married?"

"He had money – notice the house and the furnishings," she said, sweeping her arm to indicate the room."

"So what?"

"So his ex-wife was demanding money to send their son to a private school. She told him she wished he would die so the son would get his money."

CHAPTER TEN

Morrison pushed his half glasses up on his nose, his head buried in the sports section of the morning newspaper. Eight-year-old Jennifer skipped into the kitchen. "Good morning, Daddy," she sang.

He grunted in her direction.

Jennifer pushed her head under his arm, between him and the newspaper, "Daddy, you aren't paying attention."

"I'm sorry, princess. I'm checking the Mets. Had a home game yesterday."

"I had my ballet class yesterday."

He kissed her forehead. "That's nice," he said, trying to read the paper above her head.

Ruth snatched the paper out of her husband's hands. "Herb, listen to your daughter. She has important news."

Jennifer's shoulders sagged; she stuck out her bottom lip and took her seat. "He doesn't care." Tears glistened in her eyes. She crossed her arms on the table and buried her head in them.

Ruth eyes slashed into her husband. "Ask her about her ballet recital."

Herb opened his eyes wide. "Are you in the recital?" His voice was excited.

Jennifer looked up at him through thick glasses and nodded. Her lips suppressed a smile.

Morrison jumped up and swung his daughter in the air. "My little princess is a ballerina. She's in the show."

He twirled her around while she giggled. "I'm a fairy princess."

"Tell Daddy about your costume," Ruth said.

Morrison put down his daughter and squatted so he was on eye level with her.

Jennifer said, "It's beautiful – baby blue with lace and ribbons and little pearls and everything."

"That's wonderful."

"I do this." She danced across the floor, twirling with her hands above her head.

"You will be beautiful."

Ruth smiled and poured her husband more coffee.

"I'll drive you to school to celebrate," Morrison said.

"Not today, Daddy. I want to tell Marci and Chelsea on the bus. They'll be so jealous." Jennifer grabbed her backpack, kissed her parents, and ran out the door.

"She's growing so fast," Ruth said.

Morrison rubbed his chin, "I'd kill anyone who took her innocence."

"Where'd that come from?"

"That professor, the one murdered on campus. He took obscene photographs of naked girls. And his pal screws around with students. I'll never forget that coed who poisoned herself a few years back."

CHAPTER ELEVEN

Tori lay on her left side. She sighed, turned on her right side, then her back. She tried each position a second time – no use – her body was so rigid her head barely made a dent in the pillow. She did her relaxation routine and when she fell asleep dreamt about newspaper headlines. FORENSIC PSYCHOLOGIST SHOT BURGLARIZING HOUSE – YOUNG SON LEFT IN CARE OF PSYCHOTIC GRANDMOTHER. She gasped and awoke. The clock blinked 3:07. She managed to fall asleep again and dreamt she was a cat burglar caught in the act. She awoke screaming before a leering Morrison pulled the trigger. The clock blinked 4:57. She shivered. When she checked the clock a third time and it was 5:14. She gave up.

She dragged herself into the bathroom. As she brushed her teeth she glanced in the mirror. Tori could not look at herself without blushing. Thinking about Morrison catching her rummaging through Coleman's desk sent her into throes of guilt and embarrassment. She chastised herself – committing a crime to prove Morrison wrong. How could she think she would get away with such a stupid idea? At least he didn't arrest her.

She decided to grade the papers Cindy's call had interrupted the previous day. Pouring herself a cup of black coffee, she went to her home office and dialed the university to retrieve her phone messages. "Tori, where are you? This is Jacqui. I called your home and you aren't there. I need to talk to you. It's urgent. Please call me as soon as you get this message." Tori didn't have any phone messages on her home answering machine. *Sean! That boy is so polite and helpful, people think he'll give me a message – he's a preteen – he forgets.* The next three messages were from Jacqui also. Jacqui, a clinical Ph.D. student, was doing an internship at the university counseling center. *I wonder what's so important that Jacqui is calling me at home and at the university. She's a good therapist. She can handle crises without help.*

Tori checked her watch – 5:30 was too early to call Jacqui at home, but she left a message on Jacqui's office phone.

At 8:00 Jacqui called.

"Hi, Jacqui. You're in early. What's up?"

"Tori, I'm so glad you called. A student came in yesterday. She's terrified. She found Dr. Coleman's body."

"She needs to go to the police right away."

"She won't talk to the police. Can you meet with us this morning?"

"Yeah. Get her to come to your office and I'll meet you there in 20 minutes."

Tori walked into Jacqui's office a little shy of 15 minutes later. A young woman cowered next to Jacqui on a love seat. The woman was striking – long silky black hair, huge black eyes, and the clear olive skin of a middle easterner. Jacqui introduced Rashida Mahajan to Tori, who shook her hand and sat on the chair across from them.

"Rashida's worried," Jacqui explained. "She's afraid you'll tell the police who she is."

Tori leaned forward and looked into Rashida's brimming eyes. "Rashida, you are in a therapy session. Both Jacqui and I are bound by confidentiality. That means neither of us can tell anyone what is said in therapy. We can't even tell anyone you are a client, unless you give us permission to do so. Do you understand?"

Rashida clung to Jacqui's arm, her eyes wide. *Why is she so frightened?* Tori wondered.

Jacquie responded to Tori's unspoken question. "Rashida doesn't want her father to know she found Dr. Coleman's body. She thinks he might take her out of college and make her go home to Pakistan."

Tori nodded. "I understand. Perhaps you can tell me what happened. I'll relate it to the police without telling them who you are."

Rashida looked at Jacqui who patted her arm. "Would that work for you?"

Rashida nodded.

Tori said in a soft voice, "You've had a terrible trauma and I promise I'll be quick." Tori took Rashida's hands in both of hers until she got eye contact. "Okay? Let's start. Why did you go to Dr. Coleman's office Tuesday morning?"

Rashida looked at Jacqui before answering Tori. Her voice was shaky and she trembled. "I had an appointment with Dr. Coleman."

"What happened when you got there?"

"I knocked. There was no answer, but the door opened a little bit. I looked in. He was leaning on his desk. I thought he was asleep. I called, but he didn't wake up. So I touched him." Rashida shuddered. She pulled her hands away from Tori and buried her face in them, weeping. Jacqui handed her a tissue. Rashida wiped her eyes but the tears kept flowing. She said, "He was cold, so...so...so... I knew ... " She sobbed.

"Okay, okay, Rashida, don't think about what you saw in the office. Why were you going to see Professor Coleman?"

Rashida's eyes darted up and around the room, she sniffled. "He told me to." She hesitated a little too long. "For extra help." Tori's clinical instincts warned her Rashida was not being forthright. *What is she holding back?*

"Were you doing poorly in his class?" Tori asked.

"Oh, no, I was getting an A." Rashida raised her head and sat up straight.

"If you were getting an A, you did not need extra help," Tori said. The nasty photographs she'd unearthed in Brad Coleman's drawer resurfaced in her mind. Rashida blushed. She looked down and played with the damp tissue which began snowing onto the floor.

"Rashida, you went to Dr. Coleman's office because you were hoping to have a relationship with him, isn't that so?"

Rashida shrugged.

"He would have affairs with coeds, wouldn't he, Rashida?" Tori asked. "And you thought it would be cool if you had an affair with him."

Looking down, Rashida nodded, her cheeks bright pink.

"That's why you don't want your father to find out, isn't it?"

Rashida nodded again.

"Were you dating Dr. Coleman?" Tori asked.

"No!!!" Rashida paused and then said in a softer voice, but emphatically, "No! We never went out."

"Did Dr. Coleman ask you for a date?" Tori asked.

"Sort of... you know, he said he'd give me 'personal' attention." She put emphasis on the word *personal*. "He winked when he said it. He said he'd get my poems published in the student journal. He told me to call him Monday."

"What did he say when you called?"

"He told me to come to his office yesterday morning." Rashida hesitated, and then said, "He said we could make poetry together." A single tear wound its way down to Rashida's chin, where she wiped it off with the back of her hand.

Gimme a break, Tori thought.

CHAPTER TWELVE

Spring sunshine lured students onto campus – walking, bicycling, skating, and skateboarding. They hurried to classes or meandered in small groups engaged in conversations interspersed with laughter. One energetic threesome tossed a Frisbee. Morrison raised his eyebrows at a shorts-clad couple in lust making-out on the grass of Turlington Plaza.

"Bit early for that?" he asked.

"Not when you're 18," Dottie replied.

Morrison ambled along with a swagger, while Dottie restrained her habitual fast stride to match his pace. They headed to the English Department in Rolfs Hall, a collegiate gothic style building in the university's Historic District. A melancholy atmosphere enveloped Morrison and Dottie as they entered the Hall. The somber mood suppressed their conversation and neither spoke a word as they climbed the ancient wooden stairs to the third floor.

An altar strewn with roses had materialized in front of Coleman's office. Morrison picked up a rose – a card saying "Michelle Riley" was tied to it with a black ribbon. "Must be a student," he said. The other roses also bore cards with names and black ribbons. A poem on black-rimmed paper was tacked to the bulletin board. Morrison sighed and shook his head. "Get the names," he told Dottie. He ran his fingers through his thinning hair and removed the crime tape before unlocking the door.

Observing mounds of paper, Dottie moaned. "Why do we have to go through all this junk?"

"Stop bitching. I'm not gonna be embarrassed again by that shrink finding stuff."

"Any idea where the nude photos she found came from?"

"Yeah. Coleman took them – by his fireplace."

"She's already found the photos and letter from his ex-wife. Why do we have to go through his office?"

"Detectives search. That's how we find stuff about the vic."

Ja, Führer, Dottie thought as she started to give her usual exaggerated salute.

"Cut that Heil Hitler shit," Morrison snapped.

Did I say that out loud? Dottie thought as she looked at Morrison. He was searching through papers with his back to her. She sat, opened the middle drawer in Coleman's desk and began exploring its contents. She felt a tap on her shoulder and looked up to see Morrison with his finger to his mouth. He pointed to the door with his drawn gun. The knob was turning very slowly. As the door edged open a hand came from behind it. The hand had its thumb folded over three curled fingers and the index finger pointing like a gun. Dottie noticed the index finger had a well-manicured pink fingernail.

"Don't shoot," Tori said, raising her hands with a big smile. "We can't keep meeting like this, Morrison."

"You're gonna get killed sneaking around," Morrison said. Putting his gun away, Morrison turned to Dottie, "Where's your gun? You could've been killed if she'd been the murderer."

Dottie pulled on her ear lobe and looked down. "I don't have it today. I didn't think I'd need it."

"Always carry. Never know what can happen." Turning hostile eyes on Tori, Morrison demanded, "What the hell you up to? Think we can't search Coleman's office?"

"Chill out, Morrison," Tori said. "I'm trying to help. I thought you'd want to know about the student who found Coleman's body." She related what she knew about Rashida without revealing her identity.

"What's her name?" Morrison asked.

"She doesn't want anyone to know who she is."

"Fuck what she wants. I need to question her," Morrison said.

Tori stuck her chin out. "Counseling sessions are protected by confidentiality. I can't reveal anything she doesn't want me to. She had nothing to do with Coleman's death. It was the first time she met with him."

"We're investigating a murder."

"What are you going to do – shoot me?" Tori asked.

"He would if he thought he could get away with it," Dottie said. "Cut it out you two – we're on the same team."

"The team from hell," Morrison said with a scowl. "Sorry."

"Forgiven. What'd you find?" Tori asked.

"I found Coleman's Smartphone," Dottie said and whistled. "It must have set him back megabucks."

"What the hell's a Smartphone?" Morrison asked. "Hear them advertised. What do they do – answer your calls for you?"

Dottie chuckled. "They're phones with connectivity and…"

"Speak English, for Christ's sake – what's connectivity?" His voice was edgy.

"It can connect to the Internet. It's like a small computer. Generation Xers use them to keep appointments and phone numbers."

"What good's it? It's too small to read," he said.

"It's got loads of info. See here's the entry for Tuesday, April 13th: '7:30 a.m. tennis - SD, 9:30 – R.M.'"

"What's R. M.'s full name?" Morrison asked.

"Doesn't say. I also found a plaque from the Boys & Girls Club of Alachua County. It thanks Coleman for mentoring boys and helping them with their homework."

"Coleman wasn't all bad," Tori said. "What about you, Morrison? Did you find anything?"

"Some student, Russell Mills, wrote Coleman. He begged for a… let's see…a late withdrawal. Dad lost his job at Georgia-Pacific," he jerked his head in the general direction, "you know, in Palatka. Then his mom got a mental breakdown. Mills had a job lined up. He wanted Coleman to let him retake the course so he could graduate."

"Any response from Coleman?" Tori asked.

"Let me see…" After shuffling through the papers he said, "Listen to this. 'You know the rules – notify the professor prior to the end of withdrawal. Take responsibility for your actions. If you don't graduate, that's your problem.'" Morrison read some more papers. "Mills was hot. Wrote last week and said Coleman would, quote 'regret it if he didn't change his grade.'"

"Doesn't look good for Mills – threatening Coleman a week before he was killed," Dottie said.

"Nah. Nobody kills over a grade," Morrison said. "Besides, Coleman can't change the grade if he's dead."

"Keeping a student from graduating is motive for murder," Dottie said. "We should interview Russell Mills."

"Go ahead. I'm not wasting my time."

Tori went to the door. "See you later. I've got to get to class."

When an hour of searching produced no additional information, Morrison pronounced the search complete. Dottie stuck the Smartphone in her backpack.

"That official issue?" he asked.

"Sure," she said pointing to the Sierra Club logo.

Morrison snorted.

Morrison and Dottie proceeded to the English Department's main office where Betty Lou Hancock, dressed in black, was holding court with a cluster of students, many of whom wore black armbands. Seeing the officers, Betty Lou dismissed her entourage with a flick of both hands. As the students gathered their belongings, Dottie asked Betty Lou how she was holding up. With more of a grimace than a smile, she responded, "I'm a tough old bird."

Aside from her blood-shot eyes and the puffiness in her wrinkled face, she did seem in good shape. Dottie gave Bettie Lou a 'thumbs up.'

"Where's that nice Dr. Vincent this morning?"

"In class," Morrison said.

"What have you found?" Betty Lou asked, sticking her chin out at Morrison.

Morrison said, "Just started investigating. We get info, I'll give it to the university."

As Morrison turned his back to watch the students leaving, Betty Lou stuck her tongue out at him. The students giggled, but muffled their snickers when Morrison glared.

Dottie erased her grin as Morrison turned toward her. She covered her amusement by asking Betty Lou for the department's telephone message book.

CHAPTER THIRTEEN

Using the English Department's phone message records, Dottie set up an Excel spreadsheet of callers, messages, frequency and dates of calls to Brad Coleman. Leaning back in her chair she surveyed her work, took a gulp of Coke and a bite out of a humongous dark Hershey bar. *Ah, comfort food!*

She worked backward from the day of Coleman's death. *Coleman received mucho calls – primarily from women, presumably coeds looking for assistance with coursework or hoping to score with the professor. I'll have to check each one. No wonder Morrison let me take the message book. This work is too dull for the Führer.* After forty minutes, she had quite a list. She'd also finished the Coke and devoured 900 calories of chocolate. It was high calorie and tedious work. *The Führer is sticking me with all the grunt work,* she grumbled to herself. *I'll beat him at this game – I'll find the connection.*

She sat back and reviewed her spreadsheet. Rashida Mahajan called once on Monday. *Aren't those the initials for the appointment with Coleman for 9:30 Tuesday?* She checked. *Bingo! I bet she's the coed who found Coleman's body.* Sitting with arms folded, Dottie pondered, *Should I tell Morrison who she is? No, I'll keep that tidbit to myself. If he interviews her, she'll clam up. It's better if Tori deals with her. She can get information from Rashida and pass it on to us.*

Dottie noted Dean Kohlberg called Coleman with increasing frequency up to a couple weeks ago, when the messages stopped. She thought, *Strange. Why would the Dean of Arts and Sciences be calling a junior faculty member? Maybe she had the hots for him?* Dottie chuckled at her little joke. *The aloof and snobbish Dean Hilary Kohlberg in a sexual liaison with smoking Brad Coleman?* Then she berated herself – *that's sexist!*

'Janet' called Coleman a lot in October. A couple of months later the messages added, "I said you wouldn't talk to her," initialed as all the messages were by B. L. – Betty Lou. *Nasty way to end a romance – have your secretary tell your lover you won't take her call. But it was effective. Janet's calls stopped.*

Among the phone messages were a few from David Harrison. *He's an attorney in town,* she thought. *I'll give him a call.* Some sporadic messages from DeMaio and from Trish Acosta -- ones you'd expect a friend and a lover to send – *nothing of consequence.* The Director of the Boys & Girls Club called periodically. One call asked for advice about your college scholarships. *Your college scholarships? What's that about?* Messages from Russell Mills provided nothing useful. A few long distance calls – his mother, a book publisher, two male friends, some woman from Atlanta. Messages dealing with college business were scattered among the others. *Damn, there's nothing to indicate why someone would kill Brad Coleman.*

Dottie added the names on the roses outside Coleman's office and appointments in Coleman's Smartphone to her spreadsheet. The names overlapped except for a series of meetings with H. H. *Strange, there weren't any phone messages from anyone with those initials.* Dottie checked the campus directory but found no one with the initials H. H. with any relationship to the English Department. *Who was it? Or was it some kind of code?*

At least she could move on to something more interesting. She uploaded the erotic photographs of young women from Coleman's computer. She selected the clearest facial photograph of each of the young women and cropped the photos so the faces were all that showed. She printed out the five faces – she would get Betty Lou to identify the women without letting on about the suggestive photographs. On a whim she searched the computer for any photographs that Coleman might have erased. Dottie found a series of photographs of a dark haired woman. She looked a little older than the other women. She restored the photographs and cropped the best facial view. *Who is she? Why did he erase these pictures?* She wondered.

CHAPTER FOURTEEN

While Dottie Epstein enhanced the faces from the erotic photographs and organized Coleman's phone messages and contacts, Morrison drove Tori to interview Coleman's girlfriend. Trish Acosta rented an apartment in a small rooming house on the edge of the student ghetto. Magnolia trees on either side of the walkway were heavy with huge white blossoms, while azaleas of every hue hugged the porch of the newly painted house nestled on a well-groomed lawn. Morrison stopped on the walkway to examine the confederate jasmine. He took a deep breath and said, "Smells like spring."

Tori said, "That's rather poetic."

"I'll be the next Adam Dalgliesh," he said.

Wondering whether he was putting her on, she asked, "A fan of BBC Mystery?"

"Never miss it. Dalgliesh's my favorite." Morrison smiled. They climbed the steps to the front door. Morrison knocked and Trish Acosta opened the door. Tori thought Trish was stunning, not as drop dead gorgeous as DeMaio had described her, but beautiful. Long tanned legs extended from white shorts to bare feet with bright pink toenails. A violet tee shirt the same color as her eyes stretched across a full bust.

Morrison introduced himself and Tori before asking, "Can we come in?"

Trish stepped aside, motioning them to a small sitting room with fashionable furnishings, their small proportions perfect for the little room. The rest of the apartment consisted of a kitchen and alcove bedroom. Tori noted that the living area was devoid of personal touches with the exception of a lace-framed photograph of a dark-haired little girl holding a baby. She thought, *everything's so clean and bare. It's like she doesn't intend to stay very long. She isn't making it homey.* Trish followed Tori and Morrison into her sitting room and sat on a small loveseat with one leg tucked under her other thigh.

"What is it you want?" Trish asked. Tori thought she was composed for someone getting an unscheduled visit from the police the day after her boyfriend was poisoned.

"You're Brad Coleman's girlfriend, right?" Morrison asked.

"That's right. Have you found who murdered him?" Trish clenched her fists and crossed her arms under her breasts.

"Afraid not," he said. "Maybe you can tell us something to help."

Tears began to trickle down Trish's face. Tori grabbed tissues from her purse and sat next to the younger woman on the loveseat. Tori ran out of tissues before Trish exhausted her supply of tears. Trish pulled a tiny handkerchief from the pocket in her shorts and dabbed her eyes. She unfolded the handkerchief and blew her nose in a lady-like manner. Then she sat back and stared into space for a moment. Without warning, she began talking non-stop. "Brad spent Monday night with me. He sat right where you are," Trish said to Tori, "his head in my lap. He recited poetry to me." She looked at her lap as if she could see his head resting there. There was no need to ask Trish questions. She was wired and prattled on. Tori diagnosed Trish's excessive talking as a reaction to the trauma of Brad's death. Babbling was her defense mechanism. As long as she was speaking, the pain could not overpower her heart.

After listening for some minutes Morrison asked, "Why'd Coleman cancel his tennis date with DeMaio yesterday?"

Confusion spread across Trish's face. "Brad didn't cancel tennis. He played tennis with Steve yesterday morning."

"Could he have changed his plans?" Tori asked. "Steve says Brad called him Monday night and canceled."

"Brad didn't call Steve Monday night. He was with me all evening and didn't make any calls. He told me he was meeting Steve when he left Tuesday morning."

Tori said, "Tell us about your relationship with Steve."

"I was Steve's graduate assistant in the fall." She shrugged. "I still am for that matter."

"You went to the movies with DeMaio and invited him to stay the night. Is that correct?" Tori asked.

Trish snorted. "I didn't do any inviting," she said with irritation. "Steve DeMaio has a cave man mentality. When he wants a woman he bops her over the head and grabs her."

Morrison lowered his head and looked at Tori over his half glasses. She nodded.

"Why did you switch your affections from Steve to Brad?" Tori asked.

"When I dated Steve, we saw a lot of Brad." Trish sighed. "Brad was suave and gentile – Steve's diametric opposite. One night Steve and I had a fight and I stormed out. I didn't know where to go and ended up at Brad's. Brad listened while I poured my heart out. We had some wine and the next thing I knew we were kissing and... one thing led to another and..." She lifted and dropped her right shoulder.

Trish stared ahead, eyes focused inward. After a moment she said, "When I told Steve about me and Brad, he went ballistic – throwing things and screaming. He terrified me. I tried to leave. He grabbed me and wouldn't let me go. He said he wasn't angry with me. He blamed Brad for seducing me." Trish shook her head and said, "I never thought Steve would be so vindictive."

"You think Steve DeMaio killed Brad?" Tori asked.

"What else can I think? Steve was furious when I dumped him for Brad." She looked at Tori with big violet eyes, rimmed in red.

"Tell us about the fight you had with Steve," Tori said.

"What fight?"

"You said you went to see Brad because of a fight with Steve." Tori's clinical insight was tapping, trying to get into her conscious thoughts. Trish was hiding something.

Trish put her hands to either side of her head and looked down. Then she raised her head. "You know I can't remember what that fight was about. We had so many conflicts."

Morrison asked, "Where were you Tuesday morning?"

Trish turned to face him. "I left the same time Brad did – about 7:15. I take an aerobics class Tuesday mornings at 7:30 at the Gainesville Spa – you know, while Steve and Brad play tennis. I started the class after I began dating Steve." She put her left hand to her mouth, clutching her stomach with her right arm. "Oh my God. They're not going to play tennis any more." Trish put her head down on her arm and began to sob. Tori put her arm around Trish's shoulders. Trish whimpered what seemed like 20 minutes, but was closer to two or three, before looking up. "I'm all right. I'm sorry. I thought I was all cried out."

"What can you tell us about Brad's involvement with the Boys & Girls Club?" Tori asked.

"Brad was great with teenage boys. He mentored a couple of them at the Boys Club. He was trying to get them into Sante Fe Community College in the fall. He set up a scholarship fund for the boys. He didn't tell anyone he funded it."

Morrison asked, "Who wanted Coleman dead?"

"Brad tormented Winston Whitherspoon, a professor in the English Department. Said he was out of date with current academic approaches. Whitherspoon tried to stop Brad from getting tenure. But, that poor old soul couldn't hurt anyone. He doesn't have a killer instinct. Besides, the argument became moot when Brad got tenure." Trish paused. "I can't think of anyone else. The students love Brad. The kids at the Boys & Girls Club adore him. Who would want to hurt him?"

Tori asked, "Trish, did Brad seem down or depressed?"

"No. Why do you ask?"

"I want to understand how he felt."

"Are you implying he committed suicide?"

"That's a possibility."

"No. It is not a possibility. He loved life."

After the interview Morrison and Tori climbed into the squad car, deep in separate thoughts.

"What'd you think of her?" Morrison asked.

Tori bit her bottom lip. "Something doesn't ring true."

"What?"

"I don't know – intuition."

"What? Think 'cause you're a shrink you can read people's minds?"

Tori glared. "I am trained to understand people. I observe their body language. It tells me a lot about people."

"Body language – that's bullshit."

Tori fumed. "Did you pick up her comment about a tiff with Steve DeMaio?"

"Yeah, told you he was lying."

"She might be the one who's lying."

"Why would she lie?" Morrison asked.

"I don't know. But how could she forget the first conversation she had with Coleman – her lover?"

"How do you know she doesn't remember it?"

"I asked her about her conflict with DeMaio. It led to her first intimate talk with Coleman – the night they became lovers. Women reminisce over those things. She should remember every word spoken that night."

"Yeah, yeah, if you say so," Morrison said, with a shrug. After a couple seconds, Morrison said, "We can check her alibi."

Tori asked, "But motive? Why would she kill her lover?"

"Damned if I know. You're the one said something didn't ring true. Whatever the hell that means."

CHAPTER FIFTEEN

Morrison was quiet on the drive to campus. He took a quick cruise through the parking lot near Rolfs Hall. Not finding an empty space, he parked in a spot reserved for campus vehicles. Tori bit her tongue to keep from commenting on his illegal parking. Then she thought, *why should I avoid offending the arrogant bastard?* She said, "If I parked here, I'd get a ticket. You cops think rules were made for lesser people."

Morrison got out of the car and leaned across the top. "I park here to do my job."

"So would the people working in Rolfs Hall." Tori walked toward the building.

Morrison caught up with Tori. "You picking a fight?"

Tori took a deep breath. "Yes, sorry. Parking on campus is a pain."

He stuck out his hand. "Truce?"

She shook his hand and they walked to the English Department office. "I think some woman killed Coleman to get even," she said.

"Get even for what?"

"For whatever the prick did." Her voice was heated.

Morrison stopped walking, turned toward her and raised his right eyebrow, "'prick'? Did the good doctor say 'prick'?"

She groaned. "You're not going to lecture me about using obscenities like my mother does are you?"

"No, I'm not going to lecture. I'm amazed a nice lady like you knows words like 'prick.'"

Palpable gloom engulfed the area around Coleman's office like thick morning fog. Melancholy descended on Morrison and Tori, smothering their joking repartee. Flowers on the floor in front of Coleman's office had proliferated, as had poetry taped to his door. Literature students had converted their grief into verse and rhyme and laid it at the altar to their fallen professor. Photographs of Coleman with students had materialized on the bulletin board by his door. Morrison and Tori observed the shrine without comment as they walked down the hall to the department office.

Betty Lou Hancock was in a funk, quietly weeping, as were many of the students congregated in the department office. The heavy woman in the corridor from the previous day, wearing similar stretch pants and a different blousy top, huddled in a corner comforting a pale blond. A recovered Rashida whispered with Betty Lou while the pink earringed Shakespearean fan and a female student hovered around Betty Lou's desk listening to Rashida and the secretary. Looking up at the visitors, Betty Lou dismissed the students. Rashida's eyes opened wide at the sight of Tori with the detective; but true to her ethical requirement to maintain confidentiality, Tori pretended she didn't know Rashida.

In a soft voice, Tori asked, "How are you doing, Ms. Hancock?"

Betty Lou sniffled. "Bless my soul, I'm trying to make it."

Tori asked Betty Lou about Coleman's relationship with Trish. Betty Lou repeated DeMaio's and Trish's descriptions of the sequential relationship Trish had had with the two friends. "Steve fell for Trish and never got over Brad stealing her."

Morrison gave Tori a knowing look. She did not concur with his assumption and shook her head. She thought, *Steve wouldn't get upset over losing a girlfriend.*

"Who else's got something against Coleman?" Morrison asked,

"Winston Whitherspoon. Brad and Whitherspoon were always at each other's throats. If they weren't arguing face to face, they were bad-mouthing each other to anyone who'd listen."

"Whitherspoon fought with Coleman?"

"Oh Lordy, yes. He hated Brad. He shouted a stream of threats at Brad in the cafeteria."

Morrison cocked his head. "Threats? What kind of threats? Say he'd kill him?"

"No... no, not exactly. I wasn't there, but it was juicy gossip for days. Whitherspoon screamed at Brad. Said he'd see him terminated or something. He swore if he didn't get Brad, his girlfriend's husband would."

"Do you think Whitherspoon killed Brad?" Tori asked.

"Whitherspoon's a dried up old prune. He hasn't got the gumption."

"What's this girlfriend's husband about?" Morrison asked. "Who's this girlfriend?"

"Janet was Brad's student." Betty Lou grimaced. She shrugged her left shoulder.

Morrison narrowed his eyes. "They had an affair?"

"Not my business." She snapped. "They were two consenting adults."

Tori gave Morrison what she thought was a withering look and then asked about the newly canonized saint of the English Department with a less antagonizing question. "I'm sure you wouldn't ask anything like that. And, if it weren't for the circumstances, we wouldn't ask either. But people talk. What did they say about Brad and Janet? Were they having an affair?"

"That's the rumor." Betty Lou crossed her arms and sat back in her chair.

"And Janet's husband found out?"

"Lordy, yes!" Betty Lou sat forward, leaning her lower arms on her desk. "He roared in here like a lion after fresh meat. He said he was going to blow Brad off the face of the earth. Now, there was a man who could kill someone. He had a loaded gun and carried on like a wild man. Old Whitherspoon went crazy – kept egging him on. He yelled, 'Go ahead and blow his head off – you'd do the world a favor.'"

"You call the police?" Morrison asked.

"No. Brad begged me not to call campus police. The husband calmed down and Brad took him to his office."

"What happened?"

"A while later, they come out of the office looking grim. The husband's gun was nowhere in sight, but Brad was shook up. He told me *never* to put a call from Janet through to him."

Tori heard the familiar ring and groped in her purse to get her phone. She flipped it open, "Hi, Kiddo, I'll be home in about an hour." She put the phone back. "Sorry for the interruption – it was my son." She turned to Betty Lou. "What about Janet? Did you see or hear from her again?"

"Did I ever. She called all day, but I wouldn't put her calls through. She dropped out of college."

"What's Janet's last name?"

"Pillsbury. Janet Pillsbury."

"What's her address?" Morrison asked.

Betty Lou looked up Janet's address on her computer, but said, "I don't know if she's still living there. I heard she and her husband divorced."

"What about Janet's husband?" Tori asked.

"He's the pharmacist at Norton's Pharmacy."

Morrison and Tori looked at each other, both thinking – *access to poison.*

"Oh, yes, one last question. What can you tell us about Brad's ex-wife?" Tori asked, keeping her voice neutral.

"Brad wasn't ever married."

Tori told her about the letter from Coleman's ex-wife. Betty Lou shook her head and looked at Tori incredulously. "I can't believe it. He told me everything. Are you sure he was married? And you say he had a child?"

"That's what the letters said."

Betty Lou wrinkled her brow and shook her head.

Morrison asked, "Where's this Whitherspoon?"

"Whitherspoon's all but lives here – has no life," Betty Lou said, still shaking her head. Absent-mindedly, she checked her faculty schedule. "He'll be back from class. His office is down the hall, third door on the right."

CHAPTER SIXTEEN

When Morrison knocked on Dr. Whitherspoon's office door, the elderly professor eased it open. Tori thought Winston Whitherspoon resembled nothing as much as a walking cadaver. He was medium height and emaciated, his pasty skin tinged yellow, his sparse white hair plastered across his pate with something greasy. The ancient professor's rumpled navy blazer hung from his frame as if on a hanger and his red striped bowtie was loose around his scrawny neck. Tori could not imagine this fragile, almost antique, man holding the attention of boisterous college students. When Morrison showed Whitherspoon his badge, the professor's eyes became pinpoints. He opened his door further, and waved his hand toward some chairs, "Come in, officer. I've been expecting you." His voice was high pitched and weak.

Whitherspoon's office had institutional furnishings similar to those in Coleman's office, but no spirit or vitality relieved the drabness of his Spartan cell. Whereas Coleman's office was alive with sunshine, open windows, green plants, bright posters, Whitherspoon's was a mausoleum with a musty smell, dusty books, yellowed poetry in ancient frames, dilapidated chairs, and dark blinds blocking sunshine and repelling spring.

Ignoring their prior agreement that Tori would handle interviews on campus, Morrison jumped in. "Why'd you expect us?"

"Don't pretend you are unaware of my antagonistic relationship with Professor Coleman. Everyone on campus knew Brad Coleman and I abhorred each other. We had frequent public altercations."

"You hated Coleman, so you poisoned him?" Morrison asked.

"You certainly come right to the point, Detective. I'm sorry to disappoint you, but, no, I did not kill Professor Coleman. Although I won't pretend I'm sorry he's dead."

"You threatened Coleman," Morrison said.

"You need to get your facts straight, Detective. I did not threaten to *kill* Professor Coleman. I threatened to block his tenure or get his contract terminated for moral turpitude." Whitherspoon formed a steeple with his bony fingers.

"He got tenure, so you got rid of him."

"I cannot say the idea never crossed my mind, but I did not poison him."

Tori gave Morrison a pointed look and asked, "Dr. Whitherspoon, do you know anyone who wanted Brad Coleman dead?"

"I'll list them for you," he said, counting on arthritic fingers. "First, that husband who terrorized him with a gun, the coeds with whom he terminated liaisons, husbands or paramours or fathers of coeds he seduced, students in his class who weren't getting good grades because they declined advances from their professor, and last, but not least, our esteemed dean."

Whitherspoon took out a pressed and folded handkerchief with which he patted his brow, despite no evidence of sweat on his forehead. He put the still pristine handkerchief back in his pocket, licking his lips and puffing out his sunken chest. He re-formed the steeple.

"Do you mean Dean Kohlberg?" Tori asked.

Whitherspoon nodded with a smirk.

Morrison interjected, "Your dean wanted Coleman dead? Why?"

"Why don't you ask her," Whitherspoon sneered, "or her friend Mary Rantala."

"Dr. Whitherspoon," Tori said, "this is the first time anyone has alleged Dean Kohlberg had a motive to kill Dr. Coleman. Why would she kill him?"

Whitherspoon jerked to attention. "I did not say she killed him. I'm tenured, but I am not bulletproof. I am not going to implicate my dean in murder." Professor Whitherspoon straightened his askew bowtie with shaky hands.

"You already implicated her," Morrison said.

"I misspoke. I didn't mean to imply the dean had animosity toward Coleman. After all, she got him tenured."

"Dr. Whitherspoon, you withhold information in a murder investigation, I'll take you to the station and discuss it with you there," Morrison said, waving his sausage-sized finger in the old professor's face.

"I told you, I misspoke," Whitherspoon whimpered. He pulled out his handkerchief again and patted his now dripping brow. He need not have bothered. His forehead was damp again before he could replace the handkerchief in his pocket. His hand was trembling. He stood, his face ashen, hands clutching his chest and made a croaking sound before toppling over his desk.

"Holy Shit!" Morrison jumped up, checked the pulse in Whitherspoon's neck and yelled, "Call 911." Morrison lifted Whitherspoon and draped him across the desk like a withered rag doll, sending pens and papers flying. He started CPR. Tori grabbed the desk phone and dialed 911, giving them the information about Whitherspoon.

Morrison's face reddened and a vein beat prominently in his forehead, as he tried to resuscitate the old man. "Stay with me you old fart," Morrison said while pushing on Whitherspoon's chest. "Dr. Whitherspoon, do you hear me?" Morrison breathed into Whitherspoon's mouth while closing his nostrils with his fingers.

Tori worried Morrison might have a heart attack, also. Every muscle in her body was taut and her fists were clenched as she watched Morrison's efforts. *Where is that rescue team?* Finally, she heard sirens. She breathed, not realizing until then that she'd been holding her breath. When voices in the hall approached, Tori opened the door and got out of the way of the medics. They pushed a stretcher into the office and Morrison stood aside. The medics fastened an oxygen mask to Whitherspoon's face. Then they lifted the scarecrow of a man onto the stretcher and started some intravenous fluids before whisking him out of the office.

CHAPTER SEVENTEEN

Morrison and Tori, relieved to leave the melancholy of the English Department and trauma of Whitherspoon's collapse, walked to meet Dottie at the Police Department. Exiting the English building they stepped onto a vibrant campus: students rushing to evening classes, strolling hand and hand, playing Frisbee, shouting greetings, and performing collegiate rites of spring. Morrison rubbed his ears as they passed a group blasting rock music. "Why do kids play music so damn loud?" he asked.

"So other students will notice them. It's sort of a mating ritual."

"A mating ritual? Who wants to mate with someone who'll be deaf by 35."

"College kids are attracted by music."

"Are they deaf?"

"Not yet, they aren't."

They exchanged grins. Despite knowing each other for months – ever since the chief asked the Crisis Center to conduct psychological autopsies for the department – Morrison and Tori had never spent time together. He considered her fluff without substance and she avoided the gruff detective who denigrated psychological autopsies, not to mention psychology in general.

Tori and Dottie watched Morrison who stood at the white board where he'd listed all the suspects in Coleman's poisoning: Steve DeMaio, Jimmy Pillsbury, Janet Pillsbury, Trish Acosta,

Unknown Student who found body (he'd given Tori an evil look while writing this), Winston Whitherspoon, Dean Hilary Kohlberg, Russell Mills, Betty Lou Hancock, Coleman's ex-wife, Davis Gibson. Dottie had tacked the faces she had cropped and enhanced of the women in the photographs Tori had found in Coleman's house.

"I asked Betty Lou to identify any of the photographs she could." She tapped the photo Tori recognized as Rashida. "She said this is the coed who found the body, but she doesn't remember her name."

"She's the coed I interviewed. She swore she'd never been involved with Coleman." Tori shook her head. "I knew she was not telling me everything, but I thought she was holding back her desires about Coleman. I was concerned about her trauma; I didn't question her truthfulness about dating him.

"Yeah, yeah, she lied to you, Doc." Morrison said. "So much for body language." He turned to Dottie, "Who're the others?"

"This is Janet Pillsbury," Dottie said pointing. "This is Jennifer – Betty Lou doesn't remember her last name. This is Cathy, she graduated a couple years ago. She doesn't recognize this one."

"That last one is Trish Acosta," Tori said.

"Coleman tried to erase all the photographs of her," Dottie said. "I was able to recover them."

"Why'd he do that?" Morrison asked.

Tori said, "Maybe he was serious about her."

"Or she found them and made him erase them," Dottie said.

"That's a more likely scenario." Tori pushed her hair behind her ear and directed her question to Morrison. "What do you think about Whitherspoon?"

"I don't like the old coot, but you didn't have to give him a heart attack," Morrison said.

"Me?" Tori asked. "You're the one who pounced on him."

"He had a heart attack?" Dottie asked. She looked from Tori who lowered her head to Morrison.

He shrugged. "Don't know yet. Collapsed during our interview. Medics took him to Shands." He turned to Tori. "I'm kidding you, but you got a way of bringing excitement to a case." Morrison smirked. Tori glared at him. Morrison said, "Tell us about Whitherspoon, you're the shrink."

"I agree with Betty Lou. He hasn't the gumption to kill."

"Did he hate him enough to kill him?" Dottie asked.

"Yeah. But the hatred was eating him up, not being directed at the source," Tori said. "He didn't attempt to hide his animosity toward Coleman or pretend he was sorry about his death. But, he didn't collapse when we questioned him about Coleman – he collapsed when we asked him about the dean."

"He's hiding something," Morrison said.

"You're right. He knows something about Dean Kohlberg."

Dottie said, "The telephone message book had a bunch of calls from Dean Kohlberg to Coleman. Starting in November there were two or three, maybe more a week until the last week in March. That week there were eight to ten messages, but no more after Friday March 26th."

"Why would the Dean of Arts and Sciences call a young faculty member?" Tori asked.

"Maybe they got something going, you know, an affair," said Morrison. "Coleman was a womanizer."

Dottie almost choked on her Coke.

Tori laughed. "Have you met Dean Kohlberg?"

"No, why? What's so funny?"

"The thought of Coleman with that vitriolic harridan. Wait 'til you meet her," Dottie said.

CHAPTER EIGHTEEN

Tori walked into the sunny kitchen nook where her twelve-year-old son was scarfing down a mammoth bowl of cereal while playing with his X-Box. Sean looked up with Tori's green eyes. His dark hair, so like his father's, sent images of her ex-husband flashing across her mental screen and she felt an icy vise clamp her heart. She swallowed, trying to regain her composure, kissed Sean on the forehead and ruffled his curly hair.

"Hey, don't mess my hair."

"Sorry." She poured herself some coffee.

"That stuff stinks. Why do you drink it?"

"Same reason you're drinking Coke. It wakes me up," Tori said.

"Coke doesn't taste like kerosene."

She sipped her coffee. "Aunt Cindy called yesterday."

He grinned. "What's she up to?" He stopped eating and concentrated on his X-Box, which was sending out beeping noises.

"She's getting married."

"Isn't she married to Uncle Derrick?" He asked, attending to his beeping X-Box.

Tori threw her hands in the air, "That's Aunt Cindy."

"Aunt Cindy's hot."

"What do you know about hot?"

Sean shrugged and hunched over his cereal. Beep, beep, went the X-Box.

64

Tori gritted her teeth, determined not to complain about her son's X-Box. "I might be late this evening," she said as she got herself some yogurt and granola.

"What about our racquetball game?"

"I can't play tonight."

"Why not?"

"I'm doing a psychological autopsy."

"That's cool."

"Since when is a psychological autopsy cool?"

"Haven't you seen the *Profiler*?" Sean asked. He let go of his X-Box and looked at his mother.

"What?"

"It's this cool TV show about this forensic psychologist. They call her Sam. She's a profiler. She, you know, works for the FBI in Atlanta. She gets into people's heads."

Tori sighed. "Sean, I'm not a profiler."

"You're a forensic psychologist, aren't you?"

"Yes, but psychological autopsies are done on the victim."

"So who got offed?"

"Sean!"

"What?"

"I'm talking about a person – a human being – who was murdered," Tori said.

"Are you helping the cops find the perp?"

"You watch too much TV."

"Was he shot?"

"He was poisoned and I used to date his best friend."

"Matt?"

"No. I still date Matt. His friend's name is Steve DeMaio."

"The Arnold Schwarzenegger look-alike with the beard?"

"Yeah."

"He was cool. Not stuffy like Matt." Sean picked up his X-Box and the beeping started again.

"Matt's not stuffy."

Sean rolled his eyes. "Says you."

Tori finished her coffee. "See you tonight."

"Why you going so early?"

"I'm going to the gym before class."

"Too busy to play racquetball with your son, but you can play racquetball with Gladys." Sean stuck out his lower lip.

Tori thought, *He knows my weak spots, and how to give me a guilt trip.*

"Sean, you can't play racquetball now; you'd be late for school."

"So write me a note."

"Forget it. We'll play racquetball later in the week."

"You're afraid I'll beat you again."

Tori reached to ruffle his hair, but pulled her hand back. "That'll be a cold day in hell."

CHAPTER NINETEEN

Tori's pal Gladys Reinhart was the director of the campus Counseling Center. They played racquetball once or twice a month and met for lunch more frequently. Gladys was warming up on the court when Tori got there. They exchanged a few volleys and Gladys won the serve. Holding the ball in the air before she served, Gladys said, "I've got information about your psychological autopsy."

Caught off guard, Tori had trouble returning the ball. When Gladys got the point, Tori said, "Not fair. What information?"

"A couple of coeds came for counseling. They were traumatized by their relationships with Brad Coleman."

"Tell me more."

"Serve, girl, I'll tell you later."

Tori served and both women concentrated on the match. When Tori got the point, she held the ball and looked at her friend with a questioning look. "Who are the coeds?"

"You know I can't tell you names. I'd violate confidentiality."

"You think one of your clients murdered Coleman?" Tori asked.

"No. Absolutely not. Serve the ball, girlfriend."

Tori served and Gladys missed the shot. Tori held up her hand and asked, "What do you know?"

"Coleman used women. One might have cracked and become violent."

"Tell me," Tori said.

"Let me finish beating your ass. I'll tell you over orange juice," Gladys said.

After Gladys beat Tori in a close game, Tori said, "Congratulations. But, I'll get you next time."

"In your dreams, girl."

A few minutes later the women plopped into chairs in the coffee shop, breathing hard and dripping perspiration.

"I don't remember getting this winded last year," Gladys said. "It can't be age, can it?"

"Not a chance, girlfriend," Tori said. "Tell me about Coleman and your clients."

"Coleman taught creative writing and poetry. He encouraged students, more precisely psychologically coerced them, to write about intimate experiences."

"Writers are supposed to write about what they know, aren't they?" Tori asked.

"Yeah, yeah, but situations and settings familiar to the writer, not intimate details of their love lives. That's what Coleman wanted."

"So what?" Tori asked.

"So, female students got better grades if they described negative interactions."

"So far he didn't do anything worse than use poor judgment, maybe he was into voyeurism," Tori said.

"His assignments weren't the problem. Coleman used them to seduce students."

"No way! You're kidding!"

"I wish I were. Coleman belittled one client's relationship with her fiancé. When she tried to defend him, Coleman brought up negative things she'd written. He praised her forgiving nature and sensitivity. Then, ostensibly to help her write better, he invited her to his house."

"His house? Come on. She must have suspected something. No one is that naive." Images of naked girls on the cushions in front of Coleman's fireplace seeped into her head.

"It isn't as obvious as you think. Coleman held class presentations and poetry readings at his house. Students were flattered to get invited."

68

"He invited this naive coed to his house and seduced her?" Tori asked.

"Right. But the story doesn't end there. She fell in love. As soon as she broke her engagement, Coleman ditched her."

"The callous S.O.B. He enjoyed the pursuit, the conquest, but not the relationship. He enjoyed breaking hearts. Maybe he was a woman hater – just shy of a rapist," Tori said.

"He was attractive and charming enough to seduce women instead of raping them, but his motivation was the same – he wanted to dominate women."

"Why didn't they complain to someone?" Tori asked. The explicit photos resurfaced in her mind. "I hope I don't already know the answer."

Gladys looked into Tori's eyes as if she could read her thoughts. "He took revealing photographs of the women. He threatened to send them to their parents or boyfriends or the faculty if they told anyone."

"I was afraid that was the reason. I found some of those photos in his house. They were more than revealing – they were very explicit." Tori pulled on her earlobe. "There's another possibility. You know, sometimes a man who engages in a series of affairs is a latent homosexual, unaware of his sexual orientation and trying to find someone to awaken true love."

Gladys rubbed her hand over her mouth and cocked her head. "I didn't know him, so I can't make a clinical diagnosis, but based on women's stories, he was interested in domineering women. I think he was more likely aggressive than gay."

"Can I talk to these women?"

"No, I'm sorry, Tori. They're too fragile emotionally."

"If this was his typical way of treating women, I wouldn't be surprised if some rejected woman killed him."

"That's a pretty strong reaction to being dumped."

"I've been through that."

"You had an affair with Coleman?"

"No. I didn't know him. I was seduced by a high school teacher. I thought he was wonderful."

"He dropped you?"

"Not before giving me a going away present."

"That's sort of nice."

"Gonorrhea is nice?'

CHAPTER TWENTY

Tori described to her class the characteristics of the disingenuous psychopath and how he or she can make a good impression on people initially. She explained how someone with this subtype of psychopathy might crave attention which can be manifested through seductive behavior. She and the graduate students discussed the psychopath for some time before Tori dismissed the class. As she gathered her notes she thought about the disingenuous psychopath – that diagnosis would fit Coleman.

After class she met Morrison at the Police Department. The overcast weather dampened her spirits like rain on the last day of a beach holiday. She muttered to herself as she and Morrison walked to his car from the department.

"Where's little Miss Sunshine?" Morrison asked.

Tori asked, "What's that supposed to mean?"

"You're usually depressingly chirpy. Why the frown?"

"I hate dreary weather."

"Couldn't put the top down on your Boxster, poor baby?"

"Let me wallow in my bad mood."

"Damn, Tori, you sound like one of them spoilt Floridians."

"I like the sun, okay?"

"You had the sun yesterday and you'll get it again tomorrow."

"What've you got against sunshine, Morrison?"

"My roses need rain."

"Your what?" Tori could not keep the incredulity out of her voice. "You grow roses?"

"Yeah. Beautiful roses. Our yard in Jersey was the size of a kid's sandbox. Dry it was a dust heap, rain turned it to mud. Couldn't grow kudzu there."

"I didn't know you were a gardener."

Morrison winked. "There's a lot you don't know about me."

Tori looked at him.

"I'm a certified master gardener," Morrison said.

"I'm impressed."

"You're from the north. This would be a great day in Jersey."

Tori sighed. "It'd be a good day in Connecticut, too."

On their drive to the dean's office, Morrison told Tori that Whitherspoon was out of the hospital and back at the university. "Had a panic attack."

"He was pretty stressed talking about the dean," Tori said. She brought Morrison up to speed about her conversation with Gladys.

"Why'd the university keep that 'pervert' as a professor?" Morrison demanded. His voice was sharp enough to etch glass. His hands clutched the steering wheel so tightly his knuckles were white.

"No one filed a formal complaint," Tori said. "He threatened to show those horrid photographs to the girls' parents or boyfriends or the faculty if they said anything." She turned to look at Morrison. "Why are you so outraged? You're more upset about Coleman's treatment of women than about someone killing him. Are you a closet feminist?"

"No – a father. Every time I think about Coleman doing something like that to my eight-year old daughter, I want to kill him myself."

A daughter. That explains his reaction, she thought. "I didn't know you had a daughter."

"Yeah, yeah, there's lots you don't know." He winked at her.

Tori thought, *that goes both ways.*

Morrison clenched his fists. "This Coleman character took advantage of coeds. If he tried something like that with my daughter, I'd have broken the bastard's neck."

I wish my father had reacted that way instead of blaming me for being seduced by my teacher, Tori thought. *I'm glad now I didn't kill the prick, but at the time I would've loved to stick a knife in him.* "I wouldn't be surprised if one of his castoffs murdered him."

"You saying he didn't commit suicide?" Morrison asked in a more normal voice.

"I'm leaning in that direction, but I need more information. Coleman's an enigma. He preyed on young women but mentored teenage boys. I talked to the Director of the Boys & Girls Club. He said Coleman volunteered a couple of days a week to work with boys living in poverty. He'd started a foundation that would give the boys scholarships if they could get into college. Coleman was helping them fill out applications."

The dean's secretary showed Tori and Morrison into the cozy office and placed a pot of coffee and some cups on the small conference table where the dean was sitting. Dean Kohlberg, a tall stately woman in her mid-forties, was not beautiful by conventional standards. Even without the extra pounds she carried, her strong features and big bones guaranteed she would never be a raving beauty. However, she exuded energy and vitality. Her quick mind and extraordinary charm increased her magnetism. It was impossible to be in a room with Hilary Kohlberg without feeling her charisma.

The dean stood to welcome her visitors. "I assume you want to discuss Professor Coleman's death."

Morrison nodded. Then he introduced himself and Tori. The dean turned to Tori. "What is a psychologist doing with a detective investigating a murder?"

Tori explained about psychological autopsies. Tori thought she saw worry cross the dean's face before she said, "Oh, how interesting." The corners of the dean's mouth turned down. "Brad Coleman will be difficult to replace." *Was she concerned about replacing Coleman or was there some other reason for her reaction,* Tori wondered.

Morrison asked, "How well'd you know Professor Coleman?"

"He was a junior faculty member so our paths didn't cross often."

Morrison narrowed his eyes. "People say you got a motive to poison Coleman."

She jerked back in her seat. "People? What people?" Her voice was testy, but she was composed.

"I'm asking the questions." It was difficult to outdo Morrison in testiness.

"Are you accusing me of poisoning Brad Coleman?" The dean locked eyes with Morrison. They stared at each other, eyes in mortal combat, neither blinking. After a few moments, she stuck her chin out and said, "Whitherspoon. Of course, that curmudgeon Winston Whitherspoon." She turned to Tori. "Have you met Dr. Whitherspoon?"

When Tori nodded, she said, "You're a psychologist. You must have seen he's unbalanced. He hates the world and everyone in it."

"When we asked Whitherspoon about your motive to kill Coleman, he had a panic attack, "Morrison said.

"Probably worried you'd find out he'd lied."

"Where were you Tuesday morning – 7:30 to 9:30?" asked Morrison.

"I'm a morning person. I get to the office about 7:15. I drove in with Mary Rantala on Tuesday. Surely, you don't think I killed Dr. Coleman." She looked down her nose at Morrison. A loud thunder clap reverberated. She turned her head toward the window where rain poured down in sheets. "I hate Florida storms."

"You called Coleman a lot," Morrison said, his eyes boring into hers.

The dean did not blink.

"We have the English Department message book," Tori said. She observed that the dean had a nervous tic below her left eye and was clenching the table with her hands. Tori asked, "Isn't it unusual for a dean to talk so often with a junior faculty member?"

Noticing Tori looking at her hands, the dean folded them on her lap. "Yes, it was unusual," Kohlberg responded. "Whitherspoon opposed Coleman's tenure. If Whitherspoon convinced others in the department to vote against him, Coleman's tenure would be denied. He'd be fired. Dr. Coleman asked my advice and assistance. With my help he received tenure and was promoted at the end of March – there was no further need for calls or meetings."

"Why was Whitherspoon angry with Coleman?" Tori asked.

"Coleman was a thorn in Whitherspoon's side. He claimed Whitherspoon was out of the main stream and taught D.W.M. literature."

"D.W.M.?" asked Morrison.

"Dead White Males," Dean Kohlberg said.

Morrison grunted and the dean raised the right corner of her mouth in a one-sided smile. "Dr. Whitherspoon maintains no one's made a meaningful contribution to English literature since the end of the 19th Century," Kohlberg said. "He thought Dr. Coleman's courses lacked substance. Dr. Whitherspoon taught Shakespeare while Dr. Coleman was teaching Zora Neale Hurston."

"Their fight was over academics?" Morrison asked.

"Not completely." Kohlberg smiled a patient smile. "Coleman enjoyed antagonizing Whitherspoon. It was a game to him."

Morrison's cell phone rang and he answered it. "Morrison." After a pause he said, "Don't touch nothing. I'm on my way. I got Dr. Vincent with me."

CHAPTER TWENTY ONE

Tori shivered. Watery blue eyes stared at her – the eyes of a dead man. When the techs noticed her and Morrison, they stopped photographing the body and stepped out of Whitherspoon's crowded office. Morrison and Tori entered. The elderly professor's body was slumped over the desk, his head resting on his left arm, ashen face turned toward the door with unseeing eyes open. The greased strands of his scanty hair had fallen away from his pate, revealing bone white skin. His bowtie was askew and his rumpled navy jacket hung on the back of his chair. Guilt weighed on Tori as she gazed at the man she'd labeled a walking cadaver living in a mausoleum. Winston Whitherspoon was no longer walking and his body was lying in his mausoleum-like office. Sheets of rain pounded against the windows.

"Any note?" Morrison asked.

"Yes sir." Jason Nolan handed him a plastic bag holding a piece of paper. Morrison read aloud: "To Whom It May Concern, I'm going to join Louisa." He looked at Tori. "Who's Louisa?"

Tori shrugged. Morrison continued reading, "Louisa and baby Thomas came to me in the hospital when I was unconscious. It was the first joy I've felt since they were killed. I can't go on alone. Bury me next to Louisa and my baby. Signed – Winston W. Whitherspoon, Ph.D."

"Formal even in death," Tori said.

"Jason, check it's his handwriting." Morrison rubbed his chin. "What's this about Louisa and his baby being killed?"

"No idea, sir," Jason said.

Morrison asked, "Find what killed him?"

Jason handed Morrison two plastic bags. "We found these on the desk and an empty glass on the floor, sir. It looks like he took an overdose of Dalmane and Mogadon."

"What're they?"

"Dalmane is a muscle relaxant and Mogadon is a sleeping pill," Tori said. "Either one would have been toxic – together they are deadly."

"That's right, ma'am," Jason said, "The prescriptions are from the hospital. I'll check for fingerprints."

"What's going on?" demanded a strident voice.

Morrison and Tori turned to see Dr. Gibson standing outside the office. They ducked under the crime tape to meet him. Morrison said, "Dr. Gibson, I'm sorry, but Dr. Whitherspoon is dead."

"Oh, my God! Was it his heart?"

"No, an overdose."

Gibson looked from Morrison to Tori. "Suicide?"

"We're trying to determine that," she said.

"Dr. Gibson," Tori asked, "can you tell us who Louisa was?"

"Louisa was Whitherspoon's late wife. It was her death that turned him into such a curmudgeon." He sighed. "Shortly after Whitherspoon joined the faculty, his wife was killed by a drunk driver. I wasn't here then, but one of the long-time faculty people told me his wife's death traumatized Whitherspoon. He resumed the motions of living, but lost all feeling."

"And baby Thomas?" Morrison asked.

"His wife was eight months pregnant when she died. I guess they were going to name the baby Thomas. Whitherspoon never mentioned his wife or child to me. According to my source, Whitherspoon found solace in Shakespeare's poems and plays. It's hard to believe, but after his wife's death, Dr. Whitherspoon's lectures were so poignant they elicited tears from students." He sighed again. "It didn't last. He never updated his lectures and years of repetition made them stale. Now students snicker instead of weeping."

"Was Dr. Whitherspoon depressed or despondent since he got out of the hospital?" Tori asked.

Dr. Gibson peered at her over his glasses as if she were the dullest star in the sky. "Dr. Whitherspoon was always depressed and despondent."

Morrison turned to Jason. "Someone checking his house?"

"We'll check it when we finish here, sir."

"I want to see his house," Tori said.

"You don't ..." Morrison stopped. "I'll take you; don't want you breaking laws."

CHAPTER TWENTY TWO

David Harrison, Esq. Dottie walked through the glass door into what was a prototype for the struggling young attorney's office. Two thrift shop chairs crowded a faux wood table displaying an imitation brass lamp and a few old issues of *Time* and *Southern Living*. A plastic-framed poster of the scales of justice hung on the wall opposite the small window. The receptionist's desk, cluttered with papers and a computer decorated with stick-um notes, dominated the room. The clock on the far wall read 11:45.

The woman behind the desk asked, "May I help you?"

"Mrs. Harrison?"

"That's right. I'm Denise Harrison, legal assistant, secretary, scullery maid." The irritation in her voice matched her expression.

Dottie said. "I'm Detective Epstein – Dottie. I called earlier."

"Yes, I remember. And I promised you my husband would be back by 11:30 because I have to leave by then. The day care center gives us a tuition break for our pre-schoolers if I help out a couple days a week." Denise Harrison clutched her purse in her lap and checked her watch. "He can't always get out of court when he wants. Please forgive him." She gritted her teeth and took a deep breath. "God knows, I'm trying to."

As if on cue, loud footsteps bounded up the stairs and a young man with a huge briefcase, a square jaw and disheveled hair barged into the office. David Harrison introduced himself to Dottie. He brushed the rain off his shoulders and ushered Dottie into his office while breathlessly apologizing to her and to his wife for being late. He blew his exasperated wife a kiss as she raced out the door.

Dottie thought, *if Morrison considers Coleman's office a mess, he should take a gander at this place.* Harrison surveyed the office and shifted a pile of papers onto the floor so he could put his briefcase on his desk. Then he took his jacket off, shook off the rain and hung it over the back of his chair, loosened his tie, and sat.

Seeing Dottie standing, examining the clutter, Harrison jumped up. "Let me get that mess off the chair so you can sit." He piled more papers on the floor.

"What you see is my filing system: urgent papers on the desk, tomorrow's work on that chair." He pointed to an overloaded side chair. "I had a secretary until two weeks ago. She found a better-paying job – left with no notice."

Putting his hands behind his head, he tilted the chair back and sighed. "Sorry – enough about my problems. What can I do for you?"

"I found your name on a smartphone and want to know if the owner was your client."

Harrison sat up and rested his forearms on his desk. "My clients have the right to confidentiality. I don't have to disclose names." He ran his hand through his unkempt thatch of hair, flicking off the remaining rain.

"Your client is dead. You won't violate confidentiality."

"Who is it?" he asked.

"Bradford Coleman. We're investigating his murder and found your name in Coleman's Smartphone," Dottie said.

"Brad Coleman, sure. I read about his death."

"Why was Coleman seeing you?"

"I represented him in a couple of things – most recently a custody dispute."

"Custody of Coleman's son?"

"No, no. Someone else's children. A guy in town sued for custody of his children. He had evidence Coleman slept with his wife prior to the divorce."

"Was this man accusing Coleman of causing the divorce?" Dottie scrunched her nose. "Is that alienation of affection?"

"Yes," he said. "It is alienation of affection, and the husband blamed Coleman for the divorce, but that wasn't the issue. The husband needed Coleman's testimony to show his wife was an unfit mother. Coleman had sex with the wife while the kids were in the house." Talking out of the side of his mouth, he asked, "Tacky or what?"

"How did Coleman become involved with the wife?" Dottie asked.

"She was his student." He shook his head. "Her husband was livid – wanted the case spread across the front page of the *Gainesville Sun*. Coleman panicked. He didn't want anyone knowing the affair broke up the marriage." Harrison grunted. "Silly me, I thought he was concerned that the gossip would hurt the wife and children – he wasn't. He was covering his ass. He was up for tenure and didn't want to jeopardize his career."

"What happened?"

"We compromised. The husband and his lawyer agreed to delay the trial until Coleman got tenure in exchange for his testimony."

"Can you give me the names of the couple?"

"I guess so. It's public information. Janet and Jimmy Pillsbury."

"Jimmy Pillsbury threatened Brad Coleman with a gun at the university!" Dottie exclaimed.

"That's right. Coleman was terrified." Harrison grinned. "It got to Coleman. He realized he was mortal and not ready to meet his maker. He'd been volunteering for the Boys & Girls Club for years. Something happened a few years back that he said 'opened his heart to others,'" Harrison said, using air quotation marks. "After the incident with Jimmy Pillsbury, Coleman set up a foundation to fund kids through college. He did it anonymously. He didn't want the boys or the club to know he was the source of the money."

"You said something happened a few years ago. What was that?"

"Don't know." Harrison put out his hands, palms up. "Whatever it was he began to volunteer for the Boys & Girls Club. He enjoyed mentoring teenage boys. Said he wished his father had given him some attention."

"He didn't want people to know he set up the foundation? That was noble of him."

"He wasn't being noble. He didn't want every charity in Gainesville knocking on his door."

"Interesting," Dottie said. "Going back to Pillsbury, what does he do?"

"Jimmy Pillsbury runs a pharmacy, the one on the corner of Main and 14th. It's not called Pillsbury. He kept the prior owner's name." Harrison ran his fingers through his disheveled hair, again. "Sorry, the name slips my mind."

"I know the pharmacy. What about his ex-wife? What's she do? I understand she dropped out of college."

"Right." Harrison sighed before continuing. "She works at that big all purpose store out on 34th St."

"Any possibility Brad Coleman continued to see Janet Pillsbury during the divorce proceedings?" Dottie asked.

"Good Lord, no! You ever hear love and hate are two sides of the same coin? She hates Coleman worse than her husband does. I can't say I blame her."

"Why's that?"

"She wanted the divorce so she could be with Coleman – that's why Jimmy went gunning for Coleman. Janet told Coleman she'd give up her children for him. He told her to forget it – he wasn't getting killed for her. She went berserk –screaming and crying and threatening to commit suicide. He hung up." Harrison frowned. "You don't think Janet Pillsbury killed Coleman, do you?"

She shrugged. "From what you say, both Pillsburys had motives." She paused before asking, "Did you handle Coleman's legal affairs, too? Did he have a will?"

"Yeah, I wrote his will, but that was two, maybe three years ago. I don't remember details."

"Do you remember if he had much in the way of assets?"

"He came from money and his granny left him a bundle. He was loaded – that's how he set up the foundation. It'll take time to find the will and review the details," he said, indicating the papers strewn around his office. "Is it all right if I get back to you in a day or so?"

"Sure. And if you think of anything you forgot to tell me, please give me a call."

Denise Harrison was long gone when Dottie passed through the reception area on her way out.

CHAPTER TWENTY THREE

The little bungalow was probably sweet and appealing 20 or 30 years ago, Tori thought, *now it's sad.* The paint was faded, the grass more brown than green and overgrown bushes were invading the windows. Grey skies darkened the already melancholy setting. Morrison pulled out some latex gloves and handed Tori a pair. "Or you got your own?"

"Don't be a smart ass."

Morrison smirked and unlocked the front door. "Don't disturb nothing. The techs haven't been here." He led the way through the dinky living room. "Feels like a funeral home or something." Morison went down the hall and opened the first door. "Good God!" Tori caught up and followed his gaze – her eyes swept over an ancient lace nightgown laid down the center of a yellowed bed spread. Propped against the lacy shams was a faded portrait of a young woman's face.

"Macabre," said Morrison. "Like *Psycho* without the body."

"It's a shrine to his dead wife." Tori shuddered. "That must be a photograph of her and I bet that was her nightgown." She looked closer. "The spread is embroidered – probably a wedding present."

Morrison leaned over the nightgown. "Look here – lace is frayed."

"Yes. And there're marks on that side of the spread – like he knelt by the bed and rubbed the lace on her nightgown. Look, the carpet is crushed there."

"A sicko."

"More pathetic than sick – poor old guy." Tori felt icy fingers grip her heart.

Wilting roses in vases adorned the nightstand. Candles and more half-dead flowers on the dresser surrounded a large photograph of a bride. "That's the woman in the photo on the bed," Tori observed. A ceramic bowl in front of the photo held ashes.

"What the hell's that?" Morrison asked.

"I'd guess the heart-broken old soul wrote messages or poems to his wife and burnt them at her altar. That looks like the remains of a recent note." She pointed to a small piece of paper almost completely burnt.

"I'll get the techs to try and recover it." He opened the top drawer and grabbed a few papers. "Poems. Hand-written. 'Ode to Louisa.'"

"How tragic."

Morrison opened the other drawers – old yellowed lingerie wrapped in tissue paper. "Holy shit!"

Tori went to the closet – a half dozen old-fashioned dresses hung above four pairs of out-dated shoes. "He left everything the way it was when she died."

A flash of lightning followed on the tail of a clap of thunder. Tori watched as sheets of rain attacked the window.

"Let's get out of here," Morrison said. They went to the next room. It looked like something out of a horror movie – a cradle shrouded with moth-holed netting, faded blue curtains, a rocking chair with matching, faded blue cushions. A teddy bear on the dresser leaned against a ceramic Peter Rabbit. Dust covered everything.

"Looks like no one's been here for 30 years," Morrison said.

"That's about right. Whitherspoon's wife and unborn child were killed 28 years ago."

Morrison opened the door to the next room. Barely larger than the tiny nursery, it held a twin-sized bed, a nightstand and a small dresser. Tori picked up a framed photo from the nightstand. "It's Whitherspoon and his wife at their wedding. He looks happy. He had a nice smile."

The melody "Can You Feel the Love Tonight" sang out. Tori grabbed her cell phone. "Hi, Kiddo. What's up?" She listened. "I

84

can't bring your book now. We're going to the department to review the case."

"What's the problem?" asked Morrison.

"Sean left his physics book at home. He needs it for class."

"No problem. We'll swing by and get it before going back to the department."

Tori related Morrison's offer with a reprimand about forgetting needed work before hanging up the phone.

"Whitherspoon must have slept in here," Morrison said. Opening the drawer of the nightstand, he picked up a worn book – "Shakespeare." He pulled out the dresser drawers – a meager supply of neatly arranged underwear, socks, and bowties. Tori opened the closet – a couple of dark blazers and a few pairs of slacks.

Morrison shook his head. "Whitherspoon had a vendetta against Coleman. With Coleman dead, he had no reason to live." He turned to Tori. "So, a suicide, Doc?"

"Or an attempt to make it look like suicide. Either way we can cross him off the list as a murder suspect."

"Not necessarily. He might've committed suicide because he couldn't handle the guilt."

CHAPTER TWENTY FOUR

When Morrison and Tori got to her house, she invited him in for coffee. Morrison sat across from her in the sunny little alcove and looked out at her patchy back yard. "No yard service?"

"Sean does the yard work. He wants to dig up the backyard, fertilize it and put in new sod."

"Likes working in the yard?"

"He loves anything to do with nature. I wanted to move to a condo, but he begged for a house with a yard. He promised to mow the lawn. He's pretty dependable."

"He interested in flowers and plants?"

"Ah! The gardener. Sean loves anything that grows."

"I'll take him to the nursery some time. Help him pick out some bushes and plant them in the yard."

"That's kind of you."

"Don't often come across kids interested in gardening. My daughter rolls her eyes whenever I talk about it." Morrison downed the last of his coffee and looked at his watch. "We better get going."

Morrison followed Tori out the front door where she had difficulty locking it. Morrison pulled on the knob and said, "Try it, now."

"You're wonderful! I always have trouble with that lock."

The twosome stood together while Morrison demonstrated how to make the lock work.

"Am I interrupting?" an icy male voice asked.

Tori started and turned away from Morrison. "Matt… how nice to see you."

"You expect me to believe that?" He glared at Tori.

Tori asked, "What are you doing here?"

"You weren't at the university so I thought I'd check here. And this is…?" The tall man's eyes, as gray and cold as a mid-winter day, ran up and down Morrison.

"This is Detective Morrison. He's… He's from the police."

Morrison stuck out his hand. Matt waited longer than appropriate before shaking the extended hand. Tori attempted to take Matt's arm, but he pulled away. She stuffed her hands in the pockets of her slacks. Matt said, "I assume you had a nice time together."

"This isn't a social visit," Morrison said. "The doc and I are working on a case."

Matt's face registered disbelief. "You work at Tori's house. How convenient."

Tori looked up at Matt. "It is about a case. I'll call you later."

Matt cast an evil eye over Morrison, glared at Tori and strode back to his car.

"A little possessive, don't you think?" Morrison commented.

Dottie and Tori sat in Morrison's office looking at the whiteboards displaying the important evidence and suspects in the case. Morrison brought Dottie up to date on Whitherspoon's death. Then he described their interview with the dean. "She was nervous."

"You got under Kohlberg's skin. Did you have to be so harsh?" Tori asked.

"This isn't a popularity contest," Morrison said, "It's a murder investigation."

"She was tense. I'm not sure if she was hiding something or was angry at the way you questioned her."

"Who cares?" Morrison paused. "By the way, you're right – Kohlberg is not Coleman's type." He wore a smug smile.

Tori was concentrating on the white board when a loud crack of thunder hit simultaneously with a lightning bolt. She started.

"Guilty conscience, Doc?" Morrison asked. "Maybe you're not cut out for breaking and entering."

Tori gulped and sat up. She took a deep breath. "I didn't break in. I had a key."

"Where'd you get a key to Coleman's house?"

Oh God, thought Tori. *I can't get Betty Lou in trouble.* She said, "If I didn't search Coleman's house you wouldn't know he kept graphic photos of his lovers or that he was wealthy and had been married before." She stood up, hands on hips and leaned toward Morrison, sticking out her chin. "You wouldn't know about his ex-wife wanting money for their kid, either. If you'd let me search Coleman's house when I asked, I wouldn't have had to sneak around."

"You can't go breaking the law and want me to cover your butt."

"Cut it out, you guys," Dottie snapped.

Jason Nolan knocked on the door and stuck his head in the office. "Sir, there were no fingerprints on the vials of medicine Whitherspoon took."

"What does that mean?" Tori asked.

"Either someone wiped off the fingerprints, or he opened them with gloves or something, ma'am."

"Shit," Morrison said. "It could be another murder."

CHAPTER TWENTY FIVE

"Lot of people hated that Coleman guy, but my money's on Steve DeMaio as the murderer," Morrison said.

"Steve DeMaio wouldn't kill over a woman." Tori retorted, looking down and thinking, *I should know, he was the most emotionless man I ever dated. Why I went out with that unfeeling chauvinist is beyond me. But I'm sure not telling Morrison about it.*

"Maybe Coleman's ex-wife killed him for the insurance," Dottie said.

"He had insurance?" Morrison asked, taking a gulp of thick black coffee.

"I don't know about insurance, but his attorney says he was loaded. Harrison's checking on the beneficiaries of his will."

Morrison started a new list on the white board: Motives – money, women. "Anything else?"

"Grades," volunteered Dottie. "Russell Mills might not be the only one who got a bad grade."

He added grades to the motive list. "Dean Kohlberg is a dead end."

"I disagree," said Tori. "She's hiding something."

"Nah, Whitherspoon spoke out of turn. Maybe he wanted to get even with her or something. When we jumped on it he chickened out. That's why the panic attack," Morrison said. "I've questioned enough people to know when someone's lying."

Dottie said, "Research shows police are no better than the average person at detecting lies."

"Bullshit!" Morrison's face flushed. Glaring, he poked a huge finger in Dottie's face. "Don't play the intellectual egghead with me. Got it?"

"Got it." She gulped.

Tori watched Dottie's face. She was crushed. She'd been trying to relay information, not lord it over Morrison. Tori had no idea he was sensitive about Dottie's superior academic background.

Morrison's flash of temper vanished as fast as it had appeared and he switched gears back to the Coleman investigation. "That Mills kid wouldn't kill Coleman 'cause he flunked him. He'd get the grade changed," Morrison said, taking another swig of coffee.

"Like how?" Dottie asked.

Tori admired Dottie's spunk. Morrison chewed her head off and she came back and challenged him. She had to have steel-plated nerves to work with that dogmatic chauvinist.

"Like going over Coleman's head. Like, you know, complaining to the chair, the dean, the president, whoever."

"It isn't that simple," Tori said. "Professors have academic freedom. No one can change a grade except the professor who gave it. Everyone else can recommend the professor reconsider the grade, but the professor can refuse to change it."

"Why have grievance procedures? It's pointless." Morrison downed the last of his coffee.

"They expect the professor to follow the recommendation, but professors are obstinate."

"So if Coleman was a prick, he has the last word?" Morrison asked.

"Prick? Did you say 'prick'?" Tori asked. "Wait 'til my mother hears what you said in front of her little girl."

"I'm sorry. Did I offend you?" Morrison asked with feigned repentance.

Dottie looked from one of her colleagues to the other, confusion on her face.

"Back to Mills' grade," Morrison said, "What good is killing Coleman? Mills's stuck with the F and the guy what can change the grade's dead."

Dottie said, "Maybe for revenge."

"Nah, no way, but you question the Mills guy tomorrow."

Dottie said, "The murderer had to have an opportunity to give Coleman the poison."

"DeMaio had opportunity – played tennis with Coleman. He knew Coleman's routine, you know, drinking Pepsi after the game. He told us that," Morrison said.

"Wait a minute. Wait a minute. Back up a bit," Dottie said. "DeMaio says he didn't play tennis with Coleman this week."

"Yeah, yeah, sure, but everything says he did. As sure as you're sitting there, he's lying," Morrison said.

"I don't know..." Tori said.

"What'd Coleman's computer thing say about Tuesday morning?" he asked.

"Tennis with SD," Dottie answered in a low voice.

"See? I'm right. Or someone else have the initials SD?"

"All right, I give you that," Tori said. "It's unlikely Coleman knew anyone else with those initials. But that doesn't mean they played tennis together."

Morrison waved her speculation aside with his huge paw. Dottie gnawed on the second knuckle on her left index finger, deep in thought. Rain pounded on the roof.

"Don't dismiss my idea – hear me out," Tori persisted. "Coleman intended to play tennis with DeMaio when he put the initials in his Smartphone. But he might have changed his mind and didn't get around to changing the initials. Or maybe he was playing tennis with another woman and didn't want Trish to know."

"You saying Coleman was cheating on Trish?" Morrison asked.

Dottie said, "The next week he had tennis on his calendar, but he didn't have any initials."

"He forgot."

"Perhaps," Tori said. "But, think about it. Trish could have met Coleman at his office and poisoned the Pepsi bottle. She knew his routine, too."

Morrison began to pay attention. "You saying Coleman was fooling around on Trish and she killed him so he wouldn't dump her?"

"It's happened before. Coleman had a reputation for dropping women who thought he loved them," Tori said.

Morrison stopped. He rubbed his jaw, deep in thought. "I don't know. She was pretty shook up about his death."

"Could have been acting," Dottie said.

Morrison poured himself more coffee and took a drink. "Didn't look like no act to me, but she couldda put it on." Morrison hesitated. Then with more certainty, he said, "But nothing says Coleman was fooling around with anyone before the day he was poisoned."

"So? Who would he tell? Trish? Betty Lou?" asked Tori.

"Trish would be the last to know Coleman was fooling around on her," Morrison said. "DeMaio said Coleman called Monday night to cancel tennis."

"So what?" Tori asked.

"So if Trish killed Coleman because he was playing tennis with another woman Tuesday morning and he scheduled it Monday night, she did a heckuva lot of planning in one night," Morrison said.

Tori's shoulders slumped. "Good point."

Dottie said, "Want to hear about my meeting with Harrison?"

Morrison nodded and she told them what she'd learned about the Pillsburys.

"Why didn't you tell us right away?" Morrison asked.

"Neither of them could have murdered Coleman," Dottie said. "They couldn't get anywhere near him to poison his drink."

"That's for me to decide, not you. I'm in charge," Morrison said.

Dottie clenched her teeth and glared.

"We've sewn this up." He smiled. "Got motive and access to poison. My deputy found both the pharmacy and the place out on 34th sell cyanide."

Tori asked, "Which one do you think did it?"

"What do you mean which one – Pillsbury," he said.

"The husband or the wife?"

Morrison crinkled his brow and looked at Tori like she was crazy. "The husband, of course."

"Why, the husband, of course?" Dottie entered the fray.

"He threatened Coleman. She was in love with the bastard. Why would she kill her lover?" Morrison asked.

"He wasn't her lover anymore," Dottie said. "Janet Pillsbury was a scorned woman – Harrison said she hated him."

"Pillsbury got what he wanted: revenge on his wife and Coleman's testimony at the custody hearing," said Tori. "Why would he kill Coleman before he testified?"

Morrison thought for a moment while he knocked back more coffee. "Maybe Pillsbury thought his wife'd come back if Coleman was out of the picture."

"Poison is the m.o. of a woman," Dottie argued.

"Men use poison, too," Morrison countered. "Pillsbury's a pharmacist. He'd use a chemical."

"What about the opportunity to plant the poison in his drink?" Tori asked.

Dottie said, "His wife majored in chemistry and she works at a pharmacy."

"Check out that phone thing of Coleman's." Morrison jerked his head at Dottie. "Doc and me'll interview Pillsbury – the husband," Morrison said. "We'll check out the wife if we don't find nothing."

CHAPTER TWENTY SIX

Morrison knew the way to the small storefront – *Norton's Pharmacy and Gifts* – it was a short distance. The weather had cleared so they set out on foot. After walking in silence for a couple of minutes, Morrison said, "Mr. Norton ran the pharmacy for years, ever since I came to Gainesville. Wonder when he sold it."

"How long have you been in Gainesville?" Tori asked.

"Since '86."

"What brought you here?"

"It's a long story."

Tori observed a cloud crossing his face. "That bad, huh?"

"Yeah."

"Are you going to tell me?" Tori asked.

"Maybe, sometime after a few beers."

Morrison stopped to look at the travel posters in the window of a travel agency. "Ever been there?" he asked, pointing to a poster of Paris.

"No, I've always wanted to see the City of Light," Tori said.

"Ah, a romantic. Let's run away together to Paris – give Matt something to worry about."

Tori gazed at his reflection in the window and he winked at her. He stuck his hands in his pockets and they walked to the pharmacy in silence.

A young man, maybe in his late 20s, possibly early 30s, stood behind the high counter in the pharmacy, counting pills into a bottle. A nerdy guy with steel rim glasses, a slight build and light complexion, he was wimpier than Tori had expected. He didn't look like he owned a gun, much less threatened someone with it. But the sign on the counter read, J. J. Pillsbury, R. Ph.

The pharmacist looked up and asked, "What can I do for you?" He had a soft voice, rural Florida bred, Tori concluded.

Flashing his badge, Morrison introduced himself and Tori. "Official business."

Pillsbury looked taken aback and asked, "Am I in trouble?"

"We've got some questions," Morrison said in an officious voice.

Pillsbury called to the teenager putting over-the-counter medications on the shelves, "Mary Ann, we're going to my office. Please watch the store." He turned to his visitors and said, "Please, come this way." He led them to the back of the pharmacy where he unlocked his office.

Pillsbury leaned against the front of his neat desk, crossed his arms and asked, "What can I do for you, Detective?"

"Questions about Brad Coleman," Morrison said.

"I thought as much."

"You got the right to an attorney."

"Do I need one?"

"Not if you got nothing to hide"

"I've nothing to hide."

"Where were you Tuesday morning from 7:30 to 9:30?"

"I dropped my children off at the day care center at 8:00. I opened the store at 8:30."

"Anyone see you open the store?" asked Morrison.

"I don't think so."

"You threatened Coleman."

"Yeah, God knows there were enough witnesses. But, I didn't kill him."

"Why'd you threaten him?" Morrison asked.

"It's a long story."

"We've got time."

Pillsbury walked behind the desk, sat on his executive chair and motioned his visitors to sit on the two small folding chairs facing him. Tori took the one nearest her and Morrison gingerly lowered his over-sized body, engulfing the rickety chair intended for someone half his size. Tori's concerns about the chair's stability were interrupted by Pillsbury's clearing his throat.

"I guess you want to know about me and Janet. Janet, she's my wife..." He put his hands out palms up. "Uh, my estranged wife... we've been...married...uh...together for 12 years – since she was 18." He stopped talking. Pillsbury's eyes brimmed. He took off his glasses, pulled some tissues out of a box on the desk, went through the motions of cleaning them, rubbed his eyes with his finger tips and replaced the glasses on his nose. Pillsbury gazed at a photograph on the desk of him and his wife.

When it didn't appear he would continue, Tori asked, "Why did you move to Gainesville?"

Pillsbury flinched at her question as if he'd forgotten they were there, but he answered in a calm voice. "Gainesville isn't far from Palatka – we can visit our families. We dreamt of owning our own business and bought this place at a reasonable price. Janet went to college to get a degree in chemistry – she was going to be my assistant."

He pulled his lips inside his mouth. Tori thought it was his way of keeping them from trembling. Again, Pillsbury seemed lost in thought, staring above their heads, but this time he came back to his story without prodding. He pushed his glasses up on his nose and said, "We had great plans." He slumped in his chair. "Then Janet took a class with Coleman. He told her she was talented and he'd help her rework her essay for publication. She was excited and flattered..." He emitted a sarcastic laugh. "She took an independent study with him."

Morrison interrupted to find out what an "independent study" was.

Tori explained, "A student works one-on-one with a professor on some project."

Pillsbury snorted. "It was Coleman's way of getting her alone with him." He frowned. "She started staying late at the U. I didn't guess what was going on until she said she was leaving me for Coleman. I begged her not to go. I told her I'd forgive everything and we'd start over. She didn't want me or my forgiveness. She told me Coleman spent two days in our house *IN MY BED* while I went to mother's funeral. *MY MOTHER'S FUNERAL*." Pillsbury clenched his fists and slammed his right one on his desk, his face was red. "Can you believe that slime ball?" He shook his head. He opened his fists and said in a lower voice, "I lost it. I grabbed my gun and stormed out of the house. I went to the university and made a helluva fuss." Pillsbury buried his head in his hands.

"What happened?" Tori asked.

Pillsbury raised his head. "I was so distraught I might have killed Coleman if there were any cartridges in the gun."

"The gun wasn't loaded?" Tori asked.

"Of course not. I've got two little children – I wouldn't keep a loaded gun in the house. That's why Janet wasn't worried. She called me a blowhard. I went to the university and yelled for Coleman. This old geezer comes and starts egging me on, telling me Coleman should be shot. He says Coleman's the scum of the earth and I would be doing everyone a favor by eliminating him. Hearing the old guy ranting brought me to my senses. When Coleman saw I'd calmed down, he took me to his office to talk."

"What did Coleman say?" Tori asked.

Pillsbury straightened his glasses, more out of nervous habit than necessity. "At first Coleman tried to convince me there was nothing between him and Janet. When I told him Janet had confessed, he swore the affair was over and promised he'd never see her again. He said their affair was a fling. He winked and said he was sure I'd had my share of women. It was all I could do not to strangle him."

The young man stared into space for a long time. Morrison and Tori were beginning to get uncomfortable when he gave a big sigh and said, "I thought I got what I wanted. I came home and told Janet what Coleman said. When she didn't believe me, I told her to call him. Sure enough, the secretary refused to put her call through. But instead of reconciling with me, she packed her bags and went to stay with a girlfriend."

Pillsbury took off his glasses and rubbed his eyes. Then he replaced the glasses and sighed again. "I cried for two days. Then I decided to get even. I hired an attorney. I didn't want my children raised by a mother who fornicated with strange men. My attorney negotiated a deal – Coleman would testify in the custody hearing if

I delayed it until he got tenure. The case is scheduled to be heard in three weeks."

"Yeah, but you got so mad at Coleman you couldn't wait," Morrison said. "You killed him."

Tori cringed, convinced Morrison was mistaken.

"I didn't kill Coleman. Why would I do that? I needed his testimony to get custody of my children," Pillsbury said.

"Maybe he went back on your agreement," Morrison said.

"I have his signed deposition."

Tori managed to intervene before Morrison asked another hostile question, "When did you get his deposition?"

"Last Thursday – the week before he died. He got tenure a week or so before."

"Do you think Janet was angry enough at Coleman to kill him?" Tori asked.

"Absolutely not!" Pillsbury said in a firm voice. "Never! Janet could never hurt a soul."

Then Morrison pounced. "You'd rather have Coleman dead than testify. Maybe your wife would go back to you if her lover was out of the picture." Morrison was warming to his role as the hardnosed bad cop.

"Coleman was out of the picture. Janet tried to call him and he rebuffed her. She was distraught," Pillsbury's voice was rising to the level of Morrison's.

"How do you know that?"

"Her girlfriend told me." Pillsbury glared at Morrison. "I'm not answering any more questions without an attorney."

"That's your right." Morrison stood. "Don't leave town without telling me."

Tori asked, "Where does your wife live?"

"She's staying at Nancy Rourke's place over on Maple Lane."

Morrison said nothing, but Tori thanked Pillsbury for his time.

Tori and Morrison walked back to the station. Tori stopped to get her cell phone out of her car while Morrison went on to his office where Dottie met them 15 minutes later. Morrison sat at his desk, head down, arms over his head. "I'm sure Pillsbury did it, but I need proof to bring him in and fingerprint him."

"Why don't we check the prints I have on him?" Dottie asked.

"Wha..?" Morrison turned toward her in amazement.

"I stopped in the pharmacy after you left and asked for a brochure on breast cancer. Pillsbury found one and handed it to me."

Morrison gasped, "Is that what they taught you at that fancy college? Go around the law and plow over the rights of honest citizens?"

Tori blushed. "I phoned Dottie and suggested she do it."

For half a second she thought Morrison was not going to test the fingerprints. Then he whooped, slapped her on the back, and choking with laughter said, "Let's get those prints checked!"

CHAPTER TWENTY SEVEN

The three colleagues waited in Morrison's office while Jason Nolan compared Pillsbury's fingerprints to those he'd found on the bottle used to poison Coleman. Morrison's desk was clear except for a phone, a pen set, and an "in and out" box holding a few papers. On a credenza behind the desk sat a pot of coffee and some mugs. *No wonder Morrison commented about Coleman's clutter,* Tori thought. *His neatness borders on Obsessive-Compulsive.* Tori looked at the mugs, *Mets, World's Best Dad, My Irish Rose, Rose-Grower.*

Morrison poured some thick, foul looking coffee into the *Mets* mug and asked, "Coffee, ladies?"

Tori said, "Not if you mean that motor oil."

"I don't drink the stuff," Dottie said.

Morrison looked from one to the other and buzzed his secretary. "Get one of them fizzy cola drinks for the officer." He looked at Tori. "What about you, Doc?"

"May I have some bottled water, please?"

Morrison crushed a couple of bills into Barbara Jean's hand.

"It won't take long to tie this up," he said, after his secretary left.

"He didn't do it," Tori said.

Morrison looked at her in disbelief. "You're the one told Epstein to get the damn fingerprints."

"To prove he didn't do it."

"Bet you lunch at Burritos Bros. his fingerprints match."

"Make that the Purple Porpoise and you're on," Tori said.

When Barbara Jean brought Dottie's Coke and Tori's water, the two women thanked her. Dottie popped the can and took a gulp.

"That guy's guilty as sin," Morrison said. "Kept hesitating – making up stuff as he went along."

Tori shook her head. "He wasn't making things up. He was emotional. He was trying to control his feelings." She opened her bottle of water and took a sip.

"Hogwash!"

"She's a psychologist," Dottie said.

Morrison stood, hands on hips, glaring at Dottie. "What's this psychologist shit? You said no one can detect a lie."

Dottie looked across the desk at her boss, stuck her chin out and said in a measured tone. "I said cops are no better than lay people. Psychologists are trained to read people. Besides, how would Pillsbury get access to Coleman's Pepsi? Coleman wouldn't take a drink from someone who'd threatened to kill him."

"She's got a point," Tori said. "Besides, Coleman gave Pillsbury everything he wanted."

"You don't get men." Morrison said, shaking his head at the two women. "You take a guy's woman you take his manhood. Guys don't forgive and forget."

"He didn't forgive Coleman or his wife, he was getting revenge," Tori said. "The story would be all over the media and everyone would know Coleman sexually harassed Janet."

Morrison said, "Having it in the paper or on TV isn't good enough. A man wants his honor back."

"Yeah, in the old days a man could kill his wife if he caught her with a lover and not be arrested." Dottie gave Morrison a nasty look.

"Yeah, right." Morrison returned Dottie's evil stare. In a voice that could chill a drink, he said, "Should've kept that law."

Tori looked askance. "Surely, you don't mean that."

"I mean it." Morrison's face was red and Dottie pretended to look at something out the window, while he fumed and sat back behind his desk. He hesitated a couple seconds before grumbling, "No, I don't." He looked down. "Don't tell my wife what I said."

They had suspended hostilities by the time Jason came to the door and said, "Pillsbury's prints don't match those on the bottle, sir."

Dottie said, "Damn! Where do we go from here?"

Morrison winked. "Tomorrow I take you to the Purple Porpoise for lunch."

"Why don't we go now for an early supper?" Dottie said.

Morrison rubbed his hand over his mouth. "I can't."

"You taking Ruth out?" Dottie asked.

"Sort of. We're going to a ballet recital."

"A *WHAT*?" Tori asked.

"My daughter's in a ballet recital," he said with an embarrassed smile, "She's a fairy princess."

CHAPTER TWENTY EIGHT

Dottie checked her watch – 4:17. If she went to Russell Mills' house, she might catch him after work. The brightening day raised her spirits and she let loose a song as she drove. Just as well no one could hear her loud tune – it was off key. She drove east out S.R 20 past Hawthorne and turned north on S.R. 21 to Keystone Heights. She drove past Barnes Road, but found it after she made a u-turn and went back. It was a narrow, winding dirt path. Dense live oaks blocked the sun and she shivered, chilly with the top down. She searched for 2318 Barnes and spotted the number on a rusty mailbox. She turned into the driveway, a grassy area identified by tire marks, and drove through the open gate in the hurricane fence. The front yard of the small house was more dusty soil than grass, strewn with ancient appliances, empty crates, and a beat-up, once-green Ford truck on blocks. A scroungy yellow dog barked his annoyance at being disturbed by an uninvited visitor. She hopped out of her Suzuki and bent down. Dottie hadn't lived in rural Florida for four years without learning how to befriend a hunting dog. She talked to him and scratched behind his ears. When he decided she wasn't a threat, he escorted her to the front door.

A young man stood in the doorway watching her placate his dog. His neat preppy clothes were out of place in the rundown rural setting. He looked like a college student, tall and muscular. His hawk nose kept him from being handsome, but clear hazel eyes and a smile made him appealing. "Great watch dog, huh?" He petted the dog that was jumping on him and licking his face. "Anyone trying to rob us would be licked to death." He grinned. "Hi, I'm Russell Mills." He stretched his hand out to Dottie and they shook hands. "What are you doing out here?"

"Hi, Russell, I'm Detective Epstein from the Gainesville Police. I'd like to ask you a few questions. May I come inside?"

"Sure." He opened the creaky screen door.

The door opened directly into a miniscule living room. The tidy house lacked any hint of extravagance. Russell offered Dottie the upholstered chair, which proved to be uncomfortable when she sat in the sagging seat. She observed an archway to the kitchen and one doorway. The door was ajar so Dottie could see the sole bedroom. *Russell must sleep on the couch*, she thought. *Going to college could not have been easy for him.*

"What's this about?" Mills asked, from his perch on the arm of the couch.

Dottie thought, *Either he isn't anxious or he's experienced at hiding it.* "I'm investigating an incident at the University of Florida."

"I haven't taken classes there since last summer."

"Is that the class you had with Dr. Coleman?"

"Yes, ma'am."

"He flunked you?"

"Yeah – is that what this is about – Dr. Coleman's murder?" Mills asked.

"You were upset with Dr. Coleman over your grade."

"No kidding."

"Mad enough to kill him?" Dottie asked.

"Wait! Hold on a minute. That's a big jump. I didn't kill Dr. Coleman. Why would I do that? If he were dead, he couldn't change my grade and I couldn't graduate."

"Sonny, what's goin' on in there?" A small woman came out of the kitchen, wiping her hands on her apron. If the woman was Russell's mother, she'd led a hard life. He couldn't be over 21 and she looked at least 65 with gray hair pulled into a tight bun behind a wrinkled, weathered face. Her neat dress was so threadbare it was almost transparent.

"Momma, this is Detective Epstein from the Gainesville Police. She wants to ask me some questions about Dr. Coleman."

"Is the college gonna let you graduate now he's dead?" she asked.

Russell Mills got up and walked over to his mother. He put his arm around her shoulder. "Don't worry, Momma, I'll take care of it."

Mrs. Mills looked at Dottie. "It ain't fair. Sonny worked hard and did good. It ain't his fault his daddy lost his job," she spat.

"It's okay, Momma." He kissed the top of her head. The woman looked at Dottie and retreated to the kitchen. "Don't mind my mom. She's had a hard time this year."

"Russell, where were you Tuesday morning from 7:30 until 9:30?"

"Doing chores around here."

No sense asking if anyone saw him. His parents will lie for him in a New York minute. "There're damaging letters from you to Coleman. You made hostile threats. Tell me about it."

"Sure. Could we go outside and talk, though. I don't want to upset my mom any more." He walked over and opened the complaining door.

Dottie followed Mills outside and into the woods at the side of the house. The dog barked farewell. When they were well away from the house, he said, "I took Coleman's class last summer. I was going to graduate at the end of the semester." His pace was slow, he clasped his hands behind his back. "I had a 4.0 average and a job lined up at the *Gainesville Sun*. All I needed was a degree. I went to the first two or three classes and stopped going."

"Without withdrawing – so Coleman flunked you."

"That's right. I was too distraught to think about class. Pop worked at Keystone Heights Wood and Paper Mill for 34 years. Last spring they let him go – no severance pay, no retirement, no nothing. They laid off 60 folks. It was tough for everyone, but it devastated us. By midsummer we ran out of money, and the garden didn't produce much and Momma... Momma always had a drinking problem and she..."

He shook his head and was silent for a moment. "She was drunk all the time; she sat and cried. She wouldn't get up in the morning, she wouldn't eat and she wouldn't talk, she cried and drank. Pop and I took her to the clinic in Jacksonville, but they wouldn't admit her without insurance. Pop got mad and made a fuss. They called the cops and arrested him. I didn't have money for bail. Pop was mortified. He'd never done anything illegal." The pain in Russell Mills' voice cut into Dottie's heart. Dottie made encouraging sounds as she walked with him deeper into the woods. A hawk circled over their heads. Mills stopped and looked at the bird.

"I had to take care of Momma. I took her to the county detox center. She begged me not to leave her, but I didn't know what else to do. I was afraid she'd die if I left her home. I couldn't get her to eat or anything." His voice broke and he stopped talking. A squirrel jumped on a branch above their heads, shaking the tree and startling Dottie. She cringed. Walking in the woods was arduous – the path strewn with rocks and broken branches. Russell bent down, picked up a thick branch obstructing their way and began tapping it against trees as they walked.

After a pause he said, "I didn't think about college. I couldn't. I tried to borrow money to get dad out of lockup. Pop wouldn't let me ask Momma's family and his kin have nothing. I needed a job. Pop spent three days in jail – it broke his spirit. When he found I'd put Momma in detox, he cried. I'd never seen Pop cry. Somehow it was worse than Momma crying." Anger replaced his pain as Mills described his helplessness. He took the branch he'd been playing with and cracked it over his knee. Dottie noted his muscular shoulders contracting as he broke the limb. He held one piece of the limb in each hand.

"Momma came from a good family. They disapproved of my dad. Momma and Pop wanted me to be a success so they could tell her family I graduated from college. No one in my father's family ever went to college. My mother's family thought he was dumb and I was worse.

"Pop never made much money. Momma didn't complain, but she drank. The last couple years I'd come home in the afternoon and Momma would be in bed. When she got up, she was unsteady. The professor discussed alcoholism in my abnormal psych class and I realized what her problem was. I tried to talk to Pop about it, but he wouldn't listen – he was in denial – something else I learned in psych. He said Momma gave up an easy life for him. So we all continued the way we were – pretending life was fine. I loved college and they were proud of me. Then the world fell apart."

Russell threw the two pieces of the branch against a tree, one at a time, his face full of rage. Wham! Wham! Mills' face contorted. He spit out the words. "I begged Coleman to change the grade. He said I was spoilt. He said he wouldn't feed into my overindulgence by bending rules. He was sick of students who thought the world owed them a living."

"He had no idea how hard it was for you to go to college."

"College wasn't handed to me on a silver platter like it was for him. He drove around in his red sports car, wearing designer clothes, and traveling the world. He didn't have a clue what it was like to be poor. He gave high grades to the foxy women, but flunked me because I'm supposedly spoilt. What right did that self-righteous bastard have to judge me?"

Mills picked up another thick branch and slammed it into a tree. Wham! Chips flew in every direction. Dottie's brain clicked into gear. *I'm in deserted woods with the man who probably murdered Brad Coleman. What was I thinking? I saw those threatening letters. No one knows I'm here. I'm not even sure how to get back to the Mills' house.* Dottie started back in the direction they had come.

"I was at my wit's end." Mills' voice was full of anger. "Pop was distraught with Momma in detox; but even with my job at the convenience store, we couldn't afford the clinic. We barely had enough for the mortgage and food. Then that pampered intellectual snob who never lacked for anything called me spoilt! I lost it. I sent him a scathing letter full of all my frustration. I told him a pompous, uncaring asshole had no place teaching at a university. I told him that grade would be changed...or else."

Russell Mills was raging and Dottie backed away, sizing him up. He was in good shape and outweighed her by 60 or 80 pounds. But Dottie had grown up Black and Jewish in a tough Irish neighborhood in the Bronx. She was hard and street smart. She never backed down from a fight, earning her the respect of the local gangs. There was easier prey on the streets than the wiry black girl who fought to the death. She'd also been the terror of her police academy class.

She was pretty sure Mills didn't have a weapon. His slim-fitting slacks and short-sleeved shirt didn't leave a place to hide one. She was not wearing her gun today. She came here on the spur of the moment. She thought, *That would make the perfect epithet on my tomb, "I wasn't thinking."* Her hope was to give him a scrotyshot.

Russell grabbed her upper arms above her elbows, immobilizing her arms against her body. "Do you have any idea how much I hated Coleman?" Mills asked as he tightened his grip, murder in his eyes.

CHAPTER TWENTY NINE

"Sean, I'm home." Tori dropped the bags on the kitchen table. "Come set the table for dinner."

The pre-teen bounced into the kitchen, "Hi, Mom."

He hugged his mother and she looked at him, thinking, *he's as tall as I am.*

"What's for dinner?"

"Boston Chicken."

"Another gourmet meal prepared by the next Julia Child."

"Cut the sarcasm." She grinned. "Set the table for three."

"Who's coming for dinner, Mom?"

"Matt."

"Oh."

"Aren't you the enthusiastic one?"

"God, Mom. He's so *wet*."

"What's wet?"

"You know – limp, dull…"

Headlights flashed across the kitchen windows. A moment later the doorbell rang. "Go answer the door and mind your manners."

"Yes sir, Mom."

Matt, dressed in a blue polo shirt and pressed khakis, strolled into the kitchen. "Hello, gorgeous." He kissed Tori on the cheek. "Thanks for calling. I'm glad you set me straight about the big detective. I didn't realize you had come from a death scene and stopped to get Sean's book for him."

"Sorry for the misunderstanding, Matt. Glad you could make dinner."

Matt handed her a bottle of wine.

"Pinot Grigio. Thank you – perfect with chicken," Tori said.

"May I sniff the screw top?" Sean asked.

"Sean!" Tori said. "I told you to cut the sarcasm." She was not smiling.

"Don't be hard on him. He's quite funny," Matt said, squeezing Tori's shoulders.

"Sit down. We don't want the food to get cold," Tori said, giving Sean a stern look she hoped would halt his caustic remarks. Tori unpacked the food, placed the chicken on a platter and passed it to Matt. As he served himself some chicken, he asked, "Sean, what did you learn in school today?"

Sean reached for the mashed potatoes, heaping them on his plate. "Nothing."

"Sean, you must have learned something," Tori said, mentally sending him a message she was going to kill him as soon as Matt left.

"I had in-school suspension."

"*WHAT??*" Tori asked.

The phone rang.

Sean jumped up. "Saved by the bell."

Tori said, "Let it ring." But Sean was already answering it.

"Hi, Nana."

Tori closed her eyes and took a deep breath. Matt patted her hand.

"Nana wants to talk to you, Mom." Sean smirked.

"Tell her we're eating."

"I did. She says it won't take long and it's important."

Tori grimaced and walked to the phone. "Hi, Mom."

"I've been calling all day. Where were you?"

"Nice to hear your voice, too."

"Cut the sarcasm."

Tori thought, *damn, I've become my mother. And my son talks to me the same way I talk to her.*

"Sorry, mother. Why were you calling?"

110

"Your sister needs you."

"Why does she need me? She has all those husbands at her beck and call."

"Tori, I told you to cut the sarcasm. You're a psychologist. You should know your sister needs you when she's going through a divorce."

"She initiated the divorce. It's Derrick who needs a psychologist."

"Derrick was abusive."

"He hit Cindy?" asked Tori. "She didn't tell me that."

"No, he didn't hit her. He was psychologically abusive. He isolated her from her family and friends. You told me that's what abusive husbands do."

"For someone isolated from people, Cindy found a new husband fast enough."

"Victoria, call your sister and talk to her. She needs your counseling."

"If you say so."

"Where were you all day?"

"I'm doing a psychological autopsy."

"Isn't the university paying you enough?"

"It has nothing to do with money, Mother. I do it to advance my career."

"No wonder you can't find another husband – working with dead people."

Tori closed her eyes and took a deep breath. "Mother, the people I work with aren't dead. We work together to find out what caused the death of the deceased person."

"That's morbid."

"Mother, I'm a forensic psychologist. That's what I do." Tori counted to ten.

"Victoria are you there?"

"Yes, mother, I'm here."

"Stop calling me mother. You do that when you are annoyed."

No shit, Tori thought. "Sorry, Mom."

"Are you dating anyone?" her mother asked.

"I'm trying. As a matter of fact, Matt is here for dinner. So I'll talk to you later. Bye."

CHAPTER THIRTY

"Get your hands off me or I'll arrest you for assaulting an officer." Dottie used her meanest voice, while preparing to knee her assailant's privates.

Mills looked at her in a daze and stood motionless for a moment. Then he freed her arms. "Sorry, I didn't mean to scare you."

Dottie backed away from Mills, rubbing her arms.

Mills clutched his head and looked at the sky saying, "Hell, I'm venting. I didn't know I had so much emotional garbage left about that grade." He looked at Dottie, his hands out, palms up. "I didn't kill Coleman and I sure as heck didn't mean to frighten you."

"I need to get back to town." Dottie backed further away from Mills.

"Where are you going? You don't think I'm going to hurt you, do you?"

"Let's go back to the house." Dottie was using her training, assuming her "bad" stance and calming voice.

Mills walked toward Dottie with his hands up in the air. "You act like I'm a criminal. Do you think I'm threatening you? Why would I do that? I wanted you to know what Coleman was like. I hated Coleman. But he changed my grade to an "Incomplete." I'm retaking the course this summer. I've already registered."

"When did Coleman change your grade?"

"A couple days after I sent that awful letter, I realized I'd never get him to change the grade with threats. So I talked to Betty Lou Hancock. I went to high school with Johnny Hancock and Miz Hancock knows my folks from First Baptist Church. She went with me to see Dr. Coleman. He was real annoyed, but Miz Hancock told him about my circumstances and he agreed to change my grade to an "Incomplete." She brought him the forms – all filled out. He said I'd have to work harder for him than I'd worked in any other class, but I don't mind hard work. I was thrilled to get another chance."

Dottie heard Mills' dog and his house appeared through the trees. Dottie realized they were approaching the house from the other side. She breathed a sigh of relief. But, she couldn't refrain from asking another provocative question. "Why didn't you want your mother to hear our conversation if you already got the grade changed?"

"I told Momma about the grade change, but she'd be mortified if she knew I told Miz Hancock about her drinking and being in detox. I didn't tell Miz Hancock that part. Miz Hancock is sweet, but she gossips. My mom is a proud woman."

"You know I can check your story?" Dottie said.

"I hope you do. It's not a story; it's the truth."

Mills extended his hand. "I'm sorry I frightened you. I'll watch my emotions."

CHAPTER THIRTY ONE

Dottie gripped the steering wheel to keep her hands from shaking – she was having a delayed reaction to her encounter with Mills. She felt her heart thumping against her chest. A lump constricted her throat, impeding her swallowing. She couldn't catch her breath.

How could I be so stupid? What was I thinking – going unarmed into isolated woods with a murder suspect? And not telling anyone where I was going. I couldn't win in hand-to-hand combat with a man that much bigger than me.

I could say instinct told me Russell Mills wasn't dangerous, but I'd be lying. No one can tell by "instinct" who is and isn't dangerous. Theodore Bundy was able to kill a slew of young women because he was handsome and charming – like the man I followed into the woods. There's no way around it. I was careless and stupid.

She sped into town and screeched to a stop in front of the Police Department – a one-story brick building in downtown Gainesville. She rushed to the front desk where Deputy Gary Ridaught greeted her, "Decided you couldn't live without me, Dottie?"

Ridaught hit on Dottie every time he saw her. He was the last person she wanted to see.

"I'm looking for Jason Nolan," she said. Her voice was cold.

"That's an excuse to see me."

"Sure, Gary, but meanwhile, where's Jason?"

"He'll be out in a minute. When are you gonna buy me a beer?"

Usually Dottie exchanged banter with Ridaught and kept it light. Tonight she was too upset to play nice. "Gary, even if you weren't married, I wouldn't be interested."

"Uppity black bitches like you need to be taken down a peg," he snarled, turning back to his paper work.

Jason came around the corner as they were finishing their exchange. "Hey, Dottie. Flirting with Deputy Ridaught again?"

She gave Jason a scathing look before asking if he'd join her for a beer.

"This is an unexpected pleasure." Jason smiled at Dottie.

Ridaught said, "I don't suppose Kitty knows her boyfriend is going out with another woman. An uppity black bitch at that."

"Fuck off, Ridaught." Jason put his arm around Dottie, guiding her away from the front desk. "What's up? Something wrong?"

"I'll explain at Huckabee's. I need to unwind."

"You're shaking. Are you all right to drive?"

"Barely."

Dottie pulled into the parking lot behind Jason's jeep and found a space among the Ford and Chevy pick-ups and decades old American cars with faded paint and falling headliners. Chrome, tinted windows, and gigantic tires interspersed with rust and dents in the red dust of Huckabee's parking lot – Waldo's other beer joint besides the pool hall. The cedar-sided dive, built when Gainesville's Alachua County was dry, was across the county line. Smoke and honky-tonk music engulfed Jason and Dottie as they walked into Huckabee's. The low lights and smoke fumes made it difficult to find a table. Dottie said, "If there's anything to the dangers of second hand smoke, Huckabee regulars are an endangered species."

The local after-work crowd swarmed: young singles from town, people working in Starke's prisons, a few farmers, some deputies, and one or two groups of college kids. The kids were dancing the Cotton-Eye Joe while locals were doing the swing. Locals cast evil eyes at the college crowd encroaching on their territory, but the kids were oblivious. The students wore designer jeans, shiny boots, and exaggerated country shirts with fringes, embroidery, sequins, and stones, while the locals wore faded plaid shirts, well-worn boots and jeans.

Jason and Dottie made their way to a table far from the band and dance floor before ordering two beers on tap. Dottie took a big gulp and unloaded on Jason about the incident at the Mills place. Expressions of shock, concern and fear followed one another across Jason's face before he said, "At least you had a gun." Dottie flushed. Jason asked, "Didn't you?" She looked down rubbing her sweaty hands on her slacks and shook her head.

"What the hell were you thinking, Dottie? You could've been killed. You interviewed a murder suspect alone? You didn't tell anyone where you were?" Jason threw his hands in the air, "And no gun."

"Don't you think I've been telling myself the same thing?"

"It's a little late for that, Dottie. You should have told yourself before you went." He sighed. "At least Sonny Mills is a decent kid."

"You know him?"

"I met him at Billy Cameron's – a new guy in tech," Jason said. "They went to high school together. But don't change the subject. Where was your head?"

Dottie rubbed her forehead. "This was the first time Morrison let me interview a suspect by myself."

"Good job, Dottie. Morrison would have found your body and arrested Sonny."

"Fuck you, Jason!" She tossed a beer coaster at Jason, who caught it and laughed.

"I was kidding, Dottie." Jason took her hand across the table and said, "C'mon, chill out."

When Dottie smiled, he said, "You be careful, girl. I don't want you hurt."

"Me, neither."

Jason held on to her hand. He said, "Count your lucky stars. You can't let your guard down."

"I've been in Gainesville too long – I've lost my edge. I'd never have done that in New York." She eased her hand away, uncomfortable with the way Jason was gazing into her eyes.

"You can't in Gainesville either, Dottie. The world isn't a nice place."

"Thank you for being here."

Jason took her hand again. "Let me see you home."

"I'll be fine."

"I'm not worried about you. I want to go home with you."

"What about Kitty?" Dottie asked.

"Kitty and I called it quits."

Dottie scrutinized Jason. It was not concern she saw in his eyes.

CHAPTER THIRTY TWO

Without an alarm, Tori woke at 6:00 a.m., hopped out of bed, threw on her sweats and drove to campus for her 6:30 aerobics class. Like a light bulb, she was either off or on. She was never groggy upon awakening. She greeted a new day anticipating the fun it would bring. Gerry, her ex-husband, had enjoyed her high spirits later in the day, but hated her eagerness in the mornings. It took 20 minutes before he was out of the twilight zone and awake.

When she finished her workout, Tori went home to get something to eat while she cooled down before showering. Sean was yawning over his history book, resting his head against his hand, preparing for his exam.

"What's up, sport?"

"Could you turn down the cheeriness a notch?"

Tori kissed her son's head and started cutting up fruit for her breakfast. *His father's son,* she thought. "Want some strawberries on your cereal?"

"Yeah, if I don't become a smiley face."

"Who were you talking to on the phone last night?"

"Dad."

Tori turned to her son. "What did he want?"

"He wants me to visit him this weekend."

"You're kidding!"

"Mom, I gotta study."

Tori met Dottie at the 43rd Street Deli & Breakfast at 8:30. Dottie was drinking her customary Coke when Tori slid in next to her.

"You look upset," Tori said.

Dottie described the incident with Russell Mills.

"Dottie, that's horrible. Are you all right?"

"Yeah, I am now. I was a wreck last night." She looked at Tori, "You look worried yourself."

"You're observant. I'm the psychologist."

"I read people pretty well."

"My ex-husband called Sean last night." Tori sighed. "He wants him to visit."

"What's wrong with that?"

"Gerry hasn't initiated a visit with Sean since our divorce. Sean was three then – he's 12 now. I usually have to coerce Gerry into seeing his son."

"That stinks."

"Yes. He's busy screwing every woman in Atlanta. It doesn't leave time for his son."

"What's changed?"

"I don't know. He remarried a couple years ago – a high-powered attorney with a beautiful body and nasty mouth."

Dottie raised her eyebrows, "Do I detect a hint of animosity – perhaps jealousy?"

Tori blushed. "I thought Gerry and I were soul mates. We married after college and went to graduate school together. I'd never been so happy. Our lives were wonderful until I got pregnant. He wanted me to get rid of the baby. I was horrified and refused.

"When I got the job at the University of Florida, I suggested he not come with me. I thought he'd beg me to forgive him." Tori clasped her hands together and brought them to her mouth. The pain was so intense it took a moment before she could speak. "Instead, he said 'fine.' He filed for divorce while my son and I were driving to Gainesville. My whole world collapsed."

Morrison's resounding voice interrupted, saying to Dottie, "How do you drink that stuff on an empty stomach?"

"My stomach's not empty. I had a bowl of raisin bran and a banana an hour ago. Besides, it's better for you than coffee."

Morrison threw his uniform hat on the bench and slid in opposite the women. The waitress brought his coffee without his asking. Morrison came in every Friday morning for black coffee and a full cooked breakfast.

"What's with the uniform?" Dottie asked.

"For the Memorial."

Tori watched Morrison avert his eyes as he responded to Dottie. *He's lying,* she thought. *Why is he lying about his reason for wearing a uniform? He looks good in the uniform. He's a nice looking man – rugged-looking, tan and fit, even if his waistline is expanding. He reminds me of Gerry in a way.* Tori stopped herself. *Why are you comparing Morrison to Gerry? Cut that out. He's married.* She asked, "How was the ballet recital?"

Morrison's face was transformed by a huge smile. "Jennifer was great. Looked like a fairy princess. The happiest I've ever seen her."

"Proud father."

"You bet."

Morrison hoovered down his meal and said, "Epstein, check Coleman's computer. See if you missed anything. Doc and I are going to visit Mrs. Pillsbury."

CHAPTER THIRTY THREE

On the ride to their interview Morrison told Tori, "Nancy McBride Rourke's family's been in Florida for generations – came from Scotland. Nancy's father and husband are dentists." SCREECH!!! Morrison jammed on his brakes and Tori braced her arms against the dashboard to keep from slamming into it. "Damn – that's dangerous," Morrison said. "Must've fallen in yesterday's storm." He turned to Tori. "You all right?" She nodded. He negotiated the car around a huge branch blocking half the road. He reported the location of the branch to the dispatcher.

"Where was I?" He stopped at a red light. "Nancy's dad hired her husband into his practice. Rumor is old Doc McBride hired Rourke less for his dental skills than to please his daughter. Nancy thought he was 'adorable.' Sure enough, not six months later they were engaged. Been married going on four years."

"How do you know this stuff, Morrison?"

"Gainesville's a small town. Guys on the force have lived here all their lives. Make it their business to know everything about everyone."

"I hate to think what they know about me."

"You don't want to know." He glanced at Tori and winked.

Tori shivered. *What does he mean?* She worried.

Morrison pulled his squad car into the driveway behind the Rourkes' SUV. The Rourkes' large, ancient house with an index card-sized front yard was in a once prosperous section of town. In

121

a larger city it might have formed the historic district. In Gainesville, the area was home to young professionals uninterested in renovating – waiting until they could afford to move to more upscale homes. Morrison rang the front doorbell. A screen door separated the house from the porch with the wooden front door open to let in the spring breeze. Nancy McBride Rourke answered the doorbell, trying to keep a toddler from escaping into the yard. Morrison took off his hat and asked if Mrs. Pillsbury was in.

"Yes, of course. Please, come in, Officer." The toddler squawked when Nancy clutched her arm while opening the door.

"This is Dr. Vincent, from the University."

Nancy cocked her head, "Didn't I see you working out on campus?"

"Yes, I thought you looked familiar."

Nancy smiled. "I'll get Janet for you. She's in the kitchen." She carried the still squawking toddler down the hall.

An old-fashioned hat stand inside the front door held a baseball cap, a child's straw hat, and a sun visor. Two tennis rackets and a baseball bat rested in the umbrella holes and three Florida Lottery tickets protruded from the mirror's frame.

Janet Pillsbury entered the foyer, an attractive woman, but far from the beauty her husband had described. Dressed in blue jeans with a crisp striped shirt and tennis shoes, she looked as if she'd stepped out of a Land's End catalog – clean-cut and preppie. Her voice was soft and her demeanor shy. Tori introduced herself and Morrison to Janet. "We want to ask you a few questions."

"Sure, we can go into the parlor," Janet Pillsbury said, indicating the room to the right off the foyer.

Morrison shoved his uniform hat into Janet's hand, preceded her into the room and sat on a large overstuffed chair. Janet looked at Morrison with raised eyebrows, but placed his hat on the hat rack. Tori sniffed her disapproval at Morrison's behavior. *I was beginning to believe there was a heart beating in that barrel chest,* she thought. *He's an arrogant male chauvinist.* Tori motioned for Janet to go ahead and sat opposite her on the twin to Morrison's chair. Sitting forward in the chair Tori began the questioning, as she and Morrison had agreed on their ride over. "We need to ask you questions in relation to Brad Coleman's death," she began.

"I figured as much."

"I'm trying to understand Dr. Coleman's state of mind before he died. Did he ever appear depressed or moody?"

"He used to get down – he called it going into a black hole. He didn't tell anyone."

"How do you know, if he didn't tell anyone?"

"One day I called and there was no answer, so I went to his house to leave a note. His car was parked in the driveway, so I rang the bell. When there was no answer I tried the door and went in."

"And...?"

"He was lying on the couch. He had closed the drapes and was listening to depressing music. He told me to go away. He wouldn't talk. Later he told me he got these black moods and not to tell anyone."

"What was your relationship with Brad Coleman?"

"I had an affair with him. Everyone knows." Janet Pillsbury looked down at her hands.

"Mrs. Pillsbury, can you tell us how you became involved with Professor Coleman?" Tori asked in a gentle voice.

Janet Pillsbury curled a lock of hair around her finger and chewed it. She took a breath and released the hair. "I needed a course in lit last fall. Dr. DeMaio suggested I take Brad's course. He was a good teacher. For the first time I enjoyed literature and writing." Janet leaned to one side so she could pull a tissue from her jeans pocket. She patted her eyes with the tissue and pulled her legs up, hugging her knees, appearing to shrink into the corner of the sofa.

"I was a fool. I knew he screwed anything in a skirt, but I believed him when he said his feelings for me were different... special. I thought he loved me." She huffed. "He didn't. I was a challenge because I was happily married."

She put her legs down and leaned toward Tori, oblivious to Morrison. "I'd always been a nobody – the mousey girl from Palatka. When Mary Anne and Nancy told me I was lucky Dr. Coleman was interested in me, I felt important. I daydreamed about him." Janet sighed, twisted her tissue, and pulled her legs up again. "I made the mistake of writing about my fantasies for a class assignment. He didn't hand my assignment back with the others. He told me to pick it up in his office. When I went to his office, he closed the door and kissed me. He said he wanted to make all my fantasies come true. It was romantic – I crumbled. I kissed back and then... You know ..." Janet pulled her lower lip in between her teeth for a moment and patted her eyes. A grandfather clock rang the quarter hour. "We'd be together every weekday until I picked up the kids from day care. I was in love with the fantasy, not the man." She looked at Tori, "Do you know what I mean?"

When Tori nodded, Janet continued. "I was obsessed with him. At first I was terrified James would find out. Then as Brad seemed to become serious I thought about leaving James." Janet wept softly as she described her seduction. "I invited Brad to spend the night when James went to Palatka for his mother's funeral. James called and we talked while Brad was in bed with me. Brad said I was a devil with the eyes of an angel. I was flattered. Can you believe that? I was flattered because I was hurting a man whose sin was loving me." Janet wiped her eyes and stared into space. She sat scrunched up at the end of the couch, legs pulled up and head buried in her knees.

After a few moments, Tori urged her in a gentle voice, "What happened?"

Hugging her legs closer, clutching the soggy mass of tissue like a baby holding her favorite toy, Janet braced her chin on her knees, looked at Tori and said, "Brad said he wanted to spend every minute with me. Fool that I was I thought he wanted to marry me. My marriage to James was our obstacle. Brad said he wouldn't interfere with my happiness." She pushed her hair behind her ears.

Janet put one foot on the floor, her voice rising. "Brad didn't care about my happiness. I was an idiot. I told James I was leaving. James begged me not to go but I wanted my freedom. James is a good man. I thought it would be easier for him if he got mad, so I told him about Brad staying in our house during his mother's funeral. I didn't expect his reaction. He never loses his temper. But he grabbed his gun and stormed out of the house. I knew he wouldn't hurt anyone – the gun's never loaded and... and he's too gentle." Janet sighed.

"After that Brad wouldn't take my phone calls. He hung up or I'd get the answering machine. I was desperate, so I told Betty Lou it was urgent. She assumed James was after Brad again and put me through. I told Brad I'd left James. I swore my undying love for him. I said I'd give up my children to be with him."

Janet pulled her legs back up, clutching the wadded tissue in her fist, and hid her head behind her knees. Her voice became so low, they could barely hear her. She spoke into her knees. "He laughed at me. Said I was a fling. I'd had my chance at romance. He said to go back to my husband. He said he never let his heart get involved in a sexual liaison and I wasn't worth dying for."

She looked up with such sad eyes Tori felt a tightening in her heart. "He said he'd bet Dr. DeMaio that he could get me into bed. I was devastated." Janet was quiet for a minute. Then she sat up, put her legs down, her hands braced on either side of them, and her voice and demeanor hardened. "I let that *lousy bastard* seduce me for a bet. *He destroyed my marriage for a bet.* I haven't been alone with my kids in months and I might lose them. I had a great marriage, a wonderful husband and I loved him and my kids. I was doing well in college. Now I've dropped out. I can't hold my head up in town. I gave up everything for that SOB and he threw it in my face."

Morrison gave Tori a knowing look and she nodded. "So you killed Brad Coleman to get even?"

"I didn't kill him. Death is too good for that bastard – he deserved to suffer. Dr. Gibson called me a couple weeks ago. He said Coleman could be fired for moral turpitude." She lifted her right shoulder and let it drop. "He asked me to write a letter telling the administration about this incident, you know, file a grievance. He said the dean was sympathetic and Coleman would be fired."

"Did you write the letter?" Morrison asked.

"I was working on it. When I heard about Brad's death I didn't see any reason to finish, but I suppose I need to write it if I want to go back to college. I'll need a degree to support myself."

The tissue Janet had manhandled was nothing but shreds. She tried to open it, but gave up and put it on the table. "I can't get myself together," she whimpered. "Everything is so..." She put her head on her knees and her whole body shook. Morrison glanced at Tori with uncertainty in his eyes. The grandfather clock pealed the hour. Tori raised her hand as if stopping traffic and gave Janet a couple of minutes to cry before asking, "Mrs. Pillsbury, we were told you saw Dr. Coleman in March. Tell us about your meeting."

She raised her head, almost in a daze. "It wasn't a meeting. We bumped into each other downtown."

"Did you talk?"

Janet lowered her eyes. "He accused me of stalking him. I told him I'd rather meet the devil. James was a much better man than he'd ever be."

Morrison asked, "Who killed Coleman? Your husband?"

"*Of course not! Never*! James couldn't hurt a fly. That's why I didn't worry when he went after Brad with the gun. I don't know who killed Coleman, but I'm sure whoever did had a good reason."

"Mrs. Pillsbury, where were you Tuesday morning?" Tori asked.

"I was here watching Nancy's baby and toddler. She had an early appointment."

Morrison asked, "Mrs. Pillsbury, do you know how cyanide works?"

"Sure. Dr. DeMaio gave us a lecture on different poisons and did a demonstration with cyanide. Is that what poisoned Brad? It didn't say in the papers."

"Mrs. Pillsbury, you have access to drugs where you work, don't you?" Morrison asked.

"Some of them – but they're monitored. I couldn't take anything without it being recorded as missing. I know what you're getting at, but I did not kill Brad Coleman."

Morrison looked at Janet. "Mrs. Pillsbury, I'm sorry, but I've got to ask you to stay in Gainesville until this investigation is complete."

"You don't believe me, do you?"

Under his breath Morrison told Tori, "Coleman had good taste."

"So what do you think? Where do we go from here?"

"Back to the office. Check her fingerprints against those on the bottle." Morrison was gingerly putting his hat into a paper bag he had taken from the back seat of the patrol car.

Tori stared.

"I cleaned the plastic protector on the brim. When I handed her the hat, I made sure she took it by the brim. We'll get some clear prints."

Tori slapped Morrison on the shoulder. "Where did citizen's rights go? You sly.... I didn't catch on."

"Who said you can't teach an old dog new tricks?"

"You tricky old dog. Let's go check the fingerprints."

CHAPTER THIRTY FOUR

Once again, Tori waited in Morrison's office while a prime suspect's fingerprints were compared with those on the poisoned bottle. This time Tori was the one convinced the suspect was the murderer. Morrison was looking out the window while consuming the thick black substance he called coffee from his *Mets* mug. Dottie waited with them, sipping a Coke. "I was convinced he didn't take his own life until Janet told us about those black moods," Tori said.

"Doesn't that indicate a possible suicide?" Dottie asked.

"It would except...I don't know. No one else seems to think he was depressed."

Morrison said, "She said he hid it."

"Maybe she told us about his episodes of depression so we'd think he committed suicide."

"You don't think it was suicide?" Morrison asked.

"No. I think she poisoned him. She hated the bastard with good reason," Tori said.

"She felt guilty about destroying her marriage," said Morrison. "Her emotions seemed real and honest."

"I don't disagree. I think she has tremendous guilt about having an affair and hated Coleman," Tori said. "After the way he seduced and dumped her, I think she could get off with temporary insanity."

"She didn't do it." Morrison turned to face the two women.

Dottie was incredulous. "Where do you come off with that?"

"Professional experience. She isn't the type."

"What?" Tori asked. "She's too pretty to kill someone?"

"Nah, no such thing. Too smart. Why tell us about hating Coleman if her fingerprints were on the bottle."

"No way. Did you see how shaky she was?" Tori said, "She didn't think about fingerprints."

"She's had lots of time since the murder to think about the fingerprints," he said.

"Yeah. She's also had time to build herself a nice case of temporary insanity," said Dottie. "Even Tori bought her story."

"She wasn't acting crazy," Morrison said. "She told us she hated Coleman. She could've pretended she loved the bastard. All the evidence points to her ex, but she defended him. I think she was used by Coleman and resents it, but I don't think she killed him."

"Lunch at the Purple Porpoise says you're wrong," Tori said.

"Make it the 34th St. Grill and it's a deal," Morrison said.

"You're on."

Morrison lifted the receiver to answer his ringing phone. "Morrison." He listened. "Be right there."

"Someone broke into Coleman's house. You started a trend, Doc. Want to go with me?"

CHAPTER THIRTY FIVE

Tori clung to the door handle with her right hand, her left hand propped against the dashboard and both feet braced against the floorboard. Even with the seatbelt she was being tossed around as Morrison took the corner on two wheels, siren blaring. He screeched around the corner to Coleman's house and jumped from the car, hitting the street running. On shaky legs Tori followed him to the front door, where a uniformed officer met them.

"Where are they?" Morrison asked.

"Still inside – no sign of breaking and entering – they must have had a key."

Morrison glared at Tori. She had never told him where she got the key when she broke in and she was not going to give away Betty Lou. She shrugged. Morrison pulled out his gun and edged the door open, the uniformed cop behind him. In a whisper he told Tori to wait at the door. She followed them with her eyes as they went into Coleman's office. A moment later they came out and crept up the stairs. "YEEEEEEKKKKK!" women's voices shrieked. THUMP!! Tori tiptoed toward the stairs and started climbing them. "Doc, get up here – fast!" Morrison yelled.

She raced up the stairs and into Coleman's bedroom. The uniformed officer was standing with a gun trained on a young blond woman who was bawling. "Calm down. Put your hands in the air." The woman covered her mouth with her hands as she backed away from him. When she bumped against the wall she covered her head with her hands and sank to the floor where she crouched in a fetal position.

"Where are you, Morrison?" Tori asked.

"Over here, Doc. She passed out." Tori glanced around and spotted Morrison's back visible behind the bed. He was bent over something. Morrison lifted a dark haired woman onto the bed. Tori gasped. *Oh no, it's Rashida. What's she doing here?*

"She's okay. Just fainted," said Morrison. "Help Jeff with the other one. I'll give her smelling salts."

Tori crouched down beside the blond woman. She spoke in a soft voice. "It's okay. I'm Dr. Vincent. I'm a psychologist. You're all right."

The woman grabbed Tori with both arms and buried her head in her shoulder. Tori patted the woman's back. Between sobs the woman said, "I knew we'd get caught. My mother will kill me."

"Your mother won't kill you." Tori said. "What's your name?"

"Jennifer Taunton."

"Jennifer, tell me why you're here."

"I knew it wouldn't work." The blond whimpered.

"What wouldn't work?"

The blond lifted her head. Red-rimmed eyes peered at Tori. "Will we go to jail?"

"I don't know. It depends. Perhaps if you tell me what you were doing, I can help you." When the blond did not answer, Tori asked, "What were you looking for?"

The blond buried her head back in Tori's shoulder. Tori had difficulty hearing her. "Pictures – pictures of us." She sobbed, "We thought if we got them, no one would ever see them."

The obscene photos of young women – of course, thought Tori.

Morrison called, "Doc, she's coming around."

Tori patted the blond's shoulder before she stood up and went to Morrison. She whispered, "They were trying to get the pictures of them that Coleman took."

"I knew this one looked familiar. She's the one found Coleman's body."

Rashida moaned and her eyes fluttered. She looked at Tori. "Dr. Vincent?"

"That's right, Rashida. You're all right. This is Detective Morrison."

"No! No! No!" She covered her face with her hands. "You promised you wouldn't tell the police."

"She didn't tell us," Morrison said. "The alarm called us when you broke into Dr. Coleman's house."

Rashida did not move. Tears were seeping out beneath her hands and trickling down her cheeks onto the bed.

Tori turned to Morrison, "Do you have to arrest them? They were trying to get the photos Coleman took of them. They didn't break into the house."

"Coleman didn't invite them in either. They could be murderers. Or might know something about the murder."

"Let me ask them about the murder," Tori said.

Morrison threw his hands in the air. "Go ahead. But if you don't get anything, I'm going to book them."

"Rashida, did you hear Detective Morrison?"

Rashida nodded.

"You can't question them together. She's," he pointed at Jennifer, "going in the other room while you talk to Rashida."

"Jennifer, do you understand?"

Jennifer nodded and went with the officer into another room.

After thirty minutes of questioning, first Rashida and then Jennifer, Tori determined that the two women were relating the same story. The two coeds were longtime friends; each had had an affair with Coleman. Rashida was the first, but when she tried to warn her friend, Jennifer thought she was jealous. The coeds had a fight and did not speak until Coleman dropped Jennifer. Then they compared notes – he had taken photographs of both of them in obscene poses. They were terrified of what he would do with the pictures and discussed ways to get them back. On the day Coleman was poisoned the two friends had planned to meet with him in his office to ask him for the photographs. If he refused, they would threaten to go to the dean. Jennifer was late and Rashida thought her friend might already be in Coleman's office. Rashida knocked and when he didn't answer, she opened the door. Realizing he was dead, she ran out of the office screaming. She bumped into Jennifer coming up the stairs. They were afraid if they told the police about going to Coleman's office the photographs would become public. When time passed without the media mentioning the photos, they decided to get them. They knew Coleman kept the photographs in his house. Tori avoided asking where they got the key to the house – she knew.

"Are you satisfied that they were not involved in Coleman's poisoning?" Tori asked Morrison.

"Yeah. Jeff, take them downtown and get their official statements."

CHAPTER THIRTY SIX

Late morning Friday found campus as quiet as a cemetery after midnight. Tori suspected many students were taking a three-day holiday rather than going to the service. A two-hour drive to Daytona Beach and students could link up with spring breakers from every corner of the country. Sunshine, beer, outdoor concerts, limbo dancing on the beach, exuberant youths bursting with hormones, potential lovers eyeing each other, cars cruising the beach, a beautiful setting – what could be more fun? College kids celebrating the rites of spring would cram hotels, overflowing on balconies like bees swarming around a hive, waving and calling to friends and lovers.

Upon entering the auditorium Tori's suspicions were supported. Although most seats were occupied, the number of students at the memorial service would not account for the empty campus. Daytona Beach would have a large contingent from the University of Florida this weekend. Morrison spotted Dottie and led Tori to the back where she had saved them seats. Dean Kohlberg conducted the memorial. Tori's assumption that a nicely dressed middle-aged couple in the first row were Coleman's parents was confirmed when the Dean introduced them to the assembly. Tori saw no sign of Brad Coleman's son or ex-wife.

Steve DeMaio sat with the Colemans. Mr. Coleman clutched his wife's hand, but aside from a tight jaw, displayed no emotion. Betty Lou Hancock sat with her arm around Mrs. Coleman, who leaned on Betty Lou as they wept together. Trish Acosta sat near the Colemans – but not with them.

Dottie said, "Guessing by the number of faculty present, Coleman wasn't very popular."

Jabbing an elbow into her arm Morrison said, "It's not 'seemly' to talk during the service."

Dean Kohlberg said a few words, and then Dr. Gibson spoke. English majors read poetry: classics, Coleman's poems, and verses written in his memory. The highlight of the memorial was a student-produced slide show featuring their favorite professor. Bigger-than-life slides showed Coleman lecturing in a classroom, eating in the cafeteria, enjoying a student picnic, playing softball with the faculty, playing tennis with DeMaio, running with students, reading poetry in the auditorium, discussing poetry with students resting on cushions in front of his fireplace. Tori gasped and covered her mouth with her hands when she recognized the cushions. Morrison patted her shoulder, before returning his attention to the slides. A number of slides showed Coleman mentoring teens from the Boys & Girls Club, an aspect of Coleman's life Tori had heard about but not seen. Tori noticed a contingent of teenage boys seated to one side – *they must be his mentees from the Boys & Girls Club.* The student narrative for the slide show was maudlin, but sweet and nostalgic. By the end of the service, few eyes were dry. Even Tori was touched.

Most students at the service were female. Tori wondered if a disproportionate number of English majors were female, or if female students particularly liked Coleman. She guessed both were true. After the memorial, Tori watched as Trish Acosta hugged Betty Lou, said something to Coleman's parents, nodded at DeMaio, and left the auditorium by the side door.

Morrison pulled out his cell phone and listened for a minute. "Yeah, okay." Morrison scowled.

"What's up?" Tori asked.

"Janet Pillsbury's fingerprints don't match the poisoned bottle."

Tori gave him credit for not saying, "I told you so." She said, "Damn, damn, damn. I was convinced it was Janet."

Morrison winked. "Know the feeling, and you buy me lunch to boot."

Dottie raised both shoulders and spread her hands. "If it wasn't Janet or her husband, who is the murderer?"

Morrison scratched his head. "Don't know. They're our prime suspects."

Tori shrugged. "Maybe I dismissed suicide too quickly. I need to talk to his parents."

She surveyed the parents still talking with the dean. Steve DeMaio was very much a part of the family. Tori searched for Janet Pillsbury among the students in weepy clusters around the auditorium, but saw no sign of her.

Dean Kohlberg walked the Colemans up the aisle of the auditorium toward the exit. When she saw Morrison, Dottie and Tori, she excused herself and went to talk to them.

"Thank you for coming to the memorial service, I'm sure it means a lot to Brad's parents," the dean said.

Tori murmured something about attending being the least they could do and Morrison and Dottie nodded.

"Dr. Coleman's parents would like his effects shipped to their home," the dean said. "Is that possible?"

Morrison said, "No problem sending household effects, but have to keep his papers."

"When can the papers be sent?" Dean Kohlberg asked.

"Best estimate – few weeks. If we tie the case up sooner, I'll release what's not needed for trial."

"How is the investigation going?" Dean Kohlberg asked.

"Got people of interest, but no prime suspect," Morrison reported.

Morrison, Dottie and Tori accompanied Dean Kohlberg back to where the Colemans were standing, talking to students. The dean introduced them to the Colemans and the threesome gave their condolences, acknowledged DeMaio, and left.

As they exited the auditorium, the press converged on Morrison. Accustomed to handling the media, he managed to convey the impression they were close to a solution without giving any information.

CHAPTER THIRTY SEVEN

Dottie was putting down the top on her Suzuki outside the restaurant where she'd lunched with Tori and Morrison when she noticed the Holiday Inn across the street. On a whim she went to check whether the Colemans were staying there – they were. She called their room and Mr. Coleman agreed to meet her in the lobby. Mrs. Coleman was freshening up to go to Steve DeMaio's house for a student/faculty get together to reminisce about Coleman.

"It'll do Mrs. Coleman good to meet the students who loved her son," Mr. Coleman said.

A little pompous speaking of his wife as "Mrs. Coleman" and strange he called Brad Coleman "her" son, Dottie thought. *Not words a loving husband and father in a close-knit family would use.*

The senior Coleman strode into the lobby looking as if he were going to a board meeting. Of average height and sturdy build, he wore an expensive grey pin-striped suit, silk shirt, hand painted tie with matching pocket scarf, all dark, subdued, and appropriate for a memorial service. His sandy hair was graying at the temples and receding at the forehead. Dottie stood when Mr. Coleman approached her chair, extending her hand and once again offering condolences.

Coleman ignored her proffered hand and said, "If you want to console me, get the bastard who killed my son."

Dottie gulped, but regained her composure and sat down. Coleman's dark brows met in the middle of his forehead in a perpetual frown, while a blood vessel pulsed in his forehead, accentuating his ill temper. Coleman sat upright in the upholstered chair across from Dottie. He appeared ill at ease and eager to leave. He gripped the arms of the chair with his manicured hands while ordering Dottie to "get on with this investigation, so Mrs. Coleman and I can get on with our lives."

Dottie wondered, *is Coleman reacting to the loss of his son or is he upset because the death interrupted his schedule?* She let him vent his frustration before asking about his son.

"You can get all the information you need from people here without bothering his family," he snapped.

Was your son's death merely an inconvenience? Dottie willed her voice to remain calm. "I'm sure I can get information from people in Gainesville, but no one knows your son as well as you do, Mr. Coleman."

"Steve DeMaio knows him better than his family does. He's spent more time with him in the last five years."

"We've interviewed Dr. DeMaio. However, the family might see things from a different perspective. For instance, what can you tell me about Trish Acosta?"

"Who?" The dark caterpillars above his eyes bumped together. "You mean the pretty girl at the memorial service?" When Dottie nodded, he replied, "Don't know anything about her."

"Weren't she and Brad very close?"

"My son wasn't *very close* to any woman." Dottie thought the way he mimicked her words was meant to provoke, but by clutching the arms of her chair, she managed not to react verbally. She felt the muscles in her jaw tighten. After a moment, Coleman continued. "I told my son he'd need to marry if he wanted to inherit anything from his grandmother – the old hag. Worst mistake I every made. My son wasn't made for married life – he didn't understand the rules. You don't have to be faithful, just discreet. He flaunted his bimbos. Anyway, Mrs. Coleman and I got our grandson."

Coleman scrutinized Dottie's face. She thought, *He wants me to challenge him. I won't give him the satisfaction. Guess I've found Brad Coleman's role model for interactions with women. If*

Brad flaunted his "bimbos," the elder Coleman flaunted his own misguided philosophy about marriage.

"So Trish wasn't..."

"Trish wasn't anything." Coleman's voice was strong enough to carry across a boardroom table where he typically sat. "Not to my son. After his divorce he swore he'd never remarry, didn't tell us who he was screwing."

"What about Brad's ex-wife?" Dottie asked.

"Melissa was the worst kind of wife for my son – independent and self-sufficient. He should have married an old-fashioned woman. Someone content to be a wife and mother, someone so interested in spending his money, she'd overlook infidelities."

"You don't approve of his ex-wife."

"Not as a wife for my son, I don't. She'd be a good mother if she'd stop trying to be some corporate executive and devote her time to raising my grandson."

"Does she harbor any animosity toward Brad?" Dottie asked.

"Animosity? No. Why should she?"

"The former Mrs. Coleman would like to send her son to a private school, but your son was not willing to pay for it and neither are you," Dottie said. She looked him in the eye trying not to gloat.

"How do you know that?" His frown deepened. His eyes bore into hers.

Dottie smiled to herself, but did not change her expression. *I guess that got his attention. Mr. Coleman does not like someone snooping into his private affairs.*

"We are investigating your son's death, Mr. Coleman. If his ex-wife inherited money from him, she might be able to send her son to a private school."

"Bullshit! I told Melissa I'd send Bradford to that school if she'd quit work. It's up to her." He pointed a finger in Dottie's face. "And none of your business."

She narrowed her eyes. "We're trying to find your son's killer – that makes it our business, Mr. Coleman. Now – is there *anyone* who would want to harm your son?"

"That's your job to find out."

Dottie gritted her teeth. Luckily, Mrs. Coleman arrived at her husband's elbow, saying, "Is Mr. Coleman giving you the information you need, dear?"

Dottie assured Mrs. Coleman her husband had been helpful. "I wonder if I might ask you a few questions, Mrs. Coleman?"

"No, you may not," said her husband. "I've told you all you need to know."

Dottie turned, eager to distance herself from the irritable patriarch of the Coleman family. Mr. Coleman sent her off with a parting shot, "If you can't solve this case, I'll hire a detective from up *north,* one who knows what *he's* doing."

Dottie was so pissed on her drive back to the police station she felt steam was escaping from her ears. For the first time she felt sympathy for Brad Coleman. *His life must have been miserable growing up with that tyrant for a father. No wonder Brad was a misogynist. How does Mrs. Coleman tolerate that arrogant bore?*

CHAPTER THIRTY EIGHT

Crossing the quiet campus Morrison and Tori observed a couple in shorts soaking up early spring rays on the green, a dribble of students going into the library, and two heading across campus with tennis racquets. "Hey! Watch out!" Morrison shouted. At the same time Tori felt Morrison's strong arms pull her off the path. She stumbled and toppled to her knees.

"Watch where you're going, you fucking idiots!" Morrison yelled at two bicyclists racing past and calling belated apologies. Morrison helped Tori to her feet. Tori brushed off her slacks. "You all right?" He picked some leaves off her sleeve and pulled a twig from her hair.

"A little shaken, but I think I'm in one piece." Tori looked at Morrison. "Thanks." She started to walk, but felt a piercing pain as her knee give out. "OUCH!" She grabbed Morrison's arm. "My knee – it's an old ballet injury."

"Can you walk if I help?"

"Yes. Thanks."

"Damn kids. They could've killed you," Morrison said.

"What about you?" she asked.

"Hell, those skinny kids and their puny bikes would have bounced off me."

A few students toting trays were leaving with Betty Lou Hancock when Tori, leaning on Morrison, arrived at the English

Department office. "Bless my soul! What happened to you?" asked Betty Lou.

Tori described the incident with the bikes. Betty Lou said, "Them bicycles are a menace. Come in and take a load off." Betty Lou looked at the students. "Go on. I'll catch you up at the parking lot in a couple minutes." She turned back to Tori and explained, "They're bringing food to the get together at Steve DeMaio's."

Tori asked, "How're things going?"

"I'm keeping busy: wiping tears, handing out tissues, comforting students, you know." She shrugged. "Don't have time for it to sink in."

"You need to give yourself time to mourn. It's not good to bottle up your emotions," Tori said.

"The weekend'll be tough; my Joe's gonna go hunting with Ned Terwillegar, the fire chief," said Hancock. "I'm thinking 'bout going to Waycross – spend the weekend with my sister."

"That's a good idea."

"Ms. Hancock," Morrison asked, "remember a student, Russell Mills? Had a falling out with Coleman?"

"Lordy, I sure do. As God is my witness, Brad was roaring mad." Betty Lou chuckled. "Did I ever have to coax Brad to change that boy's grade to an 'Incomplete.' Poor Sonny works hard – then his daddy gets laid off and his momma goes on a binge. I pretended I didn't know his momma is an alky, but everyone at First Baptist knows about her. Amy down at detox told me, too."

"Coleman changed Mills' grade?" Morrison asked.

"He sure did."

"Okay thanks," Morrison said.

"Any time you want to know what's happening in this department, just you ask me," Betty Lou said.

"Gibson in?"

Dr. Davis Gibson greeted Morrison and Tori with a ready smile as they entered his orderly office. The hefty middle-aged man with a beard reminiscent of Ernest Hemingway stood and shook their hands. He motioned toward two Danish chairs facing his teak desk, a major upgrade from lowly professors' desks – expensive furniture being a perk for administrators. The desk was clear except for a single sheet of paper in front of Dr. Gibson and an inbox with a few items. Dr. Gibson's office, three times the size of Coleman's, displayed dozens of photographs of vintage cars.

"Refurbish cars, Dr. Gibson?" Morrison asked, looking around.

Gibson wrinkled his brow. Then he laughed. "The photographs."

Morrison nodded.

"No. My DNA doesn't contain the mechanical ability gene. Photography's my hobby and vintage car owners keep those beauties polished. They're great to photograph. I love capturing reflected images of proud owners and adjacent cars." He admired his work with a smile. Then Dr. Gibson sat behind his desk, folded his hands on his belly and asked Tori, "I hope you don't think me presumptuous, Dr. Vincent, but why are you here with the police?"

"I'm conducting a psychological autopsy."

"I've heard of that. That's where you..." He pulled on his beard.

"I'm trying to determine Coleman's state of mind prior to his death."

"How can I help?"

"Did you notice any change in Dr. Coleman's behavior or demeanor recently?"

"Like what?"

"Did he appear upset or depressed?"

Gibson snorted. "Coleman was never depressed. He specialized in upsetting everyone else. If you're talking about suicide, that's not Coleman. He thought too much of himself."

"Did he tell you about any plans he had – publishing papers, going to conferences, personal plans – was he was looking forward to anything?"

He pulled on his beard again. "Nothing I can think of."

"Who was close to him in the department?" she asked.

"Betty Lou. She was like a mother to him."

"Anyone else?" Tori asked.

Gibson shook his head. "He was not an easy man to like."

Morrison said. "Dr. Gibson, you know a Janet Pillsbury? Used to be a student of this Coleman guy."

"That's right."

"Husband threatened Coleman. That right?"

143

"Yes it is. He came storming in with a gun, threatening to blow Coleman's head off if he didn't leave Janet alone. It was quite a scene."

"You saw him threaten Coleman?" Tori asked.

"No, I was at a meeting. When I got back Dr. Whitherspoon was waiting in my office to relate the news. He reminded me of Rumpelstiltskin in the Brothers Grimm fairy tale – you know, the rascal rubbing his hands with glee. Of course, I heard about it from Betty Lou and students, too."

"You report it to the police?" Morrison asked.

"No, it wasn't necessary."

"Not necessary? Someone threatens to kill a faculty member and you don't report it to the police?" Morrison's eyes drilled into Gibson's.

Gibson lowered his eyes and stroked his beard. "Please don't misunderstand, Detective. Dr. Coleman refused to report the incident and begged me not to call the authorities."

"Yeah? Why?"

"Brad was being considered for tenure and didn't want wind of his affair with Janet to get back to the administration. Everything had quieted down by the time I got back, so I saw no harm in letting it go."

"Detective Epstein questioned you Tuesday – right? And you didn't tell her about it?" Morrison's eyes pierced further into those of the Chairman.

Gibson examined his fingernails and said, "It didn't have anything to do with his murder."

"You think a man has a gun and threatens someone who turns up murdered and it has nothing to do with his murder?" Morrison's loud voice propelled Dr. Gibson backward against his chair's back.

"I...I..."

"You did nothing – never told the cops – right? Then you suddenly call Janet Pillsbury. Right?" Morrison asked.

The Chairperson's ears turned pink. He stammered before answering, "You don't understand."

"You got that right," Morrison snapped.

"I, uh, was sure Coleman, uh, would get a terminal contract, you know, not be tenured. When he was tenured, Dr. Whitherspoon demanded I do something."

"You decided to terminate him for moral turpitude. Is that correct?" Tori asked.

"Yes. The dean and I encouraged Janet to file a sexual harassment grievance so we could fire him," Gibson said. "She was an A student before Coleman got his talons into her." His face registered his antipathy for Coleman.

"Don't you think you should've told Detective Epstein that?" asked Morrison.

Gibson lowered his eyes.

"This Pillsbury woman – she file a grievance?" Morrison asked.

"I don't suppose there's any need to now."

Tori said, "The dean didn't tell us about the grievance. I thought she supported Coleman's tenure."

The pink on Gibson's ears spread to his cheeks and he said nothing. *Searching for words? Or manufacturing a story?* Tori wondered. After a noticeable pause, Gibson responded. "The dean supported Professor Coleman's tenure, but she won't tolerate sexual harassment of students. We had proof of his misconduct and she was willing to nail him."

"The dean gets this Coleman guy tenure," Morrison said. "But not a month later she wants to get him fired?"

Gibson smirked. "She must have changed her mind. Maybe she got new information."

There was an undercurrent to his statement, but Tori couldn't identify it.

"What new information she get?" Morrison asked.

"You need to ask her." Gibson's face got very pink. He rubbed the back of his hand across his mouth.

"Think this dean killed Coleman?" Morrison asked.

Dr. Gibson's face drained of color. He sat upright and stammered, "How…How would I know?"

CHAPTER THIRTY NINE

Walking across campus, Tori leaned on Morrison's arm. She said, "Let's go get a drink."

"How can you? It's Friday night," Morrison said. "What about your son?"

"Sean's visiting his dad this weekend."

"Dad live around here?"

"No, he's an FBI agent in Atlanta."

"Son go there a lot?"

"Never."

Morrison raised his right eyebrow. "And?"

"He suddenly wants to see his son."

"When'd you get divorced?"

"Let's get a drink and I'll tell you the whole sorry tale."

"Isn't this a cozy twosome," a nasty voice accosted them.

Tori felt the color rise to her cheeks. She stopped and took her arm away from Morrison. "It isn't what it looks like, Matt. I fell."

"Listen, fella, Doc and I are like… coworkers," Morrison said. "We're working on a case together."

Matt said, "How sweet. You walk arm in arm to discuss crime?"

"She fell. Hurt her knee. I'm helping her walk."

Tori felt Matt's eyes scan her from top to bottom. "You look all right to me."

"I'm much better, now."

"Amazing recovery," Matt said. The ice in his voice sent a shiver down Tori's neck.

"Don't be silly. Why would I lie to you about falling?"

"So now I'm silly, am I?" Matt stormed away.

"Sorry, Tori," Morrison said. "Go on. Go catch him."

"I'm not feeding into his paranoia. Let him go. He'll calm down."

Morrison offered her his arm.

"No thanks, I'm fine, really."

It was Morrison's first visit to the Purple Porpoise, Tori's favorite haunt on West University Avenue. He stood inside the entrance looking befuddled. The noise and bustle were overpowering. Morrison pushed through the crowd to sit in the back, Tori followed in his wake.

"I'm too old for this," he said, dropping into the seat.

"I won't admit it's age, but the noise gets to me, too," Tori said. "I usually come later. I forgot they have 'Sundowner' in the evenings."

"What the hell's 'Sundowner'?" Morrison asked.

"Cheap beers and 2 for 1 drinks."

"Maybe I can take the noise after all," Morrison said with a wink.

"It's the TV that gets me."

"Don't worry about that." Morrison fiddled with his keys.

"You don't care as long as you get your cheap beer."

The waitress appeared at their table and Morrison ordered a Corona with lime while Tori asked for a Mojito. Tori looked at the TV over the bar and smiled. "Thank God. Someone turned off the TV." She saw the barman turn the TV back on.

"Damn," Morrison said. In an instant the TV went blank. The people at the bar complained to the barman and in a couple of minutes he turned the TV on again. Morrison shook his head and aimed something on his keychain at the TV. It flickered off.

"What's that you have?"

"A TV B Gone clicker."

"God, Morrison. Do you want to get us killed?" Tori asked with a grin.

"I'll protect you." He said, "Got a gun."

The barman told the complainers the TV was not working. Morrison grinned.

"Where'd you get that device?" Tori asked.

"Ruth heard about it on NPR. She got me one. But she won't let me use it when we go out."

"Smart woman. They find out you're shutting off the TV during a game and we'll have a riot on our hands."

As soon as the waitress brought their drinks, Morrison said, "Okay, tell me about your ex-husband."

"Gerry and I fell in love in college. We married and left for the University of Rochester. I got my doctorate in psychology and he got his law degree."

"What went wrong?"

"I got pregnant."

Morrison gave her a questioning look.

"Gerry didn't want a child. Then he decided he didn't much want a wife, either. I took Sean and moved here."

"What'd he have against a kid?" Morrison asked.

"It interfered with his lifestyle. He's a party animal. He never sees Sean unless I coerce him to."

"Damned fool." He took a swig of his beer. "Why's he want his son now?"

"You know as much as I do."

Morrison shook his head. The TV came back on and Morrison picked up his keys and aimed his TV BE Gone at the TV. The screen went blank.

"People won't like you turning off the TV again," Tori said.

"Think I care?" Morrison fiddled with his keys. "What do you think Gibson was getting at about the dean?"

"I don't have a clue, but don't try to change the topic. It's your turn. Tell me why you moved to Gainesville."

"We were talking about the case," Morrison said.

"Don't dodge the question."

Morrison sighed and gulped down the last of his beer. He signaled to the waitress to bring him another. "Want another, Doc?"

Tori shook her head. "Tell me."

"I shot someone."

"In a fight?"

Morrison lowered his head and looked over his glasses at Tori. "In the line of duty."

"Isn't that what cops are supposed to do?"

"Not when it's a 13 year old kid."

Tori wrinkled her nose. "And..."

"And he was breaking into his uncle's house. He was playing a joke on him."

"Didn't the uncle recognize him?"

"Uncle wasn't home. Neighbor saw a 'man' walking around the uncle's house, looking in the windows," Morrison said, using his fingers to put quotation marks around the word, man.

"And when you got there?"

"Climbing over the back fence. I called, 'Stop, police.'"

"He didn't stop," she said.

"Right."

"So you shot him," she said.

Morrison nodded.

"Did you kill him?"

"No. Worse. Paralyzed from the chest down."

"Oh, Herb, I'm so sorry," she said putting her hand over his. "Did you get counseling?"

"Counseling can't undo what I did." After a moment he added, "Or how I feel."

The waitress placed Morrison's beer on the table.

Tori asked, "So after the incident you moved to Gainesville?"

"Not right away. I transferred to the detective unit in Jersey for awhile. Then wanted to work where they don't have much violence." After a few moments of silence, Morrison took a swallow of beer. "So who do you think killed Coleman? Steve DeMaio?"

"Nah, DeMaio wouldn't kill over a woman. I think a woman poisoned Coleman."

"Why?" Morrison asked.

"Poison is a woman's m.o. – it doesn't demand strength. Also, Brad Coleman got along with men, but was an S.O.B. to women. There's someone out there who got even with him."

"Not covering up for DeMaio or nothing, are you, Tori?"

"Why would I do that?"

"You and DeMaio were a hot item back in the day."

149

"Let's get one thing straight right now." Tori glared at him. "There is not now and never was anything between me and Steve DeMaio." Tori could feel the heat rising in her face, but she spoke emphatically.

"Maybe nothing now, but there sure as hell was something between you two," Morrison insisted. "How long'd you date this DeMaio guy?"

Tori opened her mouth, and then closed it without speaking. Her face flushed. When she regained her composure, she asked, "How do you know I dated DeMaio?"

"I told you. Guys on the force keep their nose to the ground." Morrison said.

CHAPTER FORTY

The receptionist, pocketbook slung over her shoulder, was locking her desk, when Dottie ran into the office. "Hi, Clara, anything for me?"

Clara sighed. "Lucky I like you – anyone else and I'd say no." Clara put her purse down on the desk and shuffled through slips of paper. She handed Dottie a telephone message from Harrison. "That's it."

Dottie blew Clara a kiss and said, "Thanks," before going to her desk to return Harrison's call.

"Got info on Brad Coleman's will for me?" she asked.

"Sure do. Coleman left big money for scholarships for boys in the Boys & Girls Club. He also set up a trust for his son with legal provisions so his ex-wife can't touch the money except in an emergency. Otherwise all the money goes to the son when he's 28."

"Twenty-eight? Why wait 'til the kid's 28?"

"It was Coleman's father's idea. He wanted the son to work before he had life handed to him on a silver platter, so to speak," Harrison said.

"Coleman agreed with his father?" she asked.

"Coleman didn't give an ant's fart."

"Are you saying he didn't care about his son?"

"Yeah. Besides he didn't expect to die young."

"So everything went to the son?" Dottie asked.

"Not everything. He left $125,000 to a Steven DeMaio."

"Wow! $125,000?"

"That's right."

"Any conditions?" she asked.

"No. No strings attached."

She thanked Harrison and hung up.

That inheritance did not look good for DeMaio.

Dottie switched on the light and cringed at the state of her kitchen: a week's worth of unwashed dishes precariously piled in the sink and a pair of cockroaches scuttling away from remnants of breakfast on the table. One whiff of the kitchen told her she had to clean it. Her mother would be appalled if she saw the pile of dirty dishes – some of them were growing mold. She pulled a banana peel suffering the Black Death from among the plates in the sink and dropped it into the garbage. She poured dish detergent in the sink and began her task. Once the clean dishes were in the drain board, she picked up the mail she'd been too busy with Jason to examine the previous evening. Most of it went straight into the trash.

She deserved a liquid reward to remove the lingering bitterness she tasted from dealing with Coleman's father. This was a martini night. Sipping the martini, she changed into sweats and turned on the stereo. She set her drink on the end table and collapsed across the living room chair. She picked up the novel she'd started Monday, but kept rereading the same page – she couldn't keep her mind focused. She turned her thoughts to the possible suspects in the Coleman case – one by one they were being eliminated. Meanwhile Steve DeMaio's motives were looking more incriminating. But she couldn't believe DeMaio killed Coleman over a woman. *Would he kill Coleman for the money? If he borrowed other things from Coleman, why not borrow money? Dean Kohlberg is emerging as an enigma. Why did she change her mind and try to get Coleman fired? And whose prints were on the poisoned Pepsi bottle?*

The third time Dottie checked to be sure the phone was on the hook, she admitted to herself she was hoping Jason would call. When the phone did ring, she jumped a mile.

She took a deep breath and said in a sexy voice, "Hello."

Her father's irritated voice said, "So you are alive."

152

"Is Mom all right?"

"No. She's worried out of her mind."

"What happened?"

"She hasn't heard from her eldest daughter in three weeks and doesn't know if she's alive or dead."

"I didn't realize it'd been so long." Dottie's voice was meek.

"It'd be one thing if you were a school teacher like Beth, but your job is dangerous."

"I don't get in dangerous situations," Dottie lied. "I'm a detective."

"What are you investigating?"

She gulped before answering in a tiny voice, "A murder."

Her father huffed. "Won't that make your mother feel better."

"Can I talk to Mom?"

"No, she turned in early tonight."

"Is she feeling all right?" Dottie asked.

"She had her six-month check-up. It's emotionally draining," after a slight pause while he swallowed, he said, "for both of us." He cleared his throat. "She was exhausted from the stress and went to bed early."

"They didn't find any new cancer, did they?" Dottie asked.

"No, no. There's no sign of a recurrence."

A powerful and painful image crept into Dottie's consciousness – her mother sitting in a lounge chair attached to an intravenous tube dripping poison into her arm – a scene she had witnessed too often. While destroying her mother's breast cancer, the chemotherapy nauseated her, sapped her vitality and stole her hair. Her mother's energy and strength slowly returned until the next chemotherapy session restarted the debilitating cycle. Although Dottie's mother had completed the chemotherapy sessions some years ago, the specter of a recurrence hung over their heads. Breast cancer survivors are not considered "cured" until 15 years without a recurrence. Dottie berated herself, *how could I forget Mom's appointment?* Dottie's thoughts were interrupted by her father's gruff question, "Are you there?"

"Yes. I'm sorry," she said.

"I've been calling all evening. Why don't you get an answering machine like everyone else?"

CHAPTER FORTY ONE

At 6:30 Saturday morning Tori walked into the Sunshine State Health Spa in downtown Gainesville. She limited visits to the expensive spa to university breaks when the campus exercise room was closed, but today she wanted to visit the spa Trish Acosta frequented. Tori completed her weight training regimen before talking to Dave Lambrides at the front desk. Dave was generous with training advice on Tori's infrequent visits to the spa. After bantering about exercise trends and work out equipment, she asked him about Trish Acosta, explaining her connection with the police investigation.

"Trish comes in every Tuesday and Thursday at 7:30 a.m., you can set your watch by her. Never misses a day."

"Was she here this past Tuesday?"

"Sure was."

Tori tilted her head. "How do you know? Don't you need to check your records?"

Dave flushed and cleared his throat, "No, I don't have to check my records." He hesitated and then smiled. "Trish goes to aerobics at 7:30 and if she weren't there half the guys in the class would be asking about her."

"Did she seem worried or anything on Tuesday?"

"Nope. Same as usual," Dave said.

Trish's story checked out, not that Tori doubted it would. Trish was at the spa while Coleman was playing tennis and being poisoned.

At 7:45 Tori pulled into her driveway. She picked up the newspaper on her way into breakfast. Coleman's murder was on the front page, but it didn't make the headlines today; the mayor's speech to a Black church was the top story. The Coleman article centered on the mayor's demand for a quick resolution to the "heinous crime." She chafed at the story line. *Easy to get publicity by making self-righteous demands when he's not behind the eight ball,* she thought.

She jumped into the shower and was at the 34th St. Deli by 8:30. Kathy poured her coffee as she walked to her usual seat. Dottie sat sipping her coke. Morrison was grinning from ear to ear when he joined them a minute or two later. He was bursting with news.

"Coleman's ex-wife was in Tampa a couple days before Coleman got himself poisoned. She rented a car. Was in Florida four days."

His news electrified the women more than their caffeine intake did.

"She could drive to Gainesville in a couple hours. Did she stay here?" Dottie asked.

"Don't know. She didn't use a credit card or use her real name. Cameron checked the local places. He's checking with the credit card companies to see if she used a credit card for a hotel in Tampa."

Morrison thanked Kathy as she placed his breakfast on the table and he dug in.

"She could have paid for her room in cash or stayed with Coleman," Dottie said

"We'd have heard if she'd stayed with him," Morrison said around the forkful of eggs crammed in his mouth.

"It's unlikely she stayed with Coleman, considering her animosity toward him," Tori said.

"She could have come and gone in one day," Dottie added. "This could be our lucky break."

Morrison nodded. "Yeah, we got to question her."

Tori brought up Gibson's comments concerning the dean.

"What do you think he means?" Dottie asked.

"Damned if I know. She didn't have an affair with Coleman." Morrison chuckled. "Not his type."

"What else could have happened between them?" Dottie asked.

"University politics?" Tori suggested.

Morrison shrugged while sopping up the last vestiges of egg and sausage grease with white toast.

"I don't get it. One minute she's pushing Coleman's promotion through the campus hierarchy and the next minute she's trying to fire him for sexual harassment." Dottie shook her head. "It doesn't make sense."

CHAPTER FORTY TWO

The three colleagues gathered around Morrison's desk where Dottie had set up a conference call to Coleman's ex-wife in Connecticut. When a woman answered on the third ring, Tori asked if she was Brad Coleman's ex-wife. She was.

After introducing herself, Dottie and Morrison, Tori said, "Mrs. Coleman..."

"I paid a lot of money not to be Mrs. Coleman," the woman snapped, "I'm Ms. Albright."

"I apologize, Ms. Albright," Tori said, "We're investigating the death of your ex-husband, Brad Coleman."

"What do you want from me?" Her voice was grating.

"When did you last have contact with your ex-husband?"

"Last December."

"Did Dr. Coleman express any fear or indicate someone was threatening him?"

"Someone was always after my ex-husband – a dumped lover or husband of a current one," she seethed. "He couldn't keep his fly zipped. He didn't discriminate – married, single, willing, unwilling, stranger, whore, saint, whatever."

"You sound bitter," Tori said.

A sour laugh came through the phone. "You got that right!"

"I guess, the divorce wasn't amicable," Dottie said.

"Hardly! Brad spent our married life hopping from one bed to another. When I could no longer deny it to myself, I confronted him. He laughed. When he left for work, I changed the locks and filed for divorce."

"You got custody of the kid?" Morrison asked.

"Right."

"Did Dr. Coleman keep in contact with his son?" Tori asked. "Write him? Phone him? See his son regularly?"

"My ex-husband saw Bradford on agreed visitation, two weeks in the summer and a week at Christmas. He didn't call or write." Tori thought, *Like Gerry.*

"Was he close to his son?" Tori asked.

A vicious snort exploded from the phone. "Bradford saw little of his father. When Brad visited his parents, he took Bradford along. His grandparents doted on Bradford while Brad cavorted with daughters of other Greenwich families."

"You weren't on good terms with your ex-husband?" Morrison asked.

"We weren't on any terms. I hated the sight of him. We never spoke."

Tori asked, "How did you discuss problems or concerns about your son? Or set up visitation?"

"Through his parents."

"How did Dr. Coleman act when he picked up Bradford at Christmas?" Dottie asked.

"I didn't see him."

"How did he pick up your child without your seeing him?" she asked.

"I told you I hated the sight of him. One of my brothers sent Bradford off with his father. I stayed in my bedroom. We did the same thing when he brought Bradford back. I haven't seen or spoken to my ex-husband face to face since our divorce, five years ago on July 14th. I celebrate the event every year. I'd like to make it a national holiday – like it is in France – Bastille Day."

Morrison said, "Mrs. Coleman, I mean Ms. Albright, you were in Tampa, Florida last week."

"How do you know that?"

"Ms. Albright, we're police officers. It's our job," Dottie said.

"Okay, so I was in Tampa."

Morrison said, "From April 9th through April 14th."

158

"Yes, yes, I've already said I was there." Her voice was harsh. "So what?"

"What were you doing in Tampa?"

"I have nothing to hide. I visited my sister. She goes to the University of South Florida."

"Where'd you stay?" he asked.

"At my sister's apartment. What has that got to do with anything?"

"Rent a car?" Morrison asked.

"My sister uses a bicycle around campus. Bradford and I could hardly ride with her, could we?"

"You rented a car?" Morrison asked.

"Yes, of course."

Morrison asked, "What'd you do? Where'd you go?"

"We went to local sights. You know, shopping at the outlet malls, the Dali Museum, the Aquarium, Busch Gardens. Mostly we went to the beach and talked."

"Where else? Did you leave Tampa?"

"What do you mean, did I leave Tampa? The Dali Museum is in St. Pete."

"I mean, did you drive around Florida?"

"Are you insinuating I went to Gainesville and killed Brad?"

"You got a motive," Morrison said.

"What motive? For all intents and purposes Brad Coleman was out of my life."

"With your ex dead, your kid gets a heap of dough," Morrison said.

Ms. Albright's voice rose. "In the first place, my son will not inherit any money until he's 28. In the second place, even if he did inherit money now, I wouldn't want him to have it. I saw what the life of a pampered rich boy creates. I was married to his father, remember?"

"You didn't bring Bradford to his father's funeral?" Dottie asked.

"No, he's too young. I didn't want him around sorrow and death."

Tori asked, "Have you told your son about his father's death?"

"Of course. It didn't have a huge impact. He's too young to understand death."

"Is there anything you can tell us to help with our investigation?" Dottie asked.

"I can't think of anything."

Morrison asked, "Know anyone might've wanted your ex-husband dead?"

She gave a mean laugh. "Try any of the women who've ever had affairs with him."

"Thank you, Ms. Albright. We appreciate your openness," Tori said, as Dottie switched off the speaker phone.

CHAPTER FORTY THREE

Morrison said, "I called the hotel last night, spoke to Coleman's mother. She wanted to talk."

"I spoke to her yesterday, also," Tori said. "She told me Brad contacted her a few years ago for suggestions on how he could 'give back' to the world. She suggested he mentor at the Boys & Girls Club. I also asked her about Brad's 'black moods.' She denied he ever had any."

"Janet Pillsbury was lying," Morrison said.

"Not necessarily," Tori said. "Family members don't like to think a relative committed suicide. His mother might be lying about his not being depressed."

"Bottom line? Suicide or homicide?" Morrison asked.

"I'm tending away from suicide. Mrs. Coleman told me Brad was going to Machu Picchu this summer."

"So?"

"Suicidal people don't make plans for the future."

"You did better than I did with the Colemans," Dottie said. "The father was so hostile you'd think I killed his son. He told me if we couldn't solve his son's murder that he'd hire a *northern* detective who knew what *he* was doing," Dottie said.

Tori said, "Sounds like a real charmer."

"He's worse in person," Dottie said.

Morrison looked at Tori. "You believe *Ms.* Albright?"

He emphasized the "Ms." But Tori thought it prudent not to discuss Ms. Albright's preferred title.

"She's a long shot," Tori said.

"Her story about the inheritance checks out with Harrison," Dottie said.

Morrison asked, "When'd you talk with him?"

"I called him late yesterday about the will."

"What else you haven't told me?"

"Wait a minute, wait a minute," Dottie said. "I found out after you left yesterday. I got so wound up with your news about Coleman's ex-wife, I forgot. I wasn't holding out, honest."

Morrison's voice softened and his color resumed a more natural tone. "Sorry, I've a short fuse. What else did Harrison say?"

Dottie filled Morrison in about the money Steve DeMaio inherited.

Morrison pounced on the information. "That gives him motive, opportunity and method."

Tori was confused. "What method?"

"He's got cyanide in his lab," Morrison said.

"Who's keeping information from whom?" Dottie snapped.

"Okay, okay. We're even," Morrison said. "I called Mrs. Coleman's room. She was headed to DeMaio's. I thought'd be a good time to check out the lab, you know, without DeMaio knowing. I called you but the answering machine wasn't on. Okay?"

"Okay," she said appeased. She thought, *I need to buy an answering machine.*

Morrison proclaimed, "It looks like we got our man."

"I don't think DeMaio killed Coleman," Tori said.

"Oldest motive on the books. A guy steals a man's woman, he kills for revenge."

"It's too pat," Tori said. "Besides, we don't know if his prints match those on the bottle."

Morrison said, "I'm willing to arrest him without the prints."

"I'm not," Dottie said.

"I'm in charge," he retorted.

"Don't pull rank; I thought we were in this together," Dottie said. "Humor me. Don't do anything until we check the prints."

He shrugged his shoulders. "I got enough to arrest him. If his prints don't match, I let him go."

"I'm not trying to take over the case," Tori said, "but we still have other people with motive, opportunity and possibly method."

"Like who?" he asked.

"Ms. Albright for one," said Dottie. "Whitherspoon for another. He was so upset when you interviewed him he had a panic attack. Then he committed suicide – maybe guilt was weighing on him. His office is down the hall from Coleman's and keys to professors' offices hang in the main office – labeled keys. He could get into DeMaio's office and lab as well. For that matter, any faculty member on campus could get to the keys. Everyone knows DeMaio and Coleman play tennis on Tuesday mornings."

Morrison looked at her over his half glasses, but didn't respond, so she said, "There's Russell Mills. He'd know how to get into the offices. He's friends with Betty Lou and could have gotten the key."

"You said he didn't have no motive," Morrison said.

"I'm brain storming."

"Stick with viable suspects, okay?"

"There's Trish Acosta," said Tori. "She was DeMaio's student assistant. She could get poison from the chem lab."

"Why kill her boyfriend?" Morrison asked.

Dottie said, "Maybe Coleman was going to dump her."

"Pretty flimsy reasoning," Morrison said.

"Yeah. And her story about being at the spa checks out," Tori said. "But, there's the dean. People hint she had something against Coleman."

Dottie asked, "Why would she decide to support a grievance against him after going out on a limb to get him promoted and tenured? Maybe something happened."

"Gibson said she encouraged the grievance. And that's someone else who might have a motive – Davis Gibson," Tori said. "He tried to stop Coleman's tenure."

"Okay, okay, so there're others who might've killed Coleman. What're we going to do – sneak fingerprints from everyone in Gainesville? The chief's on my ass now." Morrison got up from his desk and walked to the window, rubbing his lower back as he leaned backwards.

"Today is Saturday and no one's at the university," Tori said. "Can't your men search DeMaio's lab and office and get a sample of his fingerprints. Meanwhile we can re-interview DeMaio and keep him busy so he won't drop by the lab."

Without responding to Tori, Morrison shouted for Jason and sent him out to the university to collect fingerprint samples.

He winked at Dottie. "Go with Jason."

CHAPTER FORTY FOUR

Tori stood behind Morrison as he knocked on DeMaio's front door about 10:00 a.m. Meanwhile Jason, with Dottie in tow, checked out DeMaio's campus office and lab. DeMaio opened the door wearing khaki shorts and an open-necked polo shirt sprouting thick hair. DeMaio said, "Well, the dynamic duo. To what do I owe this unexpected, and I should add unwelcome, visit?"

Morrison said, "Questions about murder."

"Come in, come in, welcome to my humble abode." While speaking, DeMaio bowed at the waist and swept his left arm in the direction of his living room.

Tori cringed when Morrison verbalized his agreement with DeMaio's assessment. "Your abode sure is humble."

"I didn't know you were on *Southern Living's* payroll or I'd have brought in decorators," DeMaio snarled. Both DeMaio and Morrison's voices were hostile and neither attempted to hide his dislike for the other.

The sour smell of stale beer and rancid food assaulted Tori's nose. The living room was strewn with remnants of the get-together the previous night: crumpled napkins, paper plates with petrified uneaten food and a half dozen partly-full plastic cups of beer. She surveyed the apartment, wondering once more why a professor lived in squalor. She asked, "May we ask you some questions, Steve?"

"Sure, what do you want to know? I told you everything I knew last time."

DeMaio sat on the futon couch and motioned to Tori and Morrison to sit on the chairs. "Have a seat." He stretched his arms along the futon's back and looked at Tori. "What's with the slacks? You've got great legs. You should show them off."

"When I want your advice, I'll ask for it."

"You seen Trish Acosta since Coleman's murder?" Morrison asked.

"I saw her at the memorial service yesterday. Why?"

"We'll ask the questions," Morrison said in an authoritarian voice. "She come to the get-together here?"

"How'd you know about that? What're you doing? Following me?" DeMaio sat upright, fists clenched, glaring at Morrison.

Tori responded before Morrison could escalate the antagonism. "Nobody's following you. The Colemans told us about the get together."

"Yeah, old man Coleman was happy as a junk yard dog." DeMaio leaned forward with his arms braced on his thighs. He absentmindedly played with debris on the table.

Tori asked, "How did Brad Coleman get along with his folks?"

"Brad thought his father was a superhero – Spiderman in a Giorgio Armani suit. He missed the fact the man had the emotions of a marble slab. But Mrs. Coleman's a sweetheart. Why she stayed with that insensitive bastard, I don't know. Brad loved his mom but thought she was a dingbat. She acted like an airhead, but I think it was an act to save face. Old man Coleman treated his wife like a princess. Meanwhile he was screwing every babe in New England. He was discreet. He didn't want to incite his mother-in-law." DeMaio rested his arms on the back of the couch.

"His father-in-law didn't care if Mr. Coleman was unfaithful to his wife?" Tori asked.

"The father-in-law died while Brad was in high school. The mother-in-law controlled the money."

Morrison asked, "When'd she die?"

"A couple years ago, right after Brad's divorce."

"You knew Brad was married?" Tori asked.

"Sure, we told each other everything."

"Why didn't you tell us?" Morrison asked.

166

"I don't know." DeMaio shrugged. "I didn't think it was important."

"What else didn't you tell us?" Morrison asked in a hostile voice.

"Nothing, I forgot that's all." DeMaio sat up straight again. "Brad didn't talk about his marriage."

"Brad timed his divorce so he inherited the money and didn't have to share it with his ex-wife?" Tori asked, resuming the interrogation.

"Yeah, he delayed the divorce until the old woman was too sick to change her will, but before she died."

"What can you tell us about Coleman's ex-wife?" Tori asked.

"Brad said she was a looker, independent, ambitious, smart, too. She's an accountant at some fortune 500 company. Brad was not a one-woman man, he screwed around. Melissa didn't want to share, so she divorced him. Everyone was happy: Brad had his freedom, his folks had their grandchild, and Melissa had her divorce."

"Did his ex-wife hold a grudge against Coleman?"

"Is the Pope Catholic?" DeMaio asked.

"What the hell's that mean?" Morrison bellowed into DeMaio's face. "Answer the question."

DeMaio glared and turned back to Tori who asked, "Do you think she killed him?"

"Nah, she'd have done it years ago if she wanted to."

Morrison interrupted, "Coleman and you were close?"

"Yes, I told you that."

"Yeah, right. So close Coleman left you dough," Morrison said.

"Yes?" DeMaio cocked his head and smiled. "A few bucks would come in handy."

"It's more like 125 grand," Tori said.

DeMaio gasped. "Are you kidding? I thought he left everything to the kid."

"Everything except the $125,000 he left you."

"What're you planning to do with the dough?" Morrison asked, raising the specter of hostility again. Tori sent him a warning look to no avail.

"This's the first I heard about the money," DeMaio said in an equally hostile tone. "Brad didn't talk about dying, he thought he was immortal. Are you suggesting I killed Brad?"

Tori took over the questioning again, trying to defuse the growing antagonism. "Did Brad ever discuss his will with you?"

DeMaio looked into space, his eyes unfocused. When he spoke again he had calmed down – his voice was softer. "No, I'd no idea he left me money." He picked up a napkin from the pile on the table and began shredding it, paying more attention to the napkin than to his visitors.

"Why didn't Brad leave anything to Trish?" Tori asked.

DeMaio stashed the shredded napkin in a half empty paper cup and looked at Tori. "Brad didn't intend to spend his life with Trish." He watched as the beer engulfed the napkin, sending a whiff of stale beer into the air.

Tori said, "Betty Lou said Brad was settling down with Trish."

DeMaio looked at Tori. "Betty Lou thought Brad was getting married if he dated a woman more than 30 minutes. She didn't approve of Brad discarding women like shirts with frayed collars."

"He wasn't serious about Trish?"

"Sure he was serious. He seriously wanted to screw her until some new chick came along. Flames burnt out fast for Brad. He liked variety. Brad had a shorter attention span with women than a kid with A. D. D. Another week or month or so and Trish would have been last week's news," DeMaio said.

"Nice guy," Morrison said.

"Hey, they had fun while it lasted."

"You bet Coleman he couldn't get Janet Pillsbury into bed," Morrison said, his face an ad for the Avenger.

"I told Brad he couldn't and shouldn't get involved with Janet. I told him to stay away from married broads."

"There was no bet?" Tori asked.

"I didn't say that. When I told Brad he couldn't get Janet in the sack he bet me 25 bucks he could. I took the bet."

"But you were wrong."

"Yeah, I was wrong. Brad could charm the pants off chicks." DeMaio snickered. "Excuse the pun."

Morrison scowled. He asked, "Dr. DeMaio, you got a stash of cyanide in your lab, right?"

"I'd hardly call it a stash, but, yes, I keep cyanide in my lab. It's a chemistry lab, for Christ's sake." DeMaio's voice and irritation rose to match Morrison's.

"You lecture about poisons in your class?" Morrison asked.

"Yeah, yeah, it's a sexy topic. Kids love it," DeMaio said. "They fantasize about the havoc they could wreak."

"You an expert on poison?" Morrison asked.

"What is this, an attempt to get me to confess to murder?" DeMaio's voice was getting louder and more aggressive each time he answered Morrison. "I'm a chemist. Poison is a chemical. I teach about it. But I did not kill Brad Coleman." He got up from the couch and began to pace. DeMaio walked to the entrance of his exercise room, grabbed each side of the door jam with a hand and leaned into the room. He straightened up, turned and asked, "What about Janet's husband? He threatened to kill Brad."

"We're looking into that," Morrison said. He pulled his cell phone out of his pocket and flipped it open. He muttered something into the phone that Tori couldn't hear and nodded. Morrison stood up and motioned to Tori he was ready to go. Tori thanked DeMaio for his time while Morrison turned and walked out without a word.

CHAPTER FORTY FIVE

Morrison sat behind his desk and looked at Tori with a pensive expression. "You're right. DeMaio wouldn't kill over a woman; he's the coldest bastard I ever met."

"Yes. He might kill, but not for love," Tori said.

"If Coleman was like DeMaio, it's no wonder some guy poisoned him. He don't care who he screws, he'd hump a mannequin."

"He tells women where they stand with him."

"He *says* he does," Morrison said. "He tell you them rules, when you dated him?"

"I didn't date him long enough to discuss rules," Tori said in an irritated voice. "That topic is off limits."

"Oh?"

She asked, "Why didn't you tell him we eliminated Pillsbury as a suspect?"

"Haven't eliminated him. He might've paid some guy to kill Coleman," Morrison said. "Besides, I don't want people knowing cops were sneaking around getting suspects' fingerprints."

Tori thought for a moment. "If Pillsbury's still a suspect, then so is Janet."

"Guess so." Morrison sighed.

Jason and Dottie burst into the room. "Whaddya find?" Morrison asked.

"DeMaio's prints match those on the bottle," Jason said. "He's the killer."

"I don't believe it," Tori said.

"You know what else we found?" Dottie asked. "The obscene photos that Coleman took of his lovers."

"Really?"

"That's not all. Obscene photos – of preteen girls."

"C'mon, let's get the bastard," Morrison thundered.

DeMaio opened the door, "The police chief of Nottingham and Maid Marian twice in one day! What did I do to deserve this attention?" DeMaio opened his arms, but blocked their entrance into his house.

Tori thought Morrison took malicious pleasure in saying, "Steven DeMaio, you are under arrest for the murder of Brad Coleman. Sergeant read him his rights."

DeMaio stood open-mouthed for a few seconds. Then he said, "What? I didn't kill Brad. How could I? I didn't see him for days before he died."

Morrison gloated. "DeMaio, we got you dead to rights. You killed Coleman because he stole your girl. Your fingerprints are on the bottle what poisoned Coleman. You were with him Tuesday morning. You had motive, opportunity and method."

DeMaio stuttered and sputtered. "Bu... how?... That's impossible. I don't believe it."

"You are charged with keeping child pornography, as well," Dottie said.

"I'd never look at kiddie porn."

Dottie said, "We also found obscene photos of Brad Coleman's former girlfriends."

"What? No way! I've never seen any photos of Brad's girlfriends. I'm not into porn. Why look at photos when I can see the real thing?"

Tori rode back to the station with Morrison. "I can't believe he did it," Tori said, still incredulous.

Morrison patted her shoulder. "I know. You almost got me convinced."

"Couldn't his fingerprints have gotten on the bottle some other way?" Tori asked.

"Tori, give it up. He's a good liar. Don't lose sleep over him, he's not worth it."

"I don't care about him, but I *do* care if someone else is getting away with murder."

CHAPTER FORTY SIX

Thoughts bombarded Tori as she climbed into her Boxster and began the drive home. She stopped at a red light. She rubbed her chin. By the time the light changed, her thoughts had coalesced. She turned the car sharply and drove across traffic, eliciting a cacophony of horns while she made an illegal U-turn. Oblivious to the annoyance of her fellow drivers, Tori drove in the opposite direction. A few minutes later she pulled into Trish Acosta's driveway.

Trish's face registered surprise and another emotion Tori could not quite identify when she opened the front door. Her face and shoulders stiff, Trish remained behind the closed screen door. "What brings you here?" she asked. Tori thought her voice sounded defensive. "Where's the detective?"

Tori said in a gentle voice, "I thought you'd want to know that Detective Morrison arrested Steve DeMaio for Brad Coleman's murder."

"He did?" Relief spread across Trish's face, replacing the other emotions. She said, "C'mon in." She opened the screen door and gestured toward her sitting room. "Sorry, I wasn't being hospitable. Please forgive me, I'm not myself." She led Tori into the sitting area and closed the laptop sitting on the coffee table. *Why did she close the laptop so quickly – wasn't she worried about saving her work?* Tori wondered.

Dressed in black running shorts and a shocking pink sports bra, her long tresses pulled up in a pony tail, Trish explained, "I just got back from jogging." Even hot and sweaty, Trish was beautiful. "I made some lemonade, care for a glass?"

"Sure, thanks."

Trish got a glass from the kitchenette and a pitcher of lemonade from the refrigerator. She poured the lemonade and handed Tori the glass. Picking up a partly full glass from the coffee table, she sat on the couch and stretched her long tanned legs, crossing them at the ankles.

"Did you know Brad and Steve were into pornography?" Tori asked.

Trish averted her eyes for a nanosecond before responding, "Brad told me Steve was into pornography, but Brad didn't like it."

Why did she avert her eyes? What isn't she telling me? Is she trying to hide the fact Brad took photos of her?

"So they didn't share photographs?"

"Never." Trish sipped the lemonade, looking over the edge of her glass at Tori. Tori said, "I saw you at the memorial service."

"I didn't see you."

"I was in back with Detectives Morrison and Epstein. It must've been difficult viewing those photographs of Brad."

"It was awful. The worst part was seeing Brad's parents."

Trish's face crumpled and she brought her fist to her mouth. She began to whimper before bursting into tears. Trish hopped up and grabbed a few tissues from a box on the end table. As she sat on the couch next to Trish, Tori noticed damp tissues filling the wastebasket near it. She put her arm around Trish who leaned on Tori's shoulder and said, "I keep thinking it's a dream. No, a nightmare."

"It must be terrible," Tori said.

"I have horrible nightmares," Trish sobbed. "Brad is calling me. He beckons me to come to him. He holds his arms out like he's waiting for me. Then he morphs into a skeleton, his arms still out, the bones of his fingers ready to clasp my arms. He makes this horrendous cackling noise." Trish continued to cry, holding onto Tori. "I run away, but he jumps in front of me. It's so horrible. I'm afraid to go to sleep."

Assuming her psychologist persona, Tori talked as she would to a client. "I empathize. You go to college, fall in love and your lover is killed. I wish I could say something to make the hurt go away."

Hearing the familiar tune, "Can You Feel the Love Tonight," Tori took out her cell phone. "Hello? Oh, Hi, Sean. What's up?" She listened. "Have fun." She turns to Trish, "That was my son, Sean."

"I didn't know you had children. Does your husband work at the university?"

"We're divorced. Sean's visiting his father this weekend."

"You don't look happy about it."

"We divorced a long time ago." Tori shrugged and thought, *I didn't realize how much I still hurt.* She looked in the distance, remembering the cutting pain when she opened the divorce notice. She brought herself back to the present and asked, "Have you been eating?"

Trish started to smile, but her lips trembled and she pressed them together. She said, "It's sweet of you to ask. I haven't been interested in food."

"You'll handle things better if you take care of yourself."

"You're nice for someone who studies murders."

In an attempt to distract Trish, Tori looked at the photograph of two little girls displayed on the end table. "Who are the cute little girls?" she asked. She looked at Trish and back at the photo. "I'd guess the older one is you, the one with the dark hair."

Trish picked up the photograph and looked at it, tears sliding down her face. "Yes, that's me. The sweet little blond is my younger sister." Trish bit her bottom lip. "My mother died when Diane was three. I became her second mother." She looked at Tori, "Do you have any brothers or sisters?

"A younger sister."

"You must know what it's like to want to protect her and keep her from harm," said Trish.

Tori sat up. Did she know what it was like to want to protect her little sister? "I haven't felt like I needed to protect my sister since we were children."

"I'd think a psychologist would help her sister over every bump she faced in life. Are you and your sister close?"

175

"We were close in high school," Tori said.

"And now?"

"I guess I should still be protecting her."

"From what?"

"I'm not sure," Tori said.

CHAPTER FORTY SEVEN

Tori called Dottie and asked if they could get together to discuss the case. Dottie was meeting Jason Nolan at the Beer & Billiards in Waldo. "Why don't you join us?"

As Dottie hung up Morrison stopped by her desk. "Don't you have to leave to get out to the Beer & Billiards before 6:00?" he asked.

"What makes you think I'm going to the Beer & Billiards?" Dottie retorted.

He looked at her over his half glasses. "I'm a detective; it's my business to know."

"What happened to personal privacy?"

"There're no secrets in the department. You're going to the Beer & Billiards to meet Jason Nolan."

Dottie looked at her superior officer. He was more aware than she thought, but she didn't like him poking his nose into her business. She was about to tell him off when he handed her speeding ticket to her and said, "And slow down, if you don't want another speeding ticket." He patted her shoulder, "Have fun."

Tori pulled into the parking lot at the same time Dottie did. They walked into the bar together where they spotted Jason Nolan at his usual table. Jason was grinning, bursting with gossip. "I can't wait to catch you up about Junior's exploits with a hot little chick he stopped for speeding."

"Who's Junior?" Tori asked.

"Jason's older, bigger, dumber brother," Dottie said. "He's a cop in Waldo and runs the speed trap for his dad, the police chief."

Tori turned to Jason, "Your father is the Waldo police chief?"

"Yes, ma'am. Embarrassing, isn't it?"

"I didn't mean that. I... it's just... the speed trap..." Tori said.

"Sure you did," Jason said. "It's embarrassing. That's why I'm a cop in Gainesville – not Waldo."

Dottie said, "I want to hear about Junior."

"A couple weeks ago Junior stopped a UF coed, a real beauty, going back to Gainesville from north Florida," Jason said. "He ran the usual by her and she seemed interested but didn't want a quickie; she wanted to spend an afternoon together."

"Wait a minute – what's this usual stuff?" Tori asked.

"Junior uses the speed trap to catch unsuspecting women and offers to let them off if they 'pleasure him,'" Dottie said in a voice that left no doubt as to her animosity toward Junior.

"Does your father know?" Tori's eyes were wide.

"Jason's father doesn't believe him. He thinks Jason's making it up to get Junior in trouble – sibling rivalry."

Tori turned to Jason. "What happened?"

"Well, ma'am, she gave him a phony phone number. He was pissed as hell. He had her name, an unusual one – Kostulos – and checked her out at the University Registrar's office. A student by that name was on the books, but hadn't registered in four or five years. Junior was hopping mad."

Jason was laughing so hard words stuck in his throat. "The horny jerk took a day off and made some excuse to his old lady." Jason wiped the tears from his eyes with the back of his hand. "The whole department's ribbing him. He bragged about sweeping this bad kitty off her feet and she was playing with him, she wasn't even a university student." Jason grabbed his mug of beer and took a gulp.

Dottie beamed. "At last the bastard met a woman who was his match."

Their boisterous laughter drowned out the juke box and brought Jimmy, the bartender, to the table. Jason relayed the story and before long Jimmy was at the bar passing the tale along to the regulars. When they stopped laughing, Dottie reminded Jason about Junior giving her a ticket.

"Want me to try to fix it?"

"You don't have to. Morrison gave me the ticket this afternoon and told me to stay out of Junior's way."

"No kidding?" Jason pursed his lips. "Daddy reviews all the tickets before they're sent to the courthouse. He must've given it to Morrison. Daddy always had a soft spot for you."

"Right. That's why he blanches every time he sees me with you."

"Don't go on about that, Dottie. Daddy's not prejudiced. He acts tough, but he's got a good heart."

Tori turned to Jason and asked, "Do you know anything else about Coleman's murder?"

"Like what? Morrison told you everything I know, ma'am."

"I don't know. I'm upset that Morrison arrested DeMaio. I don't think he killed Coleman," Tori said.

"Are you defending DeMaio because of your relationship with him?" Dottie asked.

"No secrets in the department, huh?" Tori asked.

"Hey girl, it might bias you."

Jason asked, "Do you have something going with DeMaio?"

"God, no! I don't like Steve DeMaio," Tori said. "When I got divorced I cried for two weeks. When I met Steve DeMaio, he offered to have sex with me so I could forget Gerry." Tori's expression was a study in loathing. "His actual words weren't that polite."

"Did you take him up on his offer?" Jason asked, looking into his beer mug.

"Nah, I told him to go screw himself," Tori said.

Jason laughed. "Good for you!" After a pause he asked, "Why don't you think he killed Coleman?"

Tori shrugged. "Intuition, psychological insight." She turned to Dottie. "What do you think?"

"I agree. I checked those porno photos we found on DeMaio's computer. Someone had superimposed children's faces on the bodies from the photos Coleman took."

"Did you tell Morrison?" Tori asked.

"He said it didn't matter," Dottie said.

"Trish told me DeMaio was into porn, but Brad wasn't."

179

"He'd lie to his girlfriend about using porn," Dottie said. She asked Jason to go over what he found at the crime scene. "Maybe we missed something."

Jason explained that someone had taken the cap off and recapped the Pepsi bottle before Coleman got it. He discovered that someone had tampered with the cap when he inspected it under a microscope.

"That means the killer had the bottle for some time before he or she gave it to Coleman," Tori said. "It can't be easy to remove a bottle cap and replace it so someone opening it doesn't realize it's been tampered with."

"All he'd need is a capping tool," Jason said.

Dottie asked, "How do you know about capping tools?"

"You city girls are naïve," said Jason. "Everyone around here makes their own brew and bottles it."

"Who would orchestrate a complex plan to poison Coleman's soda and then leave their fingerprints on the bottle?" Tori asked. "DeMaio isn't stupid."

"Everyone makes mistakes, even smart people," Jason said.

Tori said, "Little kids know how to wipe off fingerprints; television cop shows have seen to that."

"Okay," Dottie said. "Where do we go from here?"

"What about DeMaio's alibi?" Tori asked. "He said he was running on campus. Do you have his route?"

"Yeah, girl. Want to meet me for a run tomorrow morning?" Dottie asked.

"Yes." Then Tori looked at her watch and said "Yikes!! I was supposed to meet Matt 30 minutes ago."

CHAPTER FORTY EIGHT

Tori hurried into the Paramount Grill where Matt was sitting at a back table looking at a half empty bottle of wine with a sour expression on his face.

"I'm so sorry," she said. When she bent to kiss him he turned his head away so she caught his cheek. *I've done it this time,* she thought.

"So am I. What's the excuse this time?" His voice sent a chill down her spine.

"Matt, you know how I am when I get involved."

He raised his eyebrows. "Silly me. I thought you were involved with me."

"I am involved with you. I'm working on this psychological autopsy…"

"Don't shit me, Tori. Steve DeMaio's been arrested for the murder."

"I'm sure he didn't do it."

"That's not the point. It's *MURDER*. M, U, R, D, E, R," he spelt it out. "There's no need for a psychological autopsy after the cause of death has been determined."

Tori sat back and took a deep breath.

"May I pour you some wine, Dr. Vincent?" their waiter asked.

Tori gave Matt a questioning look, but he averted his eyes. "Yes, please, thank you, Philippe."

"Are you ready to order?" the waiter asked.

"Give us a few minutes, please," Tori said. Tori tried to get eye contact with Matt, but he looked to the side. When she attempted to take Matt's hand, he pulled it away. She sighed. "You're right, Matt. The psychological autopsy is over."

"Then what were you doing? And why do you smell of beer?" Matt asked, letting her hold his hand.

"I had a beer with Dottie. We were discussing the case."

"I suppose Morrison was with you."

"No. Herb wasn't… You don't still think Herb and I…"

"Herb is the macho kind of guy you fall for – like your ex-husband, like DeMaio."

Tori laughed. "Herb?"

"You think I'm joking?" he pulled his hand away from Tori's.

"Herb is married with a daughter. He also thinks psychological autopsies are as scientific as faith-healing."

Matt said, "I thought this was going to be our special weekend while Sean was away with his father."

"It is." Tori looked at Matt.

Matt looked into Tori's eyes and reached for her hand. "Let's start over. Forget this little tiff. After dinner we can drive to St. Augustine and stay at that bed and breakfast by the Bridge of Lions."

Tori lowered her eyes. "I can't stay in St. Augustine tonight."

"Didn't Sean go with his father?"

"Yes."

"Look at me Tori. What's going on?"

"I'm running with Dottie tomorrow morning at 7:00."

"Call her and say you're not going."

"I can't," Tori said.

Matt glared without speaking.

"We're going to run the route Steve DeMaio said he took the morning Coleman was poisoned."

"Why? You agreed there's no need for a psychological autopsy," Matt said.

"Steve DeMaio didn't murder Brad Coleman."

"That's for the police to decide."

"Morrison thinks he did it," she said.

"What's that got to do with you?"

"I've got to prove DeMaio didn't kill Coleman," Tori said.

"Why? Are you still hung up on him?"

"No, I'm not hung up on Steve DeMaio, but I am tired of having to explain myself to you." Tori glowered at Matt, stood up and stormed out.

CHAPTER FORTY NINE

Tori tossed her purse on the couch and flopped into the lounge chair. She crossed her arms and seethed. She stood and paced. She wasn't sure whether she was more annoyed with Matt or herself. *Why do I mess up relationships? Gerry, Steve, Matt, even Cindy. Cindy,* she thought, *at least I can patch up that relationship.* She picked up the phone.

"Hi, is Cindy there?" she asked.

"Of course she's here. She's my wife. Where else would she be?"

"Sorry, Derrick. This is Tori; I'd like to speak with her."

"She can't come to the phone," he said.

"Is something the matter?"

"No. She's busy."

"It's 9:00 Saturday night. What's she doing she can't talk to her sister?"

"I said she's busy." He voice was hard.

The phone went dead. Tori held the receiver out and looked at it. *What's going on?* Tori riffled through her purse and pulled out her cell phone. She scrolled down her contact list with unsteady fingers. She dialed Cindy's cell phone number.

"Hello." The voice was low and wobbly.

"Cindy?" Tori asked.

"Yes."

"Are you all right?"

"Oh Tori – help me." Sobs coming over the phone clutched Tori's heart.

"Cindy, what's going on?"

"I told Derrick I want a divorce," she choked out the words between sobs. "Derrick said if he can't have me no one can."

"Where are you?"

"I locked myself in the guest room," Cindy said.

"Did he hit you?"

"No. I ran in here. He threw a chair at me, but I closed the door before it hit me. It slammed into the door."

"Cindy, has he ever hit you?" `

"Not really."

"What do you mean, not really, Cindy?" Tori asked. "Has he hit you or not?"

"He threw his shoe at me once."

"Cindy, call 911 right now." Tori's voice was emphatic.

"I can't. He'll kill me."

"The idea is to keep him from hurting you. If you won't call 911, call Dad."

"No. I don't want him to know. He'll kill Derrick."

"Cindy, I'm going to call Steve, Gerry's brother. He lives about 20 minutes from you. Stay on the phone with me. I'll call him on the land line."

"Derrick won't like it."

"I don't give a flying fuck whether Derrick likes it or not."

Thirty minutes later, Cindy said, "The doorbell's ringing. He opened the door. I can hear voices. Someone's talking to Derrick. He's getting loud. Oh, Tori, I should never have let you call Steve."

"Don't worry," Tori said. "Steve knows what he's doing. He's a district attorney. He deals with criminals all the time."

"Derrick is not a criminal!"

Tori looked at the ceiling and slapped her head. *Silly woman.* "Sorry, I meant he knows how to handle people who are upset."

"They're yelling." Cindy sobbed. "I better go talk to Derrick."

"Cindy, stay where you are. Keep that door locked and do not open it for anyone except Steve." When there was no answer, Tori said, "Do you understand me?"

"Derrick is threatening to throw Steve out. What should I do?"

"Stay where you are. Steve will handle it." Tori thought, *I hope to God Steve can handle Derrick without making it worse than it is already.*

"I don't hear anything," said Cindy.

"Maybe they're talking in lower voices."

"Someone's knocking on the bedroom door." Cindy called out, "Who's there?" After a moment she said, "Steve, what's happening?"

Tori could hear him say, "Everything's all right." Then, "Is that Tori on the phone?" His voice came over the phone, "Hi, sweetheart, don't worry. I'm taking your sister with me. She can stay with us until she decides what to do.

CHAPTER FIFTY

Both punctual, Dottie and Tori pulled into the parking lot at 7:05, ten minutes before their agreed upon meeting time.

"I love high achievers," Tori said. "They're always early."

"It gives us time to stretch before we run, too," Dottie said. As she pushed against her car, with one leg bent and the other extended. Dottie looked at Tori. "So how was the romantic evening with Matt?"

"There was no romantic evening and there's no Matt."

"Ouch."

"And I discovered my sister's in an abusive relationship," Tori said.

"Double ouch."

"It's my mother's fault. She told Cindy she was beautiful and should use her looks to manipulate men. She said she could get anything she wanted from men."

"Is that what your mother told you?"

Tori's laugh was bitter. "My mother used to tell me gypsies left me on the doorstep. She said I couldn't be her child, a scrawny red-head with freckles. Cindy was the perfect child; she looked like Alice in Wonderland, long blond hair and big blue eyes. My mother adored and pampered her.

"Was your mother ever nice to you?"

"That made it worse. One minute she'd tell me I was beautiful and special, the next minute she'd scream and tell me to get out of

187

her life," Tori said. "I fantasized about the gypsies coming to rescue me. I resented Cindy. My mother would ask me why I couldn't be like my sister."

"That's awful," said Dottie, "but it wasn't your sister's fault your mother was like that."

"No. Now, I realize my mother has an anti-social personality disorder, but as a kid I thought she hated me."

"So what's happening with Cindy now?"

"I'll tell you all about it after I cool down. Let's concentrate on our run."

"Whatever you say."

"DeMaio said he ran eight minute miles."

"That's what I run, so I'll set the pace," Dottie said. Tori looked at Dottie's long legs and moaned. "I'm lucky if I can do 10 minute miles."

At exactly 7:20 they began the five-mile run, following DeMaio's route. They headed west on Stadium Road passing Little Hall – no sign of human activity. The same was true of the Music Building and the Auditorium. They turned the corner, continued onto McCarthy Drive, past McCarthy Hall and the water plant. "There's no one around," Dottie said. Tori was breathing heavily and puffed out a "Yeah."

They ran by parking lots, empty fields, and the windowless psychology building, turned onto Mowry Road, past Wilmot Gardens and Lake Alice, then turned north onto Bledsoe Drive where they passed recreational facilities and fields. Turning east on Radio Road they saw the first hint of life at Lakeside Residential, a housing complex, where a couple of people were getting into cars. They passed the northern part of Lake Alice and turned onto Village Drive. At the corner was Kinder Care.

Dottie checked her watch. "7:50. Parents would be dropping kids off before classes or work on a weekday."

Tori nodded, too breathless to say anything. After another minute she stopped. She leaned over, hands on her knees. Dottie turned back. "Are you all right?"

"I'm out of breath." She puffed and breathed out hard. "And my knee is hurting from that fall. Go ahead. I'll slow down and meet you at the parking lot." Tori watched Dottie run ahead. She stretched her legs and after a couple of moments began to walk. A car pulled next to her.

"You look like you could use a ride," Matt said, through the open the window.

Tori stopped and looked, not sure how to respond.

"Let's forget last night." He smiled. "I'll drive you to your car."

Tori hesitated before getting into the car. "I'm parked by Little Hall."

They passed Dottie as they got to West University. "There's Dottie. Stop so I can tell her."

Tori opened the window and called, "Matt's driving me to the parking lot. I'll wait for you there."

Matt turned onto University. Tori said, "There are lots of cars, but no way of knowing who drove by last Tuesday. All the buildings are set back from the road and facing campus." She looked at her watch. "It's 8:10. On weekdays people would be going into the buildings."

Matt pulled the car into the left lane. "Where are you going?" Tori was confused. "I told you I parked at Little Hall. You need to turn right."

"I'm taking you back to my house for our romantic weekend." Matt reached for her hand.

Tori pulled her hand away. "I don't want a romantic weekend. I want to go back to my car."

Matt clenched his teeth, looking straight ahead. Tori grabbed the door handle. Matt jerked her arm and pulled her toward him. He slapped her with the back of his hand. Startled, she put both hands to her mouth. He said, "Don't try that again."

CHAPTER FIFTY ONE

For the first time since Brad Coleman's murder, Herb Morrison was pursuing his passion, gardening. While Ruth and Jennifer were at the synagogue, he was kneeling before the one god he worshipped, his beloved plants. He caressed one of the yellow day lilies before clipping off the dead blossom of her sister. He pulled out dry leaves from around the plant and forked out the dollar weeds trying to encroach on his beauties. When his cell phone vibrated in his pocket, his first impulse was to ignore it, but his sense of professional responsibility overcame the temptation. He leaned back on his haunches, took off his right glove, wiped his hand on his pants, pulled out his cell and grunted, "Morrison."

"I think Tori's been kidnapped," Dottie panted.

"What??"

"Tori said she broke up with Matt last night. We were running together. She stopped – her knee – and I went ahead." She took a deep breath. "She came by in Matt's car. She said he'd drop her off at the parking lot. But, when I went around the corner, I saw Matt's car turning the wrong way and she wasn't here when I got to our cars."

Morrison jumped to his feet. "Where are you?" Dottie told him. Morrison said, "Call Jason. Get the license plate for Matt's car and his address. I'll pick you up in ten minutes."

"That woman attracts trouble like sugar draws ants," Morrison ranted to Dottie as he drove to Matt's house. "Those characters she

190

dates are the dregs. First, it's DeMaio – a womanizer and a murderer. Then this Matt character – I knew that dog couldn't hunt no more. Her ex-husband must've been a lulu."

Morrison drove down Matt's street at a snail's pace. "Which one's his house?" Dottie identified the house, a small ranch, on the left. Morrison pulled around the corner and parked. "No car in the drive. I'll check out the garage."

"I'll go," Dottie said. "I saw the car."

Morrison nodded. Dottie walked to Matt's house. Within minutes she was back. "The car's in the garage."

"Call Tori's cell phone," Morrison said. "Ask where she's at. If she can talk ask if he's got a weapon."

The melody "Can You Feel the Love Tonight" played. Tori pulled out her cell phone and spotted Dottie's name before Matt grabbed her wrist and took the phone away from her. He threw the phone across the room.

Tori said, "That's Dottie. She saw me in your car."

"So what? She knows we're dating."

"I told her we broke up."

"People get back together. You told her I was driving you to your car."

"But, she knows…" Matt's ringing phone interrupted her. Tori reached for it, but Matt grabbed her wrist again. "Don't touch the phone." The answering machine picked up, "Hi Matt, this is Dottie. I'm looking for Tori. Please call me."

"Matt, Dottie knows you didn't take me to my car. Stop. Don't ruin your career."

"I'm not going to ruin my career. We are going to have a romantic weekend."

CHAPTER FIFTY TWO

When Matt did not answer, Morrison called for backup. Within two minutes, three black and whites careened around the corner and parked behind Morrison's car. Morrison sent two SWAT members to the back of Matt's house, warning them to keep out of sight, but to watch the house with their high-powered binoculars and keep their weapons at the ready. "I'll knock on the front door," he said.

Dottie interrupted. "Maybe it would be better if I knock. He knows Tori and I were running together. He won't be upset if he sees me."

"Too dangerous."

"I'm a detective, not a damsel in distress," she retorted.

"Right. I'll wait behind my car across from the house. Three minutes and I come in."

Matt did not answer the door to Dottie's knock. She called, "Hey, Matt, it's Dottie. Is Tori with you?" She tapped on the window next to the door. "Matt! Tori!" Not a sound. She tried to look into the room, but the drapes were drawn.

Morrison signaled Dottie to join him. When she was behind the car, Morrison called for the other squad cars. When the black and whites were parked in front of Matt's house, Morrison spoke into a megaphone. "Matt, we know you're in there. We know Tori's with you. Come out with your hands raised."

There was no answer.

Morrison's voice boomed, "Matt, pick up the phone. Talk to us." He turned to Dottie. "Dial his number."

Dottie dialed and listened. "No answer."

Morrison wiped the sweat from his forehead with the back of his hand. He paced behind the car. "We need the psychologist to talk to him." He ran his hands through his hair.

Dottie said, "Tori is a psychologist."

"Yeah. She's so good with people, she got taken hostage."

Jason said, "Stop bickering, you two, and find a way to get Tori out of there."

Morrison's phone rang and he checked the ID. "It's Bergman; he's scouting out the back with binoculars." Morrison clicked the button, "What do you see?"

"He doesn't appear to have a weapon. They're sitting in the living room. It looks like they're talking."

Dottie jumped when her phone rang. "It's him." She answered the call. "Okay." A pause. "Does he have a weapon?" Another pause. "Are you sure?"

Dottie turned to Morrison. "He doesn't have a weapon and she wants us to give her ten minutes to talk to Matt. She wants the squad cars to go. You and I are to stay."

Morrison closed his eyes and shook his head, but said into his radio. "Move the squad cars around the corner – be sure they're out of sight. Leave the guys in back with the binoculars. Tell us what's happening." Morrison paced back and forth mumbling and cursing. Every so often he looked at his watch. "How long's it been?"

Dottie leaned against the car watching the house, hands clenched on the car roof, perspiration dripping from her forehead. "Give her time. It's been six minutes."

"What're they doing?" Morrison asked.

"I can't see anything from here."

Morrison got in the car and called the SWAT team in the backyard. He leaned out and said to Dottie, "They're sitting, talking. Looks like this Matt is crying."

"She knows what she's doing."

"The woman's nuts! She broke into Coleman's house, I just about killed her."

"No, you didn't. Your gun isn't loaded."

"How do you know my…?"

"There they are!"

Morrison looked up to see Tori walking out of the house with Matt. Tori had Matt by the elbow, and she was guiding him down the sidewalk to the driveway. Morrison and Dottie met them halfway. Morrison said to Dottie, "Read him his Miranda Rights."

"No!" Tori held her hand up. "Nothing happened. Everything is fine."

Morrison threw his hands in the air. "Nothing happened? For Christ sake, he took you hostage."

"He wouldn't hurt a fly."

Morrison scowled at Tori. Tori flew into Morrison's arms, crying and trembling.

CHAPTER FIFTY THREE

Morrison drove a shaken Tori to her house. "You got to press charges," he said for the millionth time. "He could've killed you." He turned to gaze at Tori with sympathy and puzzlement.

"He was trying to be macho so I'd love him," she said.

"Strange idea he's got about love."

"He was convinced you and I were having an affair."

"Oh, for God's sake, you must be kidding." Morrison said. "But, I'm not kidding about pressing charges. God knows what he might've done if we hadn't got to you."

Tori swallowed. "I'm grateful you did. I was terrified. I thought everyone would stop looking when I didn't answer Dottie's calls. I can't tell you how relieved I was when I heard Dottie knock on the window and then heard you on that megaphone."

Morrison pulled his car into Tori's driveway, shut off the engine and turned to her, resting his arm on the seatback. "Tori, listen." He took her hand. "Please press charges. He's loony. Who knows what he's capable of? I might not be there next time."

Tears wound down Tori's cheek. "Herb, I can't do that. It would ruin his career."

Tori's little silver Boxster glided to a stop next to them in the driveway and Dottie hopped out, dangling the keys toward Tori.

"At least file a restraining order," Morrison said. "Keep him away from you."

"I'll think about it."

Dottie offered to stay with her, but Tori insisted she was fine. She lied. She was traumatized by the encounter with Matt. *Morrison's right, I'm horrible at relationships. I thought Gerry was my soul mate, but he felt claustrophobic and wanted his freedom. I thought Steve DeMaio was fun, but he only wanted sex. I thought Matt was a gentle intellectual, but he wanted to own me and was jealous of his own shadow. What is wrong with me? I'm a psychologist. Why can't I understand men?*

Tori spread the morning paper open on the kitchen table. The headlines read: ALLEGED MURDERER OF UNIVERSITY OF FLORIDA PROFESSOR ARRESTED. A photo of a serious-looking Morrison peered at her. *Too bad Herb's married. But, if I got involved with him I'd find he was wrong for me, too.* She thought, *Don't go there, girl.* She returned her attention to the newspaper. Quotations from faculty members sanctified Coleman following his untimely death; a professor tenured over his colleagues' objections had morphed into a valued member of the department. Tearful students missed their favorite professor, a kind mentor who could never be replaced. "Gimme a break!" she said out loud. *Why don't you interview the coeds he seduced, the women whose lives he shattered?*

Dean Kohlberg was quoted as saying Coleman was a 'unique individual.' Tori thought, *That description was open to a lot of interpretations. Kohlberg is hiding something.* Unlike her habit of reading every detail of the paper, Tori skimmed it – even skipped doing the crossword puzzle and Sudoku. Around 1:30 p.m. she gathered up the paper, put the puzzles aside and the rest of the paper in the recycling bin. *I'm not going to mope around,* she thought. *I'm not letting the incident with Matt intimidate me. I'm not going to let it change my behavior. I'm going to visit Steve DeMaio before Sean gets home.* She changed into a crisp cotton shirt and neat slacks and headed to the Alachua County Jail, north of Gainesville.

CHAPTER FIFTY FOUR

The correctional officer at the desk, Billie McCarthy, was an old timer, a rotund, fatherly man with a ready laugh. Billie was engrossed in papers on his desk when Tori arrived. She gave him a radiant smile and said, "Good morning, Officer."

McCarthy returned her smile with one equal in size. "Morning, Dr. Vincent. Haven't seen you for a while. How're you doing?"

"I'm great. How're things with you?"

"Aw, I tell you it's a hard life, Doc."

"Sure, Billie, I know how hard you work."

Billie shook his head. "It wears a man down sitting here reading the newspapers, counting the months till retirement." He laughed deep from his belly. Billie held up the Sunday paper with the article about the arrest prominently displayed. "Everyone's talking about it."

Tori leaned her arm on the desk and said, "I'd like to see Steve DeMaio."

"You can't take no statement or nothing." He looked at her through narrowed eyes.

"I realize that." She put on an innocent expression. "I want to visit, you know, as a representative of the university. Not to get information for court or anything."

"I don't know..." McCarthy was reluctant.

"I was with Detective Morrison when he arrested DeMaio. I'm sure he'd want you to let me see him. Why don't you call Herb to check?"

She hoped her bluff worked. *Using Morrison's first name will let Billie know I'm close to him. Morrison would be furious if he knew I was visiting DeMaio, but Morrison terrorizes the correctional officers and Billie thinks I'm Morrison's buddy. Poor Billie has a dilemma on his hands; either way he could be on the receiving end of Morrison's wrath.*

"Detective Morrison hates to be disturbed on Sunday," he said.

"Yeah. I bet he'd be upset, especially after working Saturday. He was so busy, he missed his gardening yesterday," she said. *Thank God Billie doesn't know Morrison rescued me this morning.*

"Well, I guess it's okay."

McCarthy hesitated another minute, then called the correctional officer on duty and told him to set Tori up in the attorney's visiting room with Steve DeMaio. The correctional officer was new and didn't know Tori. He inspected her and asked, "Why is she allowed in the attorney's visiting room? Why does she get special treatment?"

McCarthy snapped, "Do as I say. Dr. Vincent helped Detective Morrison catch this murderer."

Tori smiled angelically. McCarthy frowned at the correctional officer before he turned to Tori and said, "J. C. here will fix you up fine."

The officer shook his head at McCarthy who ignored him and buzzed open the door to the jail. Tori thanked McCarthy and stepped into the double-doored entrance. CLANG! The sound of McCarthy electronically shutting the door behind them made Tori jump. "Are you all right?" J. C. asked as the far door opened.

"Fine. The noise startled me."

CHAPTER FIFTY FIVE

Tori followed the correctional officer to the attorneys' visiting room: a cold jailhouse-green coop, bare but for a metal table with two chairs. A harsh overhead light attempted to compensate for the meager illumination coming through the glass in the steel door. Tori sat. Within two minutes J. C. came back with Steve DeMaio who was wearing an orange jump suit, handcuffed and shackled. Tori asked J. C. to remove the restraints.

"You sure you want to be alone with him with no handcuffs?" J. C. asked. "I can't prevent a sexual assault."

Tori put her hand on DeMaio's arm to silence his response to the guard. She said, "I'll take responsibility for my safety."

After the guard slammed and locked the steel door, Tori asked DeMaio to join her at the table.

"I can't sit still," DeMaio said. He paced around the room, rubbing his wrists where he had been handcuffed.

J. C. looked in the window of the interview room. Tori smiled at J. C. "You'd better sit or they'll put the handcuffs and shackles back," she said under her breath.

DeMaio sat at the table; his bravado depleted. He rubbed his mouth with the back of his hand. Then he ran his fingers through his disheveled hair. "What do you want? I was interrogated half the night. I don't have anything left to say."

"I didn't come to interrogate you."

"Oh, I get it. You want to rub it in, make fun of the professor in jail – like going to the zoo." DeMaio's bitterness was thick, an almost palpable barrier between them.

"I don't want anything of the sort, Steve," Tori said. "It doesn't look good for you."

"You think I don't know that? Morrison and his band of country bumpkins treated me like a mass murderer – and a child molester." DeMaio looked at her with red-rimmed eyes. "Do you believe me? I didn't kill Brad?"

"Yeah, I believe you."

"And I don't know where that kiddie porn came from."

"I know."

"You know?"

Tori explained how Dottie recognized the photographs from Coleman's computer. "You don't have to worry about the porn charges, but you still have murder hanging over your head."

DeMaio pushed his chair from the table and started to stand. Tori put her hand on his arm and cautioned him to stay seated. DeMaio leaned forward, clasped his hands, resting his arms on his thighs and gazed at the floor. "I don't know what to do."

"Do you have an attorney?" Tori asked.

"They told me I wouldn't need one if I had nothing to hide. I waived my right to an attorney during the interviews. I thought it would convince them I'm innocent."

"God, DeMaio, that's not how law enforcement works. They think they'll get more information if there's no attorney to warn you not to answer questions. You need to refuse to answer any more questions until you get a lawyer."

DeMaio nodded.

Tori asked, "How did your fingerprints get on the poisoned Pepsi bottle?"

DeMaio pulled his chair to the table and slammed his fist on it. "Damn!" He slammed his fist again. "They can't be my prints, I never drink that stuff."

Tori warned, "Keep your voice down and stop slamming the table."

He sighed. "I haven't had a soft drink since I was a teenager. I'm a health nut. My fingerprints couldn't be on a Pepsi bottle."

200

"Okay, okay. Let's assume someone got your prints on the bottle somehow. Someone also planted the porn on your computer. Who would want to set you up?"

"I don't know anyone who hates me that much."

"What about one of the women you messed over?"

"I haven't 'messed over' any women." DeMaio stared at Tori with sullen eyes.

"I lay out the rules before I get involved with a woman."

Tori locked eyes with DeMaio. "Always?"

"Yeah, always." His eyes did not flinch. He paused. Then he continued in a subdued voice, eyes on his hands in his lap. "A few years back a coed got upset... emotional... you know, after I'd been involved with her. I swore I'd be upfront with women I dated after that."

"Could she have tried to get back at you?" Tori asked.

"No. Not possible."

"Anything's possible."

"That isn't. She's dead."

Tori sat back in her chair and took a breath. "Want to tell me about it?"

"No. She couldn't have done this. So drop it, okay?" DeMaio's face was contorted with pain and he drummed his fingers on the table.

Tori watched him take a deep breath and asked, "Have you dumped anyone lately?"

"Trish is the only woman I've dated all year and she dropped me," he whispered. "I'm not dating anyone. I'm too busy writing a grant to cover my summer salary. I don't want the hassle of dealing with some chick at the same time."

Tori asked why he was writing a grant when he'd get some money for teaching. DeMaio explained he owed over $50,000 on his student loans.

"Steve, you don't live an affluent life. The place you rent must cost next to nothing. You've no furniture to speak of and you drive a Honda. You make a decent salary. You could pay off your student loans. What do you do with your money?"

DeMaio put his hands behind his bent head, elbows on the table, talking to a spot on the table. "My kid brother's gay. He has AIDS. His insurance ran out, and medication's expensive. My folks support him, but they're retired. Keeping him on antiretrovirals costs almost more than I make."

Tori sat back. At least she'd found out why Steve lived in circumstances bordering on poverty. *But why were his fingerprints on the bottle of poison?* She chewed on her bottom lip. DeMaio watched without speaking. She looked at him. "Who hated Coleman enough to kill him?"

He scratched his head. After a moment he said, "Janet's husband."

Tori thought, *Morrison and I wrote off Janet and her husband when their fingerprints didn't match those on the bottle. But, if the murderer planted DeMaio's fingerprints, we're back to square one – everyone is back as a suspect.* "How would he get access to Coleman's Pepsi?"

DeMaio grimaced. "He couldn't get anywhere near Brad."

"And how would he get your fingerprints on the bottle?"

"No way. I've never seen the guy."

"What about his wife, Janet?"

"Nah, Janet's a nice girl. Besides she likes me, she wouldn't set me up."

"You know her?" Tori asked.

"Of course, she's a chem. major. She's been in all my classes. Bright girl."

"So she had connections with you and Brad?" Tori asked. "Were you involved with her?"

"No. I don't mess around with married women."

"Such high morals." Tori glared.

"It's got nothing to do with morals, high or otherwise. Married women are trouble." He returned her glare. The staring contest ended in a stalemate.

He's being honest, she thought. "She's got connections with you and Coleman as well as access to the poison."

"During labs all the students have access to chemicals. If the student assistant is distracted, any other student could get to it."

"That means hundreds of students could have gotten the poison." Tori bit her bottom lip, thinking. She looked at him. "Steve, do you know who H. H. is?"

"H. H. stands for Horrible Hilary, the nickname the union gave Dean Kohlberg. But, Brad changed the nickname to Horny Hilary." DeMaio laughed. "Brad said she's a nympho."

"Brad Coleman had an affair with Dean Kohlberg?" Tori almost choked.

"Yeah. I promised to nominate him for the 'golden prick' award. The plaque would say 'His prick was powerful but not discerning.'" DeMaio's hands outlined the imaginary plaque.

"Didn't people think it odd he was dating the dean?"

"No one knew. He convinced her to keep their 'love' a secret until he got tenure." DeMaio made air quotation marks when he said love. "They never went anywhere in public."

"What about Trish? Did she know?"

"Trish was cool. Brad's career was important to him and he needed Kolhberg's support. Trish didn't like it, but she went along."

"What ended the affair?"

"Hilary had a faculty party at her house to announce their relationship. Brad didn't show."

"God, what a bastard."

"Kohlberg is a good dean and a good woman. He went too far and I told him so."

"She might have killed Coleman, if she thought she could get away with it."

"She could get even without murdering him," DeMaio said. "A dean can make life miserable for faculty. You know that."

"Didn't Coleman realize that?"

"People who grow up rich think they can get away with anything."

"Does Dean Kohlberg resent you? You knew about her affair with Brad. You were his best friend."

"Brad never told her I knew. I wasn't invited to the party when he dumped her."

CHAPTER FIFTY SIX

Tori's buns had barely touched the cushions on the couch in Dottie's living room when Dottie asked, "What'd you learn from DeMaio?"

"Dean Kohlberg is H. H. It stands for Horrible Hilary, or as Coleman renamed her, Horny Hilary."

Dottie's chin dropped. When Tori described Coleman's relationship with Dean Kohlberg, Dottie gasped. "The bastard screwed her so he could get tenure?"

"You got it."

"The S.O.B. I wouldn't blame the dean for murdering him," Dottie said.

"Coleman's behavior was rotten, but it didn't warrant the death penalty."

"He got what was coming to him," Dottie answered with fervor.

"Hey. Don't get mad at me. I agree he was an incredible bastard. His behavior was horrific."

"I'm not mad at you," Dottie said. "I'm furious that scrote used another human being – male or female – like that."

"Murdering someone isn't playing nice, either," Tori argued.

"Poisoning doesn't cause as much suffering as emotional torture."

"But death is permanent."

"Okay, so maybe killing someone is as bad as emotional abuse."

"Truce?" Tori asked. Dottie extended her hand in the air, palm forward and they high fived.

"Did you see this morning's paper?" Tori asked.

"I wanted to barf."

Tori shook her head. "Death transformed Coleman from a mediocre scholar with a penchant for seducing coeds to a shining star of the department who selflessly guided students."

"What a whitewash," Dottie said.

Tori nodded.

"How did DeMaio's fingerprints get on the soda bottle?" Dottie asked.

"I don't know. DeMaio says he hasn't drunk a soda in years."

"Maybe DeMaio handled an empty bottle or one full of something else. Then the murderer emptied it and refilled it with Pepsi."

"Yeah. I didn't think of that." Tori cocked her head. "They used DeMaio for a reason."

"Someone had it in for both Coleman and DeMaio."

"Yes, otherwise why go to the trouble of getting DeMaio's prints on the bottle when it'd be easy to get someone else's or wipe it clean. And then there's the kiddie porn planted in his office."

"Where do we go from here?" asked Dottie.

"Dean Kohlberg lied to me and Morrison. She didn't want us to know about her affair with Coleman. Whitherspoon and Gibson hinted at something, but wouldn't risk the dean's wrath by revealing her indiscretion," Tori said. "I'm going to re-interview Dean Kohlberg. Want to come?"

"I've got to watch my butt, girlfriend. The case is closed. They've got enough evidence for a grand jury indictment. Morrison thinks Steve DeMaio poisoned Coleman. He'd fire me if he found out I was trying to establish DeMaio's innocence."

"I forgot Morrison's your boss."

Dottie muttered, "I wish I could." Then added, "I *can* help you track down capping tools on the internet."

"Now we know the fingerprints were planted, we're back at square one," Tori said. "It could be anyone: Coleman's ex-wife, an ex-lover, Janet, Janet's husband, someone we haven't thought of yet."

"Coleman's ex-wife could have wandered all over Gainesville without being noticed," Dottie said. "No one, not even Steve DeMaio, has met her. No one knows what she looks like; even Coleman hadn't seen her in years. She could have changed, dyed her hair, worn a wig, put on weight or lost it. Who knows?"

CHAPTER FIFTY SEVEN

An un-spring-like chill in the air Monday morning combined with a murky sky gave little hope of the sun warming the day. Floridians are spoiled. Bright sunshine is ubiquitous so they expect nothing less and take overcast skies as a personal affront. The afternoon showers during summer don't enter the equation. They come and go quickly, cool the air and the sun is back before nightfall. But, Floridians resent day-long damp, dreary weather.

At 7:00 a.m. Tori, wearing a fleece jacket to fend off the damp air, jogged a short version of the route DeMaio ran. The area was deserted. As she walked and stretched to cool down following her three-mile run, students were heading for their 8:00 classes. Heads turned to look at her. *Perhaps someone saw DeMaio last Tuesday morning. If I prove DeMaio was telling the truth about not playing tennis with Coleman, the rest of his story becomes credible.*

After driving the few minutes home, Tori picked up the newspaper from the lawn on her way into breakfast. She read the newspaper at the kitchen table while nibbling her breakfast. The headlines focused on Steve DeMaio's arrest. An interesting event retains media attention for weeks in a small town like Gainesville that has little real news. She skimmed the article – no new information – a reshuffling of previously reported stuff. Morrison's face looked at Tori from an inside page. She missed the old coot and their morning get-togethers at the 43rd St. Deli. She'd gained insight into another side of the man whom she'd stereotyped as dull and biased. *That'll teach me to prejudge people based on limited information.*

"Checking out your photo in the newspaper?" Sean asked, grabbing his usual humongous bowl of cereal. He poured copious amounts of milk into his bowl as he sat across from his mother.

"Want some strawberries?" she asked.

"Didn't see any."

Tori washed and sliced some strawberries and handed a bowl to Sean. She stood leaning against the counter. "And my photograph is not in the newspaper," she added.

"I thought you found the perp. You know, got in his head and figured out why he did it."

"I don't get in people's heads and I don't think Steve DeMaio is the murderer."

"Why'd you arrest him?"

"Sean, I do psychological autopsies. I'm not a police officer arresting people."

"Dad says it's the same thing."

"How is your father?" Tori asked in as casual voice as she could manage with her heart beating a drum roll.

"He's great. He showed me around the FBI office in Jacksonville. It's huge."

"I thought you went to Atlanta."

"Nah."

"He works in Atlanta, doesn't he?"

"He did. He's transferred to Jacksonville," Sean said.

"What about his wife? Betsy? Is she getting a job in Jacksonville?"

Sean pointed to his mouth stuffed with strawberries and cereal. Tori waited while he chewed. She turned her back to pour coffee and compose her expression. "Well?" she asked over her shoulder.

"He's divorcing Betsy."

Tori's mug seemed to have a mind of its own. It quivered and coffee sloshed onto the counter. She used her other hand to steady it and rested the mug on the counter. She took a deep breath and was able to sip some coffee before turning to face her son.

Sean said, "Dad does exciting things."

"I'm sure he does."

Sean raised his chin and looked at his mother, "What's that mean?"

"Your father has an exciting job." She tried to sound uninterested.

Sean shoved a mega spoonful of cereal and strawberries into his mouth, as only a twelve year old boy can. He was trying to gain weight to keep up with his growth spurt. Tori ruffled her son's curls and smiled.

"Hey, don't mess my hair."

"Sorry, I forgot. Those curls are such an invitation." She sat at the table and picked at her breakfast.

Sean looked at his mother with annoyance. Then he asked, "Why don't you think Steve DeMaio murdered the other prof? You hung up on him?"

"No. I've no personal feelings for Steve DeMaio. I think he was set up."

"You've been reading too many mysteries, Mom."

Tori laughed. "I don't base my opinions on novels. I use my psychological training to examine information about the deceased."

"If DeMaio didn't off Coleman, why were his fingerprints on the bottle?" Sean asked.

"I think the murderer planted DeMaio's fingerprints on the bottle of poisoned Pepsi to implicate him. This murder was too well-planned for the murderer to forget to wipe off fingerprints."

"Why didn't Coleman taste something wrong with the soda?"

"Pepsi has a strong flavor. It camouflaged the taste and the aroma of cyanide – further evidence that this murder was well-planned."

"If DeMaio didn't kill Coleman, who did?" Sean asked.

"I don't know. I think a woman did it."

"A woman? You aren't getting sexist are you?" Sean asked as he stood up and began stuffing books and papers into his backpack. He appeared to be deep in his own world, but Tori could tell he was listening.

"A lot of reasons: first, poison is the m.o. of a woman; you don't need strength to kill with poison. Second, Coleman mistreated women, dumping them when he found a new cutie. Someone like his ex-wife could've held a grudge for years.

Coleman's ex-wife was in Florida a few days before his death and could've murdered him so her son would inherit his money."

"The TV didn't say anything about his ex-wife. Or a son."

"They didn't know about them."

"Dad says the cops have a strong case."

"They do. But the police told the media about evidence supporting their case. Detective Morrison had to arrest someone because the chief was pushing him to solve the case. Morrison admitted to me he didn't think DeMaio would kill over a woman."

CHAPTER FIFTY EIGHT

Brian Petkowski greeted Tori with enthusiasm when she entered the Registrar's office. "What can I do for my favorite shrink?" Tori liked Brian, a slim, soft-spoken man, with wire-framed glasses, and thick sandy hair worn in a pony tail down his back. He dressed in the student uniform: jeans and t-shirt with a rock group on his chest. Tori explained she wanted a list of students who had an 8:00 a.m. class on Tuesdays in Little Hall.

"No problemo."

Brian pulled up data on his computer screen; hit a few keys, and the next thing Tori knew paper was spewing out of the printer across the room. Brian tapped more keys and the printer once again danced to the tune he played. He pulled the paper out of the printer, reviewed it and handed it to Tori.

Tori was ecstatic when she saw the list. The sole 8:00 am class in Little Hall was a small seminar with 13 students and most of the students lived in the dorm near the Hall. That made sense. If you have an early class, enroll in one near your dorm.

"Brian, I can't tell you how much I appreciate this." She blew him a kiss and took off for the dorm. She crossed the campus green, overrun with book-carrying students scurrying to every corner of their academic world. The level of activity told her classes were changing. The atmosphere was charged; students were conversing as they walked to classes or gathered in groups on the green. The news about Professor DeMaio's arrest for murdering Professor Coleman was spreading across campus like a virulent virus. Gainesville was a small town and the university was an even smaller community.

Tori walked against the flow of bicyclists and skaters. She watched for rogue bicycles, remembering the one that caused her knee injury. Turning a corner she almost bumped into Laurie Bruno heading in the same direction. Laurie had attended Tori's talk on date rape a few months back and stayed to ask Tori about an abusive boyfriend. Tori had walked Laurie to the Counseling Center, where she introduced her to Gladys.

Laurie was difficult to define. One day she dressed in figure revealing spandex, the next in a Laura Ashley granny dress, another day in Liz Claiborne high style. Today Laurie disguised her rather voluptuous figure with carpenter jeans three sizes too large and a baggy t-shirt. She had recently cut her thick black hair above her ears; only someone with Laurie's clear skin, pug nose, and big eyes could still look cute. Laurie greeted Tori. She asked, "Have you heard how Professor DeMaio killed Dr. Coleman?"

"I did a psychological autopsy on the case," Tori said.

"So Dr. DeMaio did it?" Laurie clutched her books to her chest.

"The police think he did."

Laurie turned, eyes knowing, "You don't?"

"I can't discuss a case before it goes to court, Laurie."

"I understand. I can't believe Dr. Coleman is dead and Dr. DeMaio is in jail. I thought they were friends."

"Did you know them?"

"I had Dr. Coleman for an English poetry class my sophomore year. He was great. Everyone swooned when he read poetry." Laurie sighed. "What a sexy voice."

"What about Dr. DeMaio? Did you have him for any classes?"

"I didn't take chemistry. I know who he is, though. I see him around campus. You can't miss his gorgeous body."

Tori thought, *Hormones rule on campus.*

Laurie asked, "Why're you going to the dorm?"

"I need to find out if anyone saw a man jogging near Little Hall one day last week."

"Why, Dr. Vincent? What happened near Little Hall last week?"

"Nothing happened near Little Hall. Sorry, Laurie, I can't tell you any more. It's police business again. Someone needs an alibi."

"Okay, I won't pester. When was this man supposed to be jogging? I have a class in Little; maybe I saw him."

"It was Tuesday morning. Early, like 7:00 to 8:30." Tori knew Laurie was not stupid. The combination of not thinking Steve DeMaio was guilty and looking for an alibi for someone on Tuesday morning would be enough for her to figure it out. "I've a list of people with an 8:00 a.m. Tuesday class in Little Hall."

"Want me to look at the list and see if I know anyone?"

"That'd be great! Students are more open with another student than a professor."

They stopped near the main entrance to the dorm while Laurie perused the list. The melody "Can You Feel the Love Tonight" played and Tori dug her phone out of her purse. "Tori, this is Jacqui. Rashida has disappeared. Do you know where she is?"

"What happened?"

"She called two days ago – terrified. Said she had to see me right away. I canceled my other clients. She never showed up. I've called her cell phone a dozen times. She doesn't return my calls."

Tori asked where Rashida lived. "I'm at the dorm now. I'll check her room."

Tori turned her attention to a group of coeds on the steps chatting and smoking. She heard DeMaio's name bandied about but couldn't catch any specific comment. Laurie pointed to a lanky woman in black with white make-up. "Dahlia's on the list." In the long black skirt and fitted black top, Dahlia's thin body resembled a black straw. She wore black stockings and black platform shoes – the Lady Gaga look. Her white make-up made her artificially black hair look darker than ebony. Laurie introduced Tori.

Tori asked, "Would you mind answering a few questions?"

"Am I in trouble or something?" the coed asked, eyeing the professor.

"No, I'm looking for a possible witness."

"Okay, I guess," Dahlia drew out the words like molasses slipping down the side of a jar.

"Thanks. You have an eight o'clock class on Tuesday, right?"

"So what? A lot of people have classes then."

Tori smiled reassuringly. "Did you see anyone last Tuesday jogging near Little Hall."

"I never get up in time for my eight o'clock." Dahlia snickered. "I didn't go last week."

Tori thanked her and asked if any of the others had been around between 7:00 a.m. and 8:00 a.m. last Tuesday. The thought of being up at that unnatural time was absurd; the students laughed and shook their heads.

CHAPTER FIFTY NINE

Sipping her ever present Coke and nibbling on a chocolate bar, Dottie waited while her computer loaded the yellow pages so she could begin the tedious job of finding the store that had sold a capping tool to Coleman's murderer. Dottie had to proceed with caution. Morrison walked by her desk a couple times; it was only a matter of time before he'd want to know what she was doing. Her nerves were on edge. If Morrison found out she was looking for evidence that Steve DeMaio hadn't murdered Brad Coleman, he would massacre her.

Dottie looked up the cities within a two hour drive of Gainesville: Tallahassee, Jacksonville, Ocala, Daytona Beach, and Orlando. She made a list of places that sold brewing and capping equipment in each city. Starting at the top of the first list, she called each establishment, asking whether a woman had called recently about capping equipment. Most replies were along the lines of, "Lady, we get lots of calls about lots of things. What do you think we're in business for?" After three hours all she'd accomplished was determining that a capping tool was available in each city. *Where do I go from here?*

When Morrison told her he was leaving, Dottie took the opportunity to interview possible witnesses who had seen Coleman playing tennis. Perhaps someone remembered his tennis partner. *Why didn't I look for the person playing tennis with Coleman right after the murder?* She chided herself. *After almost a week, people's memories fade and they won't be able to describe his tennis partner.*

A row of houses overlooked the tennis courts on the western edge of campus. Beginning at the southern end of the block, Dottie progressed from house to house in a northerly direction, asking occupants if they had seen a blond man playing tennis early last Tuesday. She won the lottery at the fourth house. A twenty-something housewife, Jean Montgomery, said she saw people on the courts when her kids car pool picked them up for school at 8:00 a.m.

"What day?" Dottie asked.

"Tuesday."

"Who was playing tennis?"

"A young blond guy – he plays tennis every Tuesday."

"Did you notice his partner?"

The young housewife colored. "Yes. Usually, he plays with the brown haired man with the beard, but last week he was with a woman."

Swallowing to open her constricted throat, Dottie asked, "What did she look like?"

"She was good looking. Marianne, we car pool together, and I remarked about her looks." Jean raised and dropped her right shoulder. "Marianne and I play a fantasy game. We make lewd remarks about the studs playing tennis. Last week Marianne pointed out the woman when she picked up my sons. She said my guy –" Jean blushed, "she favors the blond and refers to the bearded one as mine – was missing. I joked and said she was losing her guy to competition. Maybe she remembers more."

"What is Marianne's last name and address?"

After the housewife provided the information about Marianne, Dottie asked, "Is there anything else you remember from that day – anything about the tennis players?"

Jean thought for a minute and said, "Yes... Usually they come in the red Corvette, but this time there was another car there, too."

"Can you describe the other car? Its make? Model? Color?"

"I'm not good with cars. It was a minivan, not too big – blue, nothing too fancy, but somewhat new looking. You know the kind soccer moms use for car pooling."

"Anything else you can remember about it? Anything that would identify it?"

Jean shook her head. "Sorry."

Dottie was about to leave when the housewife asked, "Why are you interested in the tennis players?"

"The blond man was the professor murdered on campus last week." Dottie said, "You were one of the last people to see him alive."

Jean gasped and covered her mouth.

Dottie continued her questioning at the other houses on the street, but found no one else who had noticed the tennis players or the cars parked by the courts.

CHAPTER SIXTY

Laurie accompanied Tori to the Resident Advisor's dorm office to find the room assignments for Rashida and the people on Tori's list. Tori asked Laurie to wait in the dorm office while she talked to Rashida. She knocked on Rashida's door. When there was no answer she knocked again. "Who's there?" squeaked a voice through the door.

"It's Dr. Vincent, Rashida. May I come in?"

The door edged open and big black, tear-filled eyes scrutinized Tori. But they were not Rashida's eyes. The young woman checked up and down the hall before motioning Tori to enter. Once Tori was inside, the coed closed and locked the door.

"I'm Dr. Vincent. I'm looking for Rashida."

"I'm Daliya, Rashida's roommate."

"I'm worried," Tori said. Rashida missed her counseling session two days ago and isn't answering her phone."

The coed collapsed on the bed, crying. "I don't know what to do."

"What's wrong?" Tori crouched on the floor next to the bed with the weeping coed. "Where's Rashida?"

"I don't know."

"What are you afraid of?"

The coed sat up and hugged herself. "Rashida got a call from her sister on Saturday. She told Rashida someone sent their father a photograph of Rashida – a nude photograph." The coed choked on her words. "Rashida and I are Pakistani. Rashida brought dishonor to her family. They are going to kill her."

"This is the United States – they can't get away with that here!"

"You don't understand." Fear defined the big black eyes searching Tori's face. "Rashida and I are like twins. We're the same size, our hair is the same, and we wear each other's clothes. Yesterday, when I went to the library, two men grabbed me – Rashida's brother and uncle. They saw me from the back and thought I was Rashida. When they realized I wasn't Rashida, they let me go. They would have killed her."

Tori hugged the coed. "Did they hurt you?"

"They threatened me if I didn't tell them where Rashida was. I said she went to Orlando."

"Did she?"

"No, I said that so they would leave."

"Where is Rashida now?"

"She left as soon as she got her sister's phone call. I don't know where she went."

"You need to get out of the dorm in case they come back. Do you have somewhere you can stay?"

"My aunt lives in town."

"Go there right now. I'll wait while you pack and take you there."

Tori drove to the apartment complex where Rashida's friend Jennifer lived. She knocked on Jennifer's door. There was no answer. She knocked again – still no response. She dialed Jennifer's number on her cell phone. "Hello," came a nervous voice.

"Jennifer, this is Dr. Vincent. I know about Rashida's father. I want to help her."

"She's afraid to go anywhere."

"I understand. I'm outside your apartment. Are you there?"

Tori saw an eye at the peek hole in the door. The door opened and Jennifer grabbed Tori and pulled her into the apartment. Over her shoulder she said, "It's okay, Rashida. It's Dr. Vincent."

A door down the hallway opened a crack. Tori saw an eye through the crack, then Rashida stuck out her head. She ran to

Tori, throwing her arms around her. "What can I do? They'll kill me."

Morrison arrived within three minutes of Tori's call; he was in the neighborhood. He listened to Rashida's story and grasped the seriousness of the situation. He promised Rashida he would see that she would be safe. He'd take her to a shelter and provide extra security at the facility until her brother and uncle were apprehended. Morrison asked, "Who you think sent the photograph to your father?"

Rashida shook her head and cried. "I don't know. Why would anyone do that?"

"Do you think it was Dr. Coleman?" Tori asked.

"He said he wouldn't show the photographs to anyone if I didn't complain about him."

Morrison asked her who had access to the photographs.

"The police," snapped Jennifer.

Morrison gave Jennifer a nasty look. He decided he couldn't get additional information from the girls about the source of the photograph and it was more important to ensure Rashida's safety than determine who sent her father the photograph. He got a description of Rashida's brother and uncle and their car before sending out an APB for the two men.

After Morrison left to take Rashida to the shelter, Tori turned to Jennifer. "Detective Morrison asked who would send that photograph to Rashida's father. Rashida could not understand why someone would do that."

Jennifer averted her eyes.

"You didn't have any idea her family would try to kill her, did you?"

"What do you mean? I didn't..." Jennifer burst into tears, covered her face with her hands and dropped into a chair. "I didn't mean to send the photo – honest. I saw it in Brad's bedroom and was jealous. I scanned it and made a copy."

"So you sent it to Rashida's father?"

"Not on purpose." She looked up, her eyes streaming. "I put it in an envelope with her father's name on it. I wasn't going to mail it." She hung her head.

"Why did you?"

220

"My mother found it and started to open it. I told her it was for Rashida's father and she took it and mailed it. I didn't think they would hurt her. I thought they would make her go home…"

CHAPTER SIXTY ONE

Tori returned to the dorm to interview students. The first two students on her list were in class. The third, Dan Schneider, was in his room. Bright, happy eyes complemented his cheerful grin. The short, stocky man with curly dishwater blond hair was in pajamas and slippers. He saw Tori eying his clothing. "I'm not a morning person." Unfortunately, he overslept last Tuesday and didn't leave until 8:15. He was in such a hurry to get to class he didn't pay attention to anything else. "I wasn't there to take notes from the beginning of class and Professor Pagliaccetti takes attendance – a lousy start to the day."

"Thanks."

He shrugged. Then his face lit up and he said, "I got the notes from Sheila Preece."

Sheila was on the list and Tori went to interview her. Sheila had earrings running up her entire left ear and a small tattoo of a ladybug on her right shoulder peeking out of a shocking pink tank top. Sheila wasn't much help. "I don't remember. I don't function well until after lunch," she shrugged her lady bug.

Tori thanked her and was about to go to the next name on the list when Sheila asked, "Did Dr. DeMaio kill Dr. Coleman?"

Tori's clinical intuition kicked in. "What do you think?" she asked.

Sheila looked at Tori, lifted the ladybug and said, "Everyone knows Dr. Coleman hits on women in his classes. Rumor is he was dropping that grad student in Chemistry."

Trying not to display her intense interest, Tori asked, "Is that so? What makes you say that? Was he dating somebody else?"

"He asked a girl in my class to meet him for coffee. She was thrilled, but someone warned her to be careful, said Coleman used coeds – screwed them and dumped them."

"Who was the woman Coleman asked to meet him?" Tori asked.

"I don't remember." Sheila squished up her face and gnawed on her bottom lip. "It was someone in my history class – an older woman. I'm pretty sure she's married. I thought she'd be dumb getting mixed up with Coleman."

"Do you remember who warned her about Dr. Coleman?" Tori asked.

"Yeah, she's got blond hair and sits in the front of the class on the right. I can't think of her name, but she said a friend of hers got burnt by Dr. Coleman. She said he was bad news and to stay away from him."

"When you think of her name, will you please call me? Immediately." Tori handed her card to Sheila and emphasized how important it was.

The next student, Patti Webster, was a tall, dark-haired Georgia peach with a silky southern accent. She was "pleased as punch" to help the police – *whatever the heck that means*, Tori thought. Tori asked about a jogger near Little Hall Tuesday morning.

Patti gushed, "I saw a gorgeous hunk jogging there last week."

"What day did you see him?"

"Gosh, it was Tuesday or Thursday. They're the days I have early class."

"Which day?"

"I'm soooo sorry. I just can't *REMEMBER*," she said throwing her arms out.

"What did the man look like?" Tori asked.

"Ohhh, ah sure remember that. He had the *GREATEST* physique." she cooed.

"What color was his hair?" Tori asked.

"Well, ain't that the dickens? I swear, I was so interested in his cute little BUTT in those TIGHT shorts, I didn't notice his hair."

"Do you remember what color his shorts were?" Tori asked trying not to show her annoyance.

"Oh, THAT I remember. They were red."

"Was he a student?" Tori asked.

"Heavens, no! He was OLD. He was like 30!" She rubbed her chin and looked up with a big smile. "He wasn't a typical runner. You know – skinny and all. He was muscular. It was WONDERFUL the way those GREAT legs flexed."

"Is there any way you can figure out which day it was?" Tori asked.

She shrugged, "I wish to high heavens I could. Days all just run together. I can't keep them straight. I'm so silly that way."

Tori thanked her, silently agreeing that she was silly. Tori disliked dealing with women who played dumb, *but maybe it wasn't an act*, she thought maliciously. *Anyway, I should be grateful; she has provided evidence supporting DeMaio's story. The jogger could have been Steve DeMaio, but it didn't help if Patti couldn't pin-point the day or remember what color his hair was.*

The next possible witness on the list was in class, so Tori climbed the stairs to Eileen Jorgenson's second floor dorm room. Eileen wasn't in, but her roommate, Amy, asked if she could help. Amy a small, emaciated, no-nonsense woman with a strident voice, wore a button down shirt and crisp khaki shorts.

Tori explained what she was looking for and asked if Eileen had gone to class that day.

"Yes, she went to class, but I can help. I saw someone. I'm a morning person. Tuesday I went to get my transcripts sent to grad school and walked past Little Hall to Tigert," she said. "I saw a man jogging near Little Hall."

"What time?"

Amy rubbed her chin and said, "Let me think." She paused, eyes looking up to the right. "I left after she got out of the shower. It must have been a little after 7:30."

Tori was grateful there were no "days all running together" for this down-to-earth woman. "Do you remember what he was wearing?" Tori asked, trying to hide her growing excitement.

"Those elastic biking shorts, black, with red running shorts over them. He had a baseball jacket tied around his waist. Had on a t-shirt, white, I think."

"What did he look like?" Tori asked.

"Brownish hair. Athletic."

"Any facial hair?"

"Hmmm...I can't remember. He might have had a mustache or a beard. I'm not sure."

"Would you recognize him, if you saw him again?" Tori asked.

"I was too far away to see his face."

Tori thanked Amy. She was convinced Steve DeMaio was jogging last Tuesday morning. The evidence might not stand up in a court of law, but it supported DeMaio's contention that he hadn't played tennis with Brad Coleman. That left Tori with another question: who had played tennis with Coleman?

CHAPTER SIXTY TWO

Opening the door to Dottie's knock was Marianne DeCourey. About 30, she was painfully thin and tall, almost gawky, until she smiled, then she glowed. "You must be the detective. Jean said you want to talk to me about the tennis players. Come in."

Dottie waded into a sea of confusion: T.V. blaring, kids cavorting, toys, papers, books, crayons strewn everywhere, and a ball flying toward the kitchen. Marianne caught the ball and yelled at the kids to turn off the T.V. "Go outside," she ordered.

Two munchkins headed toward the back door, another looked as if she might join them, following her friends with her eyes and starting to get up. The remaining children ignored Marianne until she turned off the television. Standing with arms akimbo in front of the T.V., she stared at them until they ran out the back door, slamming it behind them.

Dottie thought, *There must have been eight kids in the house.* "Are they all yours?" she asked, wide-eyed.

"God forbid! My neighbor works and her nanny is sick. I've got two preschoolers so I said I'd watch her two. Her kids are obedient and well-behaved – the ones who went out right away. The prima donna in the house behind me considers this her personal day care center. Her kids are the rowdy ones who pay no attention. My kids can go either way. Being a nursery school teacher must be hell on earth. Let's talk before the monsters reinvade." Marianne pointed Dottie to a seat at the kitchen counter adjacent to the play room and picked up a carafe. "Coffee?"

"No thanks. But I'd love something cold," Dottie said.

"Kool-Aid?"

Dottie tried not to cringe, "Water would be fine."

"Sure thing."

Marianne handed Dottie a glass of ice water and sat on a stool with one elbow braced on the counter so she could face her visitor. "What do you want to know about the tennis playing hotties?"

"Did you see the blond one last Tuesday morning?"

"Sure did."

"You're sure it was Tuesday?" Dottie asked.

"Absolutely. He's there every Tuesday."

"What did he look like?"

"Blond, tan, muscular, white shorts. He's about 30-33." She sighed, staring unfocused into the distance, a loopy smile on her face.

Good God, she's mooning over him, Dottie thought.

"Jean tried to make me believe the blond guy was the professor murdered last week."

"I'm afraid Jean was telling you the truth."

"NO WAY!" Marianne said. "Oh my gosh."

"What can you tell me about him?"

Marianne took a deep breath. "He drives a red Corvette with a faculty sticker for the university."

"You're observant." Dottie was encouraged.

"I'm a people watcher. I majored in psych and like to figure people out. You know, try to imagine what they do for a living, that sort of thing."

"What about his tennis partner? What can you tell me about him?" Dottie was testing Marianne's observation skills.

"It wasn't a him; it was a her," Marianne said.

"Can you describe her?"

"She was small, with blond hair and a nice figure. Oh, and she has kids," Marianne said.

"How do you know she has kids?"

"The blue minivan she drove had a kid's car seat in it."

"You have a good memory for details." Dottie grinned. "Would you recognize her if you saw her again?"

"I don't think so. She had on a sun visor. It blocked her face. You know the kind, those dark green ones with the Gainesville Country Club logo on it."

"Any idea about her age?" Dottie asked.

"Somewhere in her twenties, I'd guess. I think she's younger than I am and I'm 29."

"What time did you see them?"

"About 8:00. That's when I pick up Jean's sons for the carpool."

"Do you know what kind of car she drove?" Dottie mentally crossed her fingers.

"It was a Mercury Villager, a new one."

"Are you positive?"

"Sure am. I was looking for one a couple weeks ago. I visited all the car showrooms. Then my husband decided we couldn't afford one." Marianne shook her head and frowned.

"Anything else you can tell me about the car?"

"It had a parking decal for the university on the rear window, but for a student, not faculty. My husband took an accounting course at night last year, so I see the decal all the time."

Dottie was excited – she could find the car now.

CHAPTER SIXTY THREE

Ever the efficient secretary, Lauriann had attempted to elicit the nature of Tori's visit before scheduling an appointment with Dean Kohlberg. The trite excuse, "it's police business that I am not at liberty to discuss," had increased Lauriann's curiosity and she asked once more about the reason for the meeting before announcing Tori's arrival to the dean. Tori smiled and reiterated her reason for not sharing information. Dean Kohlberg nodded at Tori from behind her desk and dismissed the waiting, and ever more curious, secretary.

Tori explained she had some questions about Brad Coleman's death.

The dean tensed and said, "They've arrested Dr. DeMaio. I don't need to answer any questions." She examined papers on her desk.

"I don't believe Steve DeMaio is the murderer."

The dean sighed, walked to the conference table and sat down. She snapped, "What do you want to know?"

"Dean Kohlberg, I'll cut to the chase. You had an affair with Brad Coleman."

The dean gasped. She flushed. She turned her head to gaze out the window, her hand covering her mouth as she took a deep breath. The gloomy weather reflected her melancholia and seemed to seep into the room. She took off her glasses and rubbed her eyes. Tori had to lean close to hear the dean. Her usually strong voice was hardly audible. The dean stared out the window as if talking to herself, chewing on the stem of her glasses when she wasn't speaking.

"Brad Coleman manipulated me from the first time we met." She sighed. "He flirted with me during his initial interview." She shook her head, blushing. "You'd think by my age I could see through a blatant con job, but he was an expert." Hilary put her thick glasses back on and scrutinized Tori's face. Tori's empathy showed and the dean took off her glasses to gaze out the window as she resumed her sad chronicle.

"I saw little of him until about six months ago when he asked me for advice. He was worried Whitherspoon would prevent his tenure. We met often. Brad was witty and interesting. We frequently ended our afternoons with a glass of sherry in my office." Hilary Kohlberg swallowed and clutched her head with her hands. "One evening Brad asked me to drive him home – his Corvette was in the shop. He invited me in for a glass of wine."

She raised her eyes to Tori. "I declined. I said it wouldn't look good. He teased me – promised not to take advantage of me." She closed her eyes and said, "I was a fool. One thing led to another. I found myself in bed with Brad. I knew I'd made an awful blunder." She shook her head. "I worried Brad would lose respect for me. I was mistaken – or so he led me to believe. After that he came to my house two or three nights a week. We never went out in public. Brad said he was concerned about my career.

"No fool like an old fool, eh?" she asked as she cleaned her glasses, eyes brimming. "It's my fault our breakup was so public and humiliating. I planned a surprise party to make our relationship public. I was that big a fool," she harangued herself. "I'm 43 years old and a handsome man, nine years my junior, was in love with me."

After a deep sigh, she returned to her story. With a bitter laugh she said, "The week before the party Brad told me he was writing a paper." She turned back to the window, her brimming eyes reflecting the rainy weather, while she mutilated the stem of her glasses. "Whenever I called Brad was too busy to talk. He didn't answer my e-mails.

"The night of the party, Brad wasn't there by 9:30 p. m. He was always punctual. I called him. He said he was working on his paper. I asked him to come for a short time. Brad was sorry, he was busy. Then I heard a young woman's voice in the background. When I demanded to know who was there, Brad said I didn't own him."

Hilary looked at her hands playing with her glasses, her voice cracked. "I was stunned. I demanded he come to the party. He was cold. I couldn't believe it was the man I loved. He said, 'Hilary, we used each other. You got sex and I got tenure, don't spoil it by behaving like a shrew.'

"I don't remember what I said, but I was loud and everyone came running. Mary Rantala tried to hug me, but I pushed her away. I was humiliated in front of the faculty. I was livid and swore I'd get even."

"So you poisoned Brad Coleman?" Tori asked.

Dean Kohlberg held Tori's eyes for the first time. "No, I did not kill Brad Coleman. Death was too good for that scumbag. I wanted him to spend the rest of his life ruing the day he used me." Her voice matched her level of determination, not loud, but strong.

"How were you going to do that?"

"I tracked down a couple of women the bastard had traumatized. He'd had affairs with them, destroyed their prior relationships and dumped them. Two young women were willing to file grievances. The provost wouldn't keep Brad – tenured or not. It would leave the university open to a lawsuit. No other institution would hire him. Why take on a liability when there're so many applicants for English positions? Coleman would have been out on the street on his ass."

Tori thanked Dean Kohlberg for being so forthright with her about her involvement with Coleman.

The dean lowered her eyes. "I suppose you'll report our conversation?"

"This is between you and me. Unless you're implicated in the crime, no one need know what you told me."

"I appreciate your discretion."

Tori could see Dean Kohlberg poisoning Brad Coleman; *but would she place the blame on Steve DeMaio?* "Before I go, I have one more question. What is your relationship with Steve DeMaio?"

"Steve DeMaio? The man they arrested for poisoning Brad?"

Tori nodded.

"I didn't know he was close to Brad. He's an assistant professor in Chemistry." Kohlberg rubbed her chin. "He went up for promotion and tenure this year – excellent dossier. I don't know him, myself, but I understand he's popular. I think Mary Rantala socializes with him."

"You don't have any animosity toward DeMaio?"

"I see what you're getting at. Steve was Brad's best friend. Brad and I never socialized with anyone else. He supposedly was protecting my reputation. Not even DeMaio knew about my relationship with Brad."

CHAPTER SIXTY FOUR

Trish seemed surprised when she saw Dottie on the doorstep. "Hello. Is something the matter?" She stood in the doorway behind the screen door without making an attempt to open it.

"No, I wanted to see how you were doing."

Trish shrugged. "Everyone's been nice. Dr. Vincent came to tell me about DeMaio's arrest and Detective Morrison called after she left to tell me, also. They were both nice."

Trish opened the screen door, saying, "I'm sorry, I'm not being polite. Would you like to come in?"

Dottie followed her into the small sitting area. She was searching for a way to broach the topic of Coleman's female tennis partner when she spotted the newspaper on the coffee table opened to a story about the murder. She gestured toward the paper, "It isn't easy to get it out of your mind is it?"

Trish folded up the newspaper and put it in a magazine rack. "It doesn't make any difference what's in the newspaper. Brad's death is always on my mind."

Dottie noticed suitcases on the bed in the little alcove where Trish slept. "Are you leaving Gainesville?" she asked, pointing to the luggage.

"Yes, there's nothing holding me here. I've withdrawn from my classes, I can't concentrate. Everything reminds me of Brad. I'll start at another university in the fall."

"When are you leaving?"

233

"As soon as possible. Detective Morrison said I need to testify at the grand jury – sometime early next week. I can't seem to do anything else, so I'm packing."

"Where will you go?" Dottie asked.

"My father's house in South Carolina."

"Do you have someone to take you to the airport? I'll be happy to drive you."

"That's sweet of you, but it's not necessary. I keep a car in the garage behind Mrs. Manecke's house. She's my landlady. I don't use it much. It's easier to get back and forth to campus by bicycle and I don't have to pay for a parking sticker and find a parking place."

Dottie nodded and asked, "How have you been coping?"

"Not well. I feel guilty that Steve killed Brad because of me."

"You're sure Steve killed Brad?" Dottie asked.

"Of course, aren't you?" Trish snapped.

Trish's reaction was so quick and so vehement Dottie was tempted to demur. Instead, she plowed ahead. "I find it hard to believe Steve would kill over a woman. He isn't the romantic type. Dr. Vincent agrees with me."

Trish looked at Dottie and asked, "Who else would kill Brad?"

"We've got a number of people of interest."

"Who?"

"That's confidential." Dottie looked at Trish. "I can't imagine what you're going through. It must be unbearable."

"I keep hearing Brad's voice. I don't think I've slept a full night since..." Tears flowed from Trish's eyes and trickled down her cheeks. "Excuse me," she said. Trish walked into the alcove and grabbed a couple of tissues from a box on the night stand. She returned and sat opposite Dottie on the small loveseat. She blew her nose and said, "I never thought it'd be this hard. I expect to wake up and find it's a nightmare."

Trish sat back and tucked one leg under her other thigh. She blew her nose, breathed deeply and sighed. "I'm sorry. I thought I'd cried myself dry." She tried to smile, but accomplished a grimace.

Dottie said, "When I broke up with Eric – the man I was going to marry – I cried for three weeks. I still tear up when I think about him."

Trish nodded. "I'm going to get myself something to drink. Can I offer you something?"

"Thanks. Got something cold?"

Trish got up and walked into the small kitchen. Dottie followed while they continued to discuss a drink.

"How about some Gatorade?" Trish asked, opening the refrigerator.

"Oh, yuck! Sorry, I hate the stuff. Have you got any Coke?" Dottie asked. She looked over Trish's head, an easy task for the 6' tall detective.

Trish said, "Don't you know cola rots your teeth and dehydrates you?"

"Yeah, I know it. But I'm addicted to the stuff." Much taller than Trish, Dottie could see further to the back of the refrigerator. "Isn't that some, back there?" Dottie asked.

"Will Pepsi do?" Trish asked.

"Yeah, I prefer it to Coke," Dottie lied as she grabbed the bottle by the cap. "Don't bother with a glass; I'll drink it straight from the bottle."

"That's macho."

"I'm a cop, remember?"

"How could I forget?" Trish poured herself a glass of Gatorade.

"If this stuff is so bad for you, why do you keep it?" Dottie asked.

"I kept it for Brad. I couldn't convince him to drink healthy drinks either."

They settled back into the sitting room and Dottie asked, "Do you think there's any possibility Brad was seeing someone else?"

Trish's reaction was calmer than Dottie had anticipated. "No. I would've known."

"You mean he would've told you?"

Trish bit her bottom lip before saying, "No, I don't think he'd be forthcoming; but we spent every night together. There wasn't time for him to see anyone else."

"But he was involved with Dean Kohlberg?" Dottie asked.

Trish scoffed. "He wasn't 'involved' with Hilary Kohlberg," she said, making air quotes around 'involved.' "He had sex with her so she would get him tenure. When he got it he dropped her."

"You didn't care if Brad slept with Dean Kohlberg?" Dottie asked.

"I'd have preferred he got tenure another way, but it was his career, and his decision." Trish sighed.

"Awfully open-minded of you."

Trish sighed again. "I loved Brad, but he was far from perfect." Trish reminisced about Brad for awhile. Dottie couldn't bring herself to push Trish about other women and saw no point in asking more about Coleman's tennis partner on that fatal Tuesday. She asked, "Didn't it bother you – Brad having sex with Dean Kohlberg?"

"I knew she didn't have AIDS or another STD."

"I didn't mean STD, I meant didn't it bother you emotionally?"

Trish gave a sad laugh. "I knew he'd never leave me for Hilary Kohlberg. He'd come home from their trysts and do malicious imitations of her. He'd walk around like he was humongous, panting, begging for sex. He thought he was hilarious. I didn't appreciate his humor. I wish Brad had been nicer to the poor woman."

"You mean the way he dropped her?"

"Yes. She called to ask why he wasn't at the party. He said he was working on a paper. When I asked who was on the phone, she heard my voice and challenged him. He turned hard and cruel. I'd never seen him like that and I didn't like it. She saved his career."

"Do you think she killed Brad?" Dottie asked.

Trish cocked her head. "I thought you arrested Steve. Why are you asking about someone else being the murderer? Are you still investigating the murder?"

"Nothing official. Morrison thinks DeMaio is the murderer, but I'm not convinced. Neither is Dr. Vincent. I've found witnesses who saw DeMaio running at the time he was supposed to be playing tennis with Brad."

Trish said nothing. Dottie could see the wheels turning in Trish's brain. Dottie asked, "Did anything unusual happen the morning Brad died, before he went to play tennis?"

"No, nothing. I've gone through everything over and over in my head."

Dottie looked at her watch and said, "I need to get going. I'm supposed to meet Dr. Vincent in a few minutes."

"I understand."

"I was so involved in our conversation I haven't touched my Pepsi. Do you mind if I take it with me?" Dottie asked.

"No. I'll get you a cup with some ice."

"Don't bother. I prefer my drinks without ice."

Trish shrugged, got up, and walked Dottie to the door.

"Call me if I can do anything for you," Dottie said.

Trish watched from behind the screen door as Dottie hopped into her Suzuki Sidekick.

CHAPTER SIXTY FIVE

Still pondering her conversation with the dean, Tori walked to her car in the parking lot. Eyes on the ground to avoid puddles, Tori shielded herself with her Van Gogh irises umbrella. She raised the umbrella to look for her car. "Oh No!!' A flat tire. She pulled out her cell phone to call AAA and remembered she hadn't renewed her membership. The one time she'd had a flat, Matt had changed her tire. He'd told her not to waste her money. "Darn it."

"May I have a word?" asked the petite African American woman with a mid-sized Afro framing a pleasant face. She stuck out her hand, "I'm Mary Rantala."

Tori shook hands, "I know. I've seen you perform on campus." Mary played half a dozen musical instruments and taught music. Mary was a popular member of the music faculty and people said she approached life with the same gusto with which she played jazz.

"Got a problem?" asked Mary motioning toward the tire.

"Yes and I didn't renew my AAA membership."

"I'll change it for you. I'm an old hand at tire-changing."

Tori gasped. "You are?"

"What did you think – women can't change tires?"

"No… I guess… Why would you change my tire? I don't even know you."

"I want to talk to you." Mary put out her hand. "Keys? I need to get to the spare."

Tori unlocked the trunk and pulled out the jack and tire iron. Mary pulled out the miniature tire. "I hate these things. Why can't they give you a regular-size tire? You can go as far as the repair shop on this thing." She bounced the spare tire. "Check that the car's in gear and the emergency brake is on."

Mary squatted next to the flat tire, took off the hubcap and began loosening the wheel lug nuts.

"Why do you want to talk to me?" asked Tori, holding the umbrella over Mary.

"I know you talked to Winston Whitherspoon about Hilary Kohlberg and I want to give you a more accurate view of her. I've been friends with Hilary Kohlberg since music school." Mary maneuvered the jack under the back bumper and raised the jack. Once the flat tire was off the ground, she removed the wheel lug nuts and placed them in the hubcap.

"I see," Tori said.

As she took off the flat tire and lined up the spare tire with the protruding wheel studs, Mary said, "That old buzzard Whitherspoon sublimates his sexual urges by gossiping about other people's sex lives. He delights in spreading nasty rumors about Hilary. Contrary to Witherspoon's contentions, Hilary is not ridiculed; she is a well-respected and competent dean, and an accomplished musician and professor."

Mary Rantala doesn't know Whitherspoon's dead and thinks Whitherspoon told us a lot more than he did, Tori thought. She nodded as if she had heard the rumors.

"Hilary had sex with different men, maybe a lot of them. She's a product of the sexual revolution. The male faculty did the same thing. Those geriatric old farts chasing young skirts are the ridiculous ones – they're the ones that give the campus a bad name. Hilary never seduced a student or had an affair with a married man. Not like the male professors who leave their wives of 20 or 30 years to marry a cute coed during their mid-life crises. The coed marries her dream professor when he's in the prime of life, a few years later the coed is stuck with a husband past his use-by date with an expanding gut, drooping jaw line and poor eyesight."

Laughing at Mary's all too accurate description, Tori said, "Tell me about the dean's relationship with Brad Coleman."

"Coleman was an ambitious, Machiavellian cad," Mary said as she screwed on the wheel lugs and tightened them with the tire iron.

"I agree," said Tori. "What Brad Coleman did to Hilary Kohlberg was despicable. Do you think Dean Kohlberg hated Coleman enough to kill him?"

Without a nano-second's hesitation, Mary Rantala stood up and said, "No! She hated him, but she didn't kill him. She had worse things in store for that bastard." Mary Rantala described the same scenario the dean had related earlier: getting former students to file grievances against Brad Coleman. Mary lowered the jack, then tightened the lugs some more.

"Would a sexual harassment grievance be worse than death?" Tori asked.

"Being fired for sexual harassment is the kiss of death for an academic in the current climate. Professors used to get away with it, but not any more." Mary put the flat tire in the trunk along with the tire iron and jack. "The college is responsible, legally and financially, for professors' behavior. Students sue colleges for mega bucks. No academic institution would hire him. It's a buyers' market in academia." She pulled out a large handkerchief and wiped her hands.

"How did you learn to change tires?"

"My mother taught me."

"She did?"

"No, I took a course. A black woman doesn't want to be stuck on a back road in Mississippi."

"Right," Tori said. "You think Steve DeMaio poisoned Coleman?"

"No, but I'd rather see him get the blame than Hilary. At least he deserves to be punished for something."

"Why don't you think DeMaio killed Coleman?"

"I've known Brad and Steve for years. Neither of them had any real feelings for women."

"You think Brad and Steve are homosexuals?" Tori asked.

"No. I'm gay and know the gay community pretty well; they weren't in it. But they didn't love women and wouldn't fight over Trish."

"You sure?" Tori asked.

"Positive. Steve blew it off when Trish dropped him; he was more confused than upset."

"Trish said they had a tiff," Tori said.

"That's not what Steve told me. According to him it came out of the blue. At any rate I know Steve and he wasn't angry with Brad, certainly not angry enough to kill him."

"So who murdered Brad Coleman?" Tori asked.

"I don't know, but it wasn't Hilary."

"Why are you so sure? Sometimes we don't know what motivates our best friends. Or are you protecting her? Are you and the dean more than friends?"

"Gay people can have straight friends," she snapped.

"Sorry."

"I'm not saying she didn't kill him because we're friends. She plotted her revenge with me. She wanted him to suffer. She wouldn't have given him a quick way out."

"Then who did it?"

"You're the forensic psychologist, I'm a musician."

Tori wasn't convinced. She knew that if she'd had the chance to get back at the high school teacher who'd seduced her she would have killed him before filing a grievance.

"I'm positive she didn't poison Coleman," Mary continued. "Hilary Kohlberg has found her niche as dean. She'll have rocky times until this incident is forgotten, but it will be forgotten. Another scandal will overshadow Hilary's indiscretion with Coleman. Faculty will retire, move to other institutions or die. The current students will graduate. Hilary was used by an unscrupulous manipulator, but she's learned her lesson. She will weather this storm."

"You think so?"

"I'm convinced of it. Particularly, now that Brad Coleman is dead."

That's what Tori thought. *The best way to eliminate the source of further gossip was to eliminate Brad Coleman.*

CHAPTER SIXTY SIX

As Tori walked into Burritos Bros., she spotted Dottie nursing a frozen Margarita and stopped a waitress to order one for herself. She sank into the seat opposite her colleague. Dottie looked up. "This weather is the pits. I didn't even put the top down on my Suzuki for the ride over." She was as gloomy as the weather.

"It didn't help your disposition, either," Tori said.

"You're no Pollyanna, yourself. Find anything?"

"A couple witnesses saw a man jogging near Little Hall. Supports DeMaio's alibi."

"I've got you trumped." Dottie sipped her Margarita with a huge grin.

The waitress handed Tori her drink and between licks of salt, Tori said, "Spit it out, girl. Don't keep me waiting."

"A woman played tennis with Coleman on Tuesday. A woman with a student parking decal for UF."

"Who?" Tori asked.

"Don't know, but it wasn't Trish. Trish is tall with dark hair and was at the spa. The tennis playing woman was a short blond with a kid."

"That woman could be the murderer or at least a key witness. She might be the last person to see Coleman alive. We need to find her."

"No shit," Dottie said. "How?"

"Don't you have access to the records of everyone on campus with a parking decal?"

"Yeah. I tried, but they keep the records by license number, not make of car. And as observant as the car-pooling mother was, she didn't remember the license number."

"Damn!" Tori said.

"My sentiments exactly"

"Can't the police get a list of license numbers for that make of car? Then you could check their list against the license numbers registered at the university."

"Great idea. You want to convince Morrison to let me do that when he's closed the case?"

"Double damn!" Tori sighed. Tori told Dottie about Rashida and her father. Dottie was appalled. Then Tori described her interviews with the dean and Mary Rantala. "They both said the same thing. Kohlberg was going to destroy Coleman's career with a sexual harassment grievance."

"What a rotten bastard. Do you think the dean killed him?"

"She had the motive..."

"You're not convinced," Dottie said.

"No, her argument about a fate worse than death was persuasive."

"Can You Feel the Love Tonight" played. Tori dug her cell phone out of her bag. "Yes?"

After a moment she said, "You're paranoid."

There was a long silence. Then she asked in an irritated voice, "What were you doing outside my house last night, anyway?" She snapped her cell phone closed and took a deep breath.

Dottie questioned Tori with her eyes.

"Matt says Morrison is following me. He said he saw his car parked outside my house last night."

"What would Morrison be doing outside your house?"

"Nothing. Matt thinks Morrison and I are lovers."

Dottie laughed. "Why would he think that?"

"He's so conceited he can't believe I'd drop him unless I was seeing someone else."

"Be careful, he might be stalking you."

"Don't worry. He's learned his lesson," Tori said. "What about the capping tool?"

243

"I found places in Jacksonville and Ocala, one in Tallahassee and a couple in Daytona Beach that sell brewing equipment, but no one was helpful."

"Where would you go to get a capping tool if you were the murderer?"

"Out of town, someplace they wouldn't know or remember me. Someplace I could go and get back in a day without arousing suspicion."

"That description fits all those places," Tori said. "Probably not Ocala, it's not far enough."

"Where do students go on weekends?" Dottie asked.

"A lot of students go to Jacksonville for the Jaguar games."

"Jacksonville's got a couple of navy bases, so there's a market for capping tools," Dottie said. "There're two places in Jacksonville that sell brewing equipment."

"I'll take a ride there tomorrow and check them out," Tori said.

"Want company? I have the day off."

"Yeah. That'd be great."

CHAPTER SIXTY SEVEN

The sky was deep blue with a scattering of puffy white cotton floating toward the east when Tori left to pick up Dottie. *Sunny days are dazzling when they replace overcast weather*, she thought. Tori's good mood returned with the sunshine. She put the top down on her Boxster. It was chilly, but the sun would soon warm her. She picked up Dottie right at 8:00 a.m.

As they drove up 301 toward Jacksonville, Tori said, "I think we're being followed."

"Pretend you don't notice. I'll pull down my mirror and act like I'm putting on lipstick." After pulling down the visor, Dottie observed the road behind them. "Which car?"

"That black Acura has been behind us since Gainesville. Every time I slow down, it does too."

"Is it Matt's car?"

"No."

"When this light turns green, turn into that side street."

She did. "It's still following us."

"Turn right at the next street."

Tori's car careened around the corner followed by the Acura. "Pull into the post office."

Tori did as she was told and the Acura kept going. She took a deep breath.

"Was is Matt?" Dottie asked.

"I couldn't see who was driving."

"I wish you'd press charges against Matt. Then you wouldn't have to keep watching over your shoulder."

"He won't do anything like that again."

"Says you."

Both sides of SR 301 displayed wires: cable, phone, and electric – a southern wire-scape. The railroad tracks peeked in and out, conspicuous among the anemic growth of trees clipped to spare the sacred wires. Tori shuddered. "It's so isolated anything could hap..."

Tori slammed on her brakes. SCREECH!! She turned the wheel to the right. The car skidded. BANG!! The air bag blocked her view. "What happened?" Dottie asked from behind her air bag.

"Someone cut me off. My brakes didn't work."

Tapping on her window drew Tori's attention. She turned to see Bob McAllister, a Gainesville detective. She opened her window.

"Are you all right, Dr. Vincent?"

"I'm shook up, but all in one piece." She turned to Dottie as the air bags deflated. "You okay?"

"The same." She looked out past Tori and asked, "What are you doing here, McAllister?"

"I'm going to Jacksonville. I was behind you and saw you skid off the road and into the gulley. There's a garage 100 yards up the road. Help me push your car up there."

Twenty minutes later the mechanic brought out a tube. "Your brake lines were cut."

McAllister, who insisted on staying with them until the car was repaired, said, "Let me see that." He turned to Tori. "Who knew where you were going today?"

"No one." She hesitated. "No one, but my son." She laughed. "He dislikes my rules, but not enough to get rid of me."

"This is no laughing matter, Tori," Dottie said. "You know Matt was outside your house last night. You need to get a restraining order on him."

"Or let Morrison arrest him," added McAllister.

"How do you know about what happened with Matt and me?" Tori asked McAllister. Before he could answer she said, "I know. There're no secrets in the department."

CHAPTER SIXTY EIGHT

After the brakes were repaired Tori and Dottie took the back roads into Jacksonville instead of the highway, crossing railroad tracks and going through Baldwin. Trailers and small houses on the outskirts gave way to shops, antique stores, and larger houses along with at least four churches.

"Isn't it lucky McAllister was behind us," Tori said.

"Yeah, but odd."

Approaching Jacksonville off the main route was like driving through the backstage area where the food warehouses, steel yards, welding firms, lumber companies, and tractor trailers hide. Billboards proliferated and small houses peeked from the foliage. The outskirts did not advertise the waterfront city well: boarded-up stores, fast food outlets, convenience stores, and gas stations converted into sales outlets. Within minutes Tori and Dottie were downtown on landscaped streets among glass and steel.

Dottie said, "I'd be more relaxed if you would do something about Matt."

"We don't know for sure he's the one who cut my brake lines."

Dottie lowered her head and peered at Tori over her sunglasses. "You wouldn't be in denial would you?"

A skinny woman with platinum hair and gobs of make-up was reading a magazine when Tori and Dottie entered Brewmasters. A bottle of nail polish and ten newly painted fingernails indicated the woman's intended level of productivity for the day. At a snail's pace she turned her attention to them, as if customers were an intrusion on her personal space. "Want something?"

Tori made her request.

"I can't remember everyone who comes in," she whined keeping her eyes on the magazine while blowing on her wet nails.

"We thought so few women look for capping tools you might remember," Dottie said.

"There ain't many women do capping," the blond said without taking her eyes off the magazine.

"Would you remember if a woman bought such a tool recently?" Tori asked.

The woman's eyes traveled up and down Tori, her left eyebrow raised. "I don't remember no women buying 'such a tool' recently," she said, mimicking Tori's accent and choice of words.

"What a charmer," Dottie said, when they left. "It's a wonder they stay in business."

"I suspect if we were guys, we would've gotten more attention. But, maybe we're asking an impossible question. Perhaps there're so many customers she can't remember them."

"They weren't doing a thriving business today," Dottie observed.

"Right. Maybe it would help if I had a photograph."

"A photograph of whom?"

Tori shrugged. "I've no idea. I was hoping to get an idea from them."

They hopped back in the Boxster and Dottie punched the next address into the GPS to track a path to the other place selling capping tools.

Tori said, "My optimism is fading."

CHAPTER SIXTY NINE

Tori parked in the strip mall and the two women walked into the store with resolve, introduced themselves, and this time Dottie explained their mission. Despite her best smile, the young man dismissed her request and went back to stocking the shelves behind the counter. Crestfallen, they turned to leave. A voice from the backroom called out, "What are you looking for, ladies?"

A robust middle-aged man with ruddy complexion, tortoise shell glasses, and a big grin appeared. He greeted them. "Hi, I'm Bart Hoffman. What can I do for you?"

Dottie explained again.

"The welcoming committee is my son and heir," Mr. Hoffman said, placing his arm around the young man behind the counter and squeezing his shoulder. In contrast to his son's scowl, the proprietor wore a pleasant expression.

Tori thought, *Dottie must have spoken on the phone to the surly young man.*

"Do you remember a woman from out of town buying a capping tool recently?" Dottie asked, returning Mr. Hoffman's huge smile.

"Sure do. I commented to myself how she was merely interested in capping. Everyone has questions about brewing, but not that little lady. She didn't want to talk about it." Hoffman put his arms out with the palms up. "Why would you cap something you weren't brewing?"

"That's great! When was she here?" Tori asked.

Hoffman rubbed his chin. "Must have been a couple a weeks or so ago."

"That's the time frame we're looking at," Tori said. "Can you describe the woman?"

He scratched his head over the left ear. "I'll tell you what I can remember. If Cal over there," he pointed to his son, "had been here, he could tell you everything about her down to her shoe size."

Cal grunted at his father and went into the backroom. The proprietor frowned, his eyes following his son. "He'll lose the business, sure as I stand here."

"What did the woman look like?" Dottie asked.

"She was a real piece of eye candy, that one. Young, I'd guess in her twenties. She had a nice shape, beautiful skin, a lovely smile. She wore tan slacks and a silk blouse. Oh, and she was wearing dark glasses and a scarf on her head."

Tori thought, *Either Mr. Hoffman has an exceptional memory or he's as interested in eye candy as he says his son is.* She asked, "Do you remember what color her hair was?"

"Dark, not a blond, but the scarf covered most of her head, so it's hard to say. I caught a glimpse when she straightened her head covering."

"What about her face?" Tori asked.

"What I could see around the sunglasses was beautiful. Like a porcelain figurine."

He went on a tangent about his late wife and how lovely she was as a young woman. His eyes filled with tears.

"Did the young woman have any distinguishing characteristics?" Dottie asked.

Hoffman pulled on his nose and looked off in the distance as if he could visualize the customer. "No, none I can recall. You know, it's been some time." Then he discussed his fading memory and how difficult it was to grow old. As he began a discourse on his father's memory, Tori asked, "Was she from around here?"

"No." Hoffman said, "No, she was from out-of-state. She called before she came to be sure I had what she wanted." He admitted he watched her drive away and her car did not have Florida tags.

Tori continued her questioning before Mr. Hoffman could introduce a new topic. "What kind of car was she driving?"

"I don't remember. I'm not good with cars. Now Cal there, he…"

"Any chance you remember her name?" Dottie interrupted.

Hoffman laughed. "My kids accuse me of not remembering their names. I'm great with faces, but somehow names don't stick. Maybe I have a charge slip for her." He returned to describing his absent-minded father. After a couple of minutes, Dottie reminded him about the charge slips. He said he inherited his father's problems with concentration. Calling Cal to take over in the store, "and don't frighten customers away," he led them through the door behind the counter to his office where he opened a huge file drawer.

Hoffman filed his charges alphabetically by date. Tori asked him to check for charges by Albright, Coleman, Kohlberg, Pillsbury, Mahajan, and Acosta. None of those names was in his records.

Dottie and Tori exchanged confused looks. *Who else could it be?* Tori thought. "Would you look up Mills and Hancock, please," she asked. No luck.

"How about Taunton? Tori asked.

"Who's that?" asked Dottie.

"The woman who broke into Coleman's house with Rashida. The one who sent the photograph of Rashida to her father."

Mr. Hoffman said, "Sorry, no Taunton either."

"Would you mind if I look through the receipts?" Tori asked. "Maybe I'd recognized a name."

"I'm sorry, but I'm responsible for those credit card numbers and I take my responsibility seriously. I can't let anyone, even someone as sweet as you, look through the files."

"Is there any chance she paid by check?" Dottie asked.

"I don't accept out of town checks. I'm sure she charged her purchase."

"What about cash. Could she have paid cash?" Tori asked.

"No. I chat with customers while waiting for the charge to go through. If she paid with cash, she would have been in and out so fast I wouldn't have had a chance to observe her."

They thanked Mr. Hoffman.

"If you think of anything else, would you call me?" Dottie handed Mr. Hoffman her card.

"Sure. I wish I could be more help."

"Thanks, again," Tori said as Mr. Hoffman walked them to the door.

Tori got behind the wheel of her Boxster and said, "We couldn't have found someone more accommodating than Mr. Hoffman."

"Yeah, if he'd been any more helpful we would've had to stay the night in Jacksonville," Dottie said. She put her hand on Tori's arm. "Tori, that green SUV that pulled out behind us…"

"Yeah?"

"I'm sure it was outside when we left Brewmasters."

"What should I do?"

"Keep driving. See if you can slow down so we can get behind it and I can get the license number."

No matter how slow Tori drove, she couldn't get behind the SUV. It turned off as they got on I-10. "I'm over-reacting, but better safe than sorry," Dottie said.

"I'm stymied," Tori said. "I'm sure the woman buying the capping tool killed Coleman. But Mr. Hoffman didn't have the name of any of our suspects."

"Maybe it was the woman playing tennis with Coleman," said Dottie. "The witness said she was blond, but maybe she wore a wig when she made her purchase."

"She attempted to hide her identity with sunglasses and a scarf. But if she was so intent on not being recognized, why would she charge her purchase?" Tori asked.

CHAPTER SEVENTY

It was close to 5:00 when Tori dropped Dottie off.

"I'm going to meet Jason at Huckabees. Why don't you come with me?" Dottie asked.

"I can't. I haven't had dinner with Sean for days. I'm beginning to feel like an unfit mother."

"I forgot you have a son."

"I almost did, too." *I haven't thought about Sean most of the weekend or today,* she thought. *What kind of a mother am I?*

After teaching her Psychopathology class Wednesday morning, Tori drove to Nancy Rourke's house. Something about her last visit tugged at her subconscious; her clinical insight was tapping on her shoulder, saying 'pay attention.' It was something she couldn't bring to her conscious mind, but somehow she knew it was important. When she pulled into the driveway, it became clear. She rang the doorbell and Nancy opened the door.

"Hi, Dr. Vincent. I'm sorry, Janet's at work," she said. "She won't be back until late this afternoon."

"That's all right. I want to talk to you," Tori said.

"Me? Why? What about?" Her eyes shifted from Tori to the ground and back.

"May I come in?" Tori asked.

Nancy moved aside.

"You're a student at the university, too, aren't you?"

"Yes," Nancy said. "That's how I met Janet."

"You know Steve DeMaio was arrested for the murder of Brad Coleman?"

"So I heard. What does that have to do with me?"

Tori walked to the hallstand and picked up the tennis racket leaning against it. The Gainesville County Country Club logo was on its dark green cover.

"Is this your tennis racket?"

"Yes," Nancy said in a weak voice.

"Is it the one you used when you played tennis with Brad Coleman last Tuesday?"

"I WAS NOT..."

"Before you deny it, Nancy, we have witnesses who identified you as the woman playing tennis with Brad Coleman on Tuesday morning," Tori lied.

Nancy's weakened defenses crumpled. Ashen, the words tumbled out in one continuous stream. "I didn't kill Brad. We just played tennis. We didn't drive together. I was afraid my husband would find out. Or Janet. There was nothing between us, believe me. He saw me with a tennis racket Monday afternoon and suggested we play tennis the next morning. I said, okay."

"Go on."

"I wasn't going to have an affair with him. I love my husband. I saw what happened to Janet. But..."

"But?"

"But Brad Coleman was cute and it was flattering to have a professor interested in me. He'd invited me for coffee before, but I always turned him down. He caught me off guard Monday and I thought if I went in my own car and wasn't alone with him, it would be okay." Nancy took a deep breath and said, "Frankie will kill me if he finds out."

Tori smiled inwardly. "I'll try not to let this get out -- if you level with me."

"I don't have any choice, do I?"

"No." Tori asked, "Did Brad have his blue cooler with him when you played tennis?"

"I didn't see any cooler."

"What happened when you finished playing?"

"He asked me to go for something to drink, but I had to get back to change for class. He said I played a great game of tennis and asked me to meet him the following Tuesday."

"Did you agree to meet him?"

Nancy blushed and nodded.

"How long had you been meeting Brad Coleman?"

"It was the first time I ever saw him. Honest." She gazed at Tori with lovely blue eyes, eyes that probably beguiled Coleman. "You do believe me, don't you?"

"When did he first approach you?" Tori asked.

Nancy looked into space. "Last semester sometime. He asked me to go to his office, so he could get to know me better. I told him I was married. He was seeing Janet then and I told her he was on the prowl, but she wouldn't believe me. She thought I was making a play for him. It wasn't until he dropped her that she realized I was right. She called when she left James and I invited her to stay with us."

"And meanwhile you were seeing Coleman," Tori said.

"No, I *told* you I refused his invitations. He used women." Nancy covered her face with both hands. "I play tennis with him one time and the next thing I know, someone's killed him."

"You're probably the last person to have seen him alive."

"Oh, God!"

"Where did Brad go after your tennis game?"

"I don't know. To his office?"

"What time did he leave?"

"About 8:45. When I went to class at 9:30, I saw his car in the faculty parking lot."

"You have no idea where he was between 8:45 and 9:30?"

"No, please, please believe me. It was the one time I ever saw Brad Coleman off campus."

As Tori left Nancy's house she walked past the blue minivan in the driveway. The van and the tennis racket had been tugging at her subconscious. She went back to campus to track down the other students from the dorm who might have seen DeMaio jogging. Still no luck.

CHAPTER SEVENTY ONE

Jason Nolan was at Burritos Bros. with a Coke in his hand, when Dottie and Tori walked in at 1:30. "Afternoon, ma'am."

"Please don't call me ma'am," Tori said. "It makes me feel old."

"Sorry, Tori," Jason said. "What's happening now the notorious campus murder is solved?" he asked.

Tori said, "It hasn't been solved."

"You're not saying Steve DeMaio is innocent, are you?" Jason moaned.

"Innocent does not describe Steve DeMaio," Dottie said, "but he didn't kill Brad Coleman."

"Dottie, his fingerprints were on the poisoned bottle."

"The murderer took the cap off and recapped it," Tori said.

"Right. Steve DeMaio."

"DeMaio didn't do it," Tori insisted.

"C'mon you two, face the facts: Coleman stole DeMaio's girlfriend and DeMaio inherited megabucks," Jason said. "Two good motives – two of the best motives – love and larceny."

Dottie said, "It's too pat, Jason. Who would go to the trouble of putting poison into a Pepsi bottle, recapping it, and then be stupid enough to leave fingerprints?"

"Steve DeMaio, apparently," Jason said.

"Smart ass," Tori snapped.

"He had access to the poison," Jason said. "My poppa says, 'find a motive and opportunity and you have your murderer.'"

"DeMaio wasn't playing tennis with Coleman," Tori said.

"That's what he says," Jason retorted. "I don't believe him."

"Believe this!" Tori said, "I found the woman who was playing tennis with Coleman and she admits it. What's more, there're two witnesses who saw her with Coleman."

"What does Morrison say?" Jason asked.

"I didn't tell Morrison. I promised the woman I wouldn't tell anyone if I could help it. She's married. Happily, she claims."

"Great! DeMaio's one chance for acquittal and you hide the evidence, so this bad kitty's husband doesn't find out," Jason said.

Tori said, "You know damned well, Morrison would ignore anything that doesn't prove DeMaio did it."

"Jason, give us a break," Dottie said. "We'll reveal her name and those of the witnesses if DeMaio goes to trial. We're hoping to find the real killer before it goes that far."

"Who's the real killer?" Jason asked.

"We don't know," Dottie said. "Everyone with a motive wouldn't have opportunity or means. And people with opportunity have no motive."

"What about the hush hush tennis player?" Jason asked.

Tori said, "She swears it was the one time she saw Coleman."

"You believe her?"

"Yes. I caught her off guard," she said. "Besides, she saw how Coleman treated Janet Pillsbury."

Dottie said, "Every woman thought she could tame Brad Coleman."

"Maybe Trish Acosta suspected Coleman was seeing someone else and decided to get revenge," Jason said.

"Not likely. He saw the new woman for the first time the day he died and he invited her the day before," Tori said. "As Morrison pointed out, Trish would have had to do one hell of a lot of planning to poison him the very next morning."

"Moreover, Trish thinks Coleman played tennis with DeMaio." Dottie cupped her chin in her hands. "He didn't want Trish to know he was playing tennis with another woman. We're back to zero."

Tori looked at Dottie. "There's always Dean Kohlberg."

"Horrible Hilary!" Jason said.

Tori was amazed. "You know her nickname?"

"Yes, Ma'am," Jason said. "I went to UF. The faculty hated the way she treated the union."

Jason was appalled when Tori told him how Coleman manipulated Dean Kohlberg and the revenge she'd devised.

"Besides, the dean wouldn't be able to get close enough to poison his drink," Dottie said.

"Janet Pillsbury had plenty of motive and access to the poison," Jason said. "Do you think she bought into Dean Kohlberg's plan?"

"I think so, and she could never get close enough to poison Brad's Pepsi." Tori took a deep breath. "Neither could her husband; Brad was terrified of him."

Jason counted on his fingers. "The people able to poison Coleman's soda don't have motives, except DeMaio. Coleman played tennis with the mystery woman and had an appointment with Rashida, both had opportunity but neither had reason to kill him. He was about to change his romantic affiliation, but Trish was oblivious to that. She had opportunity, but no motive."

"That sums it up," Tori said.

Jason asked. "What about the capping tool?"

"Tori and I went to a shop in Jacksonville," Dottie said, "And Matt almost killed us. He cut the brake lines in Tori's car."

"Darn it, Tori." Jason looked at her. "You've got to press charges against him. The man's a lunatic."

"We don't know that it was Matt who cut the brake lines," Tori said.

Dottie threw her hands in the air. "There's no reasoning with the woman." She rubbed her forehead. "Anyway, the owner of the brewing store remembers a young woman buying the tool but can't remember her name. He checked the names in his receipts for the past two months for any of our suspects. None pan out."

Jason said, "She could have used a phony name."

"Not if she charged it," Tori said.

"Maybe she paid by check or cash."

Tori explained why that was unlikely.

"What about the mystery tennis player?" Jason asked. "Did you ask the proprietor to check her name?"

"No. But thanks, I'll call him," Tori said.

"Dottie, I still don't get it," Jason said. "Why would Steve DeMaio's prints be on the bottle if he didn't kill Coleman?"

"They were planted. Someone set him up."

"Maybe his was a handy set of fingerprints," Jason said.

"Not handy," Tori said. "He hates soft drinks. He's a health nut, doesn't even drink beer."

"I knew he was a freak. Anyone who doesn't like beer is weird."

"Someone had it in for both Coleman and DeMaio," Tori said. "Where do we go from here?"

Dottie said, "I've made a list of women's names Coleman kept in his smartphone. You could go over the names with Steve DeMaio."

"Will you come with me?" Tori asked.

"I can't, girlfriend. Morrison would draw and quarter me, but I've cleared it for you to visit him."

CHAPTER SEVENTY TWO

A correctional officer led the forlorn DeMaio in a jailhouse orange jumpsuit, handcuffs and leg shackles, into the visiting room. Tori convinced the deputy to remove the restraints. DeMaio didn't smart off to the officer as he had at her last visit. He started pacing. Tori appraised the deputy's reaction. He didn't seem concerned, so she said nothing to deter DeMaio's agitated movements. DeMaio's eyes jumped around the room. He looked like a caged animal – mistreated and abused. DeMaio rubbed his wrists. "I can't cope with being locked up. I'm used to exercising. I run every morning. I work out." He ran his hands through his hair as he spoke and paced.

The guard looked in the interview room window. DeMaio glanced at the guard over his shoulder and sank into a chair. "I'm sorry; I know you're trying to help. I'm going stir crazy. I feel like I'm in living in an elevator – one that doesn't stop at any floors." DeMaio's body crumpled.

"I'd feel the same way. Do you want me to bring you some weights or something?"

"I hate it when people play 'yes, but...' So excuse me for doing it. Yes, but there're three other guys in a space the size of a utility closet with two bunk beds, a toilet, and a sink. Where the hell would I lift weights?" DeMaio's eyes were wild.

"I thought the jail was required to provide exercise opportunities," Tori said.

"Twice a week we go to the yard. Not a yard with grass and flowers, mind you – a concrete slab. Not a yard outside in the world where you see birds and trees, either. The exercise yard's inside the walls. How they get off calling that a yard, I don't know. And exercise times aren't followed by a shower. If I worked out or ran, I'd go back to our steamy cell reeking of b. o. We'd mix our foul smells for two days before they let us shower." He growled, "Is depriving people of showers part of the punishment?" DeMaio leaned back in his chair, with a black look on his face.

"Pretty rough, huh?"

"The guys in my cell..." DeMaio grimaced. "Try having a conversation with two winos and a pimp. I mentioned the secretary of state's criticism of Iran's president yesterday. They looked at me like I was speaking a foreign language. They don't know what or where Iran is."

Tori nodded her understanding.

"Look on the bright side," he said. "I'm learning all there is to know about squirrel hunting."

Tori laughed. "At least you've kept your sense of humor."

"If I didn't laugh, I'd go bananas. Forget it, I'm venting."

"I have good news." When Tori told him about the woman tennis player and the witnesses, he revived.

"Great! They have to believe I'm telling the truth now." DeMaio sat up, relief spread across his face.

"Not necessarily. There's still the matter of your fingerprints on the poisoned bottle."

"Damn! How could my fingerprints get there?"

"Someone set you up. That is, unless there was something else in the bottle when you touched it. Did you store something in a Pepsi bottle – cleaning fluid, soap, anything?"

"Hell, no. I'm a chemist. People identify substances by the bottle – even if it's relabeled. A guy in grad school grabbed a bottle of Sprite and drank some before he realized someone had stored lye in it. I'll never forget what he went through."

"Yuck! Talk about one-trial-learning," Tori said. "What about students?"

"I'd flunk a student for keeping a compound in a bottle other than the one it came in." DeMaio slammed his fist on the table between them. "Damn! Who would do this to me?" DeMaio began

261

to get up from the table. He spotted the correctional officer watching him through the window and lowered himself back into his seat.

"Calm down or they'll stop our visit," Tori warned. "Now listen, Detective Epstein made a list of women whose names Coleman had in his smartphone. Let's go over the list and see if you were involved with any of them."

"Brad and I didn't date the same women." DeMaio pushed his chair back from the table, spread his legs and slouched, right arm on the back of his chair. A musty smell permeated the room.

"Maybe you dated the woman at different times. See if you recognize any names."

DeMaio nodded, but made no verbal response.

"Joan Aaron." He shook his head.

"Don't dismiss the names too quickly. Think about them before you discount them."

"I am. I remember women I date."

"Not only women you dated. Maybe you had another relationship with them – a student you flunked or something."

"Okay, okay. I didn't think about that. I'll concentrate," DeMaio said.

"Pamela Bush, Debbie Christensen, Beth Crump." DeMaio shook his head each time.

"Lisa Daniel."

"Yeah, who could forget her? – a real bimbo, but what a body. She took it hard when Brad unloaded her. She begged me to help her get Brad back. I told her I couldn't help."

"Was she angry with you?" Tori asked.

"I guess so. I wasn't getting involved."

"What happened with Lisa?"

"She went to hangouts Brad frequented. He ignored her. One night she confronted him. He introduced her to his new flame and she lost it. He told her to get a life."

"Is she a local girl?" Tori asked. "Is she still around?"

"She married a manager or something out at the Mill."

"Is she holding a grudge?"

"How the hell do I know? I date 'em, I don't try to understand them." DeMaio sat up and pulled his chair closer to the table, his face a few inches from Tori's. He reached over and grasped her arms and snarled, "I'm going bonkers! I can't deal with this!"

CLANG!! The door opened and the correctional office stepped in. "What's going on in here?"

Tori said, "It's all right, officer. Everything's fine."

The officer gave DeMaio a nasty look. "Keep your voice down and your hands to yourself, or this visit is over. Got it?"

"Yes, I get it," DeMaio said in a defeated voice. When the officer left, DeMaio said, "This is getting us no place. We're wasting our time."

"Got something else on your social calendar?" Tori asked.

"Touché!" After a slight pause, he slouched back in his chair. "Go ahead."

"Cathy Farrell, Missy Graham." He shook his head.

"Melissa Houston."

He said, "She was just a friend."

Tori leaned toward DeMaio, her eyes narrowed. "You aren't friends with the women you sleep with?"

"You psychoanalyzing me? If you're friends, you treat them differently. You know," DeMaio said, waving his right hand in the air. DeMaio looked at Tori as if she were one French fry short of a happy meal. "If you become friends, it's hard to break off when you get bored."

"Maybe if you treated them like friends they wouldn't try to kill you."

They were both on the verge of snapping. He said, "I'll mention that to Brad so he won't do it again."

"I was talking about you."

"Nobody tried to kill me!" he barked.

"What do you think they were doing putting your prints on the poisoned bottle?"

They glowered at each other. The correctional officer tapped on the window. Tori smiled at him.

"Let's get on with this," Tori said. "What about Dean Kohlberg?"

DeMaio glared but relaxed in his seat. "You know about her."

"I know about Coleman. What about you and Dean Kohlberg?"

"I didn't have an affair with the dean, if that's what you're asking."

"Betty Jolly?"

"That's ancient. I don't remember any problems between her and Brad."

"Diane Kostulos?"

DeMaio sat up, put his elbows on the table, pulled his hands together in front of his face and turned away from her.

"Diane Kostulos?" she asked again, leaning toward DeMaio.

"I heard you."

DeMaio took a deep breath before speaking in a low voice. "Diane goes back four or five years. She got clingy, so Brad told her to get lost." DeMaio took a deep breath. "She went off the deep end. Coming back from running one morning, Brad and I found a note on his front door saying, "I can't live without you. Call me or I'll end it all."

"What did Coleman do?" Tori asked.

"He wadded up the note and threw it away. I was appalled. I thought she might mean it, but he said it was a ruse." DeMaio looked at the ceiling and said, "I called her and suggested she go to the Campus Counseling Center. She said I was sweet. We chatted and she asked if she could come over. We (or more accurately, she) talked half the night. She asked to stay – she needed human contact. Brad was through with her and she was cute, so I said okay."

His eyes were on his hands clenched in his lap. "It was the dumbest thing I ever did." He shook his head. "She stayed that night and the next. We dated a couple of weeks, maybe a month. Then she tells me she's pregnant – with Brad's kid." His eyes found Tori's. "And get this – she wants me to tell him. I say, 'hell no,' that was between her and Brad. Then she drops the bomb – says I'd be a better father than Brad. I almost croaked. I tell her she's nuts, I'm not gonna be a father. She says, 'I thought you loved me.'"

DeMaio lowered his eyes and glanced at Tori from the corner of his eye. With some effort, she kept her face expressionless. DeMaio continued in a low voice. I told her she needed to learn the difference between love and lust." He looked down at his hands, his knuckles were white.

"She went ballistic: throwing things, screaming at me, yelling. Said Brad and I were two of a kind. I said, 'yeah, yeah, yeah, ain't that the truth' and tried to calm her. The guy next door came to see if I was killing her. After he left, she collapsed on my couch and cried. She said her sister told her to stay away from me.

"When she finished bawling, I told her to go home. She didn't want to leave, but I said she had to go. She asked, 'what about us?' I told her there was no 'us.' I was screwing her so she'd get over Brad. I'd made no promises. I told her all I felt for her was horn. She left." He slouched, guilt weighing on his shoulders.

"Where is she now?" Tori asked.

"Dead. She committed suicide."

Tori gasped. "She's the reason you make yourself clear whenever you get involved with women?"

"Yeah. She left a suicide note saying she couldn't face life."

"You took it hard?"

DeMaio looked her in the eye. Emotion contorted his face. "I didn't blow it off, if that's what you're asking."

"Did Coleman blow it off?"

"I guess."

"He didn't feel any guilt?"

"He said he wasn't responsible for her fantasies. But after that he started volunteering at the Boys & Girls Club."

"Is there anything else you can tell me about Diane?"

"No. Brad and I talked about her one time. It got pretty heated. He said not to let it bother me and he wasn't going to discuss it any more."

DeMaio had sad eyes. Tori hesitated and then started again with a lowered voice, "Jennifer Larson."

"She's new on campus – in my morning class. I didn't know he was involved with her."

"Does it surprise you?" Tori asked. "I mean wasn't he going with Trish?"

"Brad was never too involved with anyone to pass up a new chick," DeMaio said. "Was she the one playing tennis with Brad?"

"I promised I wouldn't divulge her name. She doesn't want her husband to know."

"You'd let me fry to protect some woman's honor?" DeMaio asked, his voice rising and his face flushing.

"No. If you go to trial, I'll give your attorney her name."

"*If* I go to trial? Don't you mean *when*?"

"If we find the murderer, they'll drop the charges and you won't go to trial."

"Are you going to find the murderer?" DeMaio asked.

"I hope so."

"Yeah, me, too." DeMaio's voice was so low she barely heard him.

She paused, trying to find her place. She was making rapid notes about the women on the list. "Let's get back to Coleman's phone directory, shall we?"

"Okay."

There was a knock on the door. The correctional officer said, "Let's go. Your time's up.

"Ain't that the truth," DeMaio said.

CHAPTER SEVENTY THREE

With heads almost touching, Jason Nolan and Dottie Epstein gazed into each other's eyes, deep in conversation at the Beer & Billiards.

"Look who's here! My little brother and his girlfriend." Junior smirked.

"Buzz off, Junior," Jason snarled.

"Is that any way to talk to your big brother?" Junior asked. "Little Miss Smart Ass don't get much chance to talk to a real man."

"Hey, Junior. How's your love life? Pick up any lovelies lately?" Dottie asked and laughed, as did half the patrons. A scarlet-faced Junior stomped to the bar.

Over his shoulder he threw back, "Loud-mouthed black bitch."

Dottie grinned while Jason scowled. "Don't let him get to you, Jason. He's a bag of wind."

Jimmy the bartender came to their table and asked, "Want another beer?"

Dottie said, "No thanks, I need a clear head. I've got to do some work."

Jason shook his head. "I've got to go to the station – I'm on the night shift." Jason turned to Dottie. "What work are you doing?"

"Going through Coleman's smartphone again," she said.

"Think you missed something?"

"Maybe. It took a long time to plan this poisoning. Maybe the murderer was a woman Coleman dated a couple years ago. I'm looking for other suspects."

"Dottie, I don't mean to frighten you, but there's a killer out there. Please lock your door, Honey."

Dottie nodded. "I've already figured that out. I'll lock my door tonight. I won't be caught off guard like I was with Russell Mills."

Knock, knock, knock. "Dottie, honey, it's me – Jason. Open the door." He waited. "Dottie!" Bam! Bam! "Dottie!" He turned the knob and pushed the door. "Darn! It's locked." He bent to peer through the space between the curtains on the door. "God Damn!!"

He backed up. Kicked in the door. Ran to where Dottie was prostrate on the floor. He bent over her and felt for a pulse in her neck. He pulled out his phone and dialed 911. "This is Officer Nolan, put me through to the fire department." He grabbed a bottle of Coke on the floor next to Dottie and sniffed it.

"Don, it's Jason. Get an ambulance to Dottie Epstein's – fast. She's been poisoned. Cyanide. Bring the antidote kit."

He lifted Dottie's head. "Can you hear me, Dottie? Honey? Open your eyes. You're going to be all right." He got her to a sitting position. "Dottie, look at me. It's Jason." He knew he needed to keep her awake. *She can survive the cyanide if she gets the antidote soon enough. She couldn't have taken the poison more than five minutes ago.* That's when he'd call to say he would be there shortly – he'd gotten his nights mixed up. He had the late shift on Friday, not tonight. He tried to get Dottie to stand. Her eyes flickered open. "That's it, Dottie. Open your eyes. You need to wake up."

She sounded drunk. "No, I can't. I need to sleep."

He slapped her face. Her eyes shot open. "Wake up." He grabbed her under the arms and lifted her to a standing position. "C'mon, Dottie. Open your eyes. Talk to me."

Her words were slurred. "Why you here?"

"That's it, baby, talk to me."

The ambulance got there in record time, but it seemed like an eternity to Jason. He turned Dottie's treatment over to the EMTs, but hovered over them. One of the EMTs put his arm around Jason and tried to get him away from Dottie. "Let them do their work, man." Jason pushed his arm away.

"Jason, stand back so they can do their job. You're in their way."

Jason moved back a foot or so and watched as they administered the antidote and checked her vital signs.

"Will she be all right?"

"She's still alive."

The EMTs lifted Dottie onto a stretcher and took her to the ambulance. "You want to go with her?" one of them asked Jason. Jason climbed into the ambulance and held Dottie's hand on the way to the hospital.

Forty minutes later Jason and Tori were sitting by Dottie's bed in the Emergency Room when her eyes flickered open. "Jason?" Her voice was faint. "Where am I?"

Jason said, "Someone tampered with the Coke in your refrigerator."

Dottie gasped. "How...? I locked the door last night."

Jason took her hand. "You started locking your door too late. The murderer got in yesterday. I've got the bottle and I'll check it out at the lab."

"You didn't touch it, did you?" she asked, her voice stronger.

"Of course, I touched it. How could I examine it without touching it? But I kept contact to a minimum. I touched the rim when I smelt it for cyanide. When I picked it up I used a plastic bag over my hand. I don't think I wiped off any prints, if that's what you're worried about."

"That's what I mean."

"I'm sure there's cyanide in the bottle. I'll call Morrison."

"No! No! Please, Jason, don't. Not yet," Dottie begged. She held his hand with both of hers. "Please. I'm getting close to someone, someone who wants me off the case."

"It could have been DeMaio," Jason said.

"No, it couldn't. Tori and I believe him. He wouldn't eliminate his only hope. Not to mention, he's in jail."

"You don't know how long the Coke's been in your fridge. I've seen your kitchen. He could've put the bottle there before his arrest."

269

"No, he couldn't. I bought the Coke Sunday after his arrest. Please, Jason, please don't tell Morrison for a few days," she begged. "Give us until Friday."

"What if something happens to you?"

"I promise I'll lock my doors and watch everything I eat and drink. I promise."

"Will you let one of my buddies stay with you tomorrow while I work?"

Dottie sighed. "Okay."

Tori stayed with Dottie for the night while Jason took the bottle back to the lab.

Dottie said, "First Russell Mills, now a poisoned bottle in my refrigerator. I feel vulnerable – violated. Am I not safe anywhere?"

"The good news is we must be close, but you need to be careful," Tori said.

"So do you," Dottie said. "Maybe it wasn't Matt who cut your brake lines."

CHAPTER SEVENTY FOUR

Jason brought Dottie home the next morning. His friend Billy Cameron was waiting at Dottie's house. "Will you be all right with Billy?" Jason asked.

"I'm fine. Don't worry. I called in sick, but I'll be fine by tomorrow." Despite her bravado with Jason, Dottie was not comfortable in her empty house even with Billy Cameron sitting in her kitchen. She locked the doors and checked the windows. Then she put her service revolver on the nightstand next to her bed.

Jason Nolan was in the office when Tori stuck her head in the door a little after 8:00 a.m.

"Hi, got a minute?" she asked.

"Yes, ma'am. Sorry, yes, Tori. I always have time for you," Jason said. "What do you want? No more poisoned Coke bottles, I hope."

Tori said, "I need a couple of favors."

"Like what?"

"I want to see the Kostulos file."

"Which file?" Jason asked.

"Kostulos, Diane Kostulos. She's the coed who committed suicide about four or five years ago."

"Oh, Diane. I remember," Jason said. "I forgot her last name. We called her 'Diane.' I worked that case."

"I thought you were in college then."

"I was. My senior year I did a practicum in the tech's office. The first crime scene I see and it's this beautiful young girl – committed suicide." Jason shook his head. "It was tragic."

"Can I see the file?"

"Sure. I'll be back. It might take awhile to find it."

Jason placed the file on his desk and began shuffling through the papers until he came to the original police report. "She took her life in her room on April 13th."

"April 13th?" Tori asked. "Does that date mean anything to you?"

"No, should it?"

"Five years ago to the day Brad Coleman was killed."

"Do you think there's a connection?"

"I don't believe in coincidences – not ones that huge." Tori leaned over the file with him.

"Look at this," she said. "She committed suicide with cyanide from the chemistry lab on campus. She told the lab assistant she was getting it for DeMaio."

"Now I remember. The inquest cleared DeMaio and the lab assistant. There was a suicide note. She had an older sister and an elderly father, her mother was dead." Jason looked through the papers. "Here it is."

Dear Daddy and Grace,

I love you so much. But the pain is more than I can bear. You were so good to me. I thought the world was a nice place. It isn't. I'm pregnant and can't bring an innocent child into this horrible world. I don't have the heart to have an abortion and I can't face bringing shame to the family. I tried to make it on my own, but I'm not like you, Grace. I'm not strong enough to go on living. Please don't hate me. I love you both. Remember me kindly. By the time you read this, I will be in a happier place."

Love forever,

Diane

Tori let out her breath. "That poor kid. She got a double whammy. First she's seduced by Coleman who unloads her and then DeMaio takes up where Coleman left off and abandons her, too. On top of everything else, she's pregnant – neither one of them cares. Talk about callous."

"She was involved with Coleman and DeMaio?" Jason asked. Tori explained.

"What assholes," he said.

"Yeah."

"Why are you helping DeMaio, then?"

"Because he didn't kill Coleman."

"Everything I hear says Coleman deserves to die," Jason said.

"Ain't that the truth," Tori said. "But DeMaio shouldn't take the blame for someone else."

"Sounds like poetic justice to me."

Tori looked at the suicide note. "Apparently, the murderer thinks so, too. What do you remember about the family?"

"Oh Gosh! It was a long time ago." Jason gazed into space, rubbing his mustache. After a moment he said, "The father was a doctor. Had a busy practice, not home much. Diane was sickly, had some blood disorder. The older sister became almost a mother to Diane after their mother died.

"It's coming back, now. The sister went to a university up north. She was about to graduate. She wrote Diane a lot."

Tori continued going through the file. "It says there were letters from her sister in Diane's effects. Where are they?"

Jason looked through the file. "They were released to the sister."

"Any idea what was in the letters?" Tori asked.

"Good gosh, Tori, that was five years ago. We didn't have the other letters, you know, the ones from Diane. The sister refused to give them to us – said they were personal. She was right, of course. I remember the older sister told Diane to get out of a relationship with someone – it could have been either Coleman or DeMaio."

"Good advice. Too bad Diane didn't take it," Tori said. "Do you have an address for the family?"

Jason flipped through some papers. "Here it is. The father lives in Beaufort, S.C."

"What about the sister?" Dottie asked.

"She was at the University of Chicago. But she would have graduated by now."

"Jason, I have another favor to ask," Tori said.

"Okay." He paused. "I guess."

She explained.

Jason frowned. "What do you expect to find?"

"Things are beginning to fall in place, but I don't want to tell you in case I'm wrong," she said. "It's pretty farfetched. Will you do it for me?"

"You know I will. Don't tell Morrison."

Tori rolled her eyes at Jason.

"I know you won't. But, if he found out he'd kill me."

"Yeah. And put the blame on me," Tori said.

"That's not funny. Be careful, huh?"

CHAPTER SEVENTY FIVE

Tori took off from Jason's office like a racer after the starting gun, jumped into her car and sped away. Tori loved to drive with the top down on her Boxster when the smell of budding trees and bushes was in the air. But today she ignored the aromas of spring and concentrated on her quest. Magnificent scenery flew past Tori's windshield unnoticed. Her mind, if not her body, was already at her destination: the Kostulos' home in Beaufort, South Carolina. If she drove like crazy she could get there by mid-afternoon. Her metabolism racing as fast as her car's engine, she was convinced she was about to solve the mystery of Coleman's murder. Twice she thought she saw state troopers following her, but although her speed exceeded the limit, they did not pull her over. She went up SR 301 into Georgia and took route 84 toward Savannah. Route 84 is interchangeable with any other blacktop route in southeast Georgia – edged with pine tree forests in varying stages of growth, interrupted every dozen or so miles by traffic lights announcing a small town. (She did reduce her speed going through the towns.) The towns had interesting, southern-sounding names: Gum Branch, Odum, Waycross, and Naylor.

She took a short turn on I-95 until she got to I-16, where she headed east toward Savannah. She wistfully bypassed Savannah, a charming southern city with parks made famous in the films *Forrest Gump* and *Midnight In the Garden of Good and Evil*. She continued north on U. S. 17 to Beaufort. The road did not differ significantly from the one she'd traveled earlier in Georgia. Large pine forests interspersed with little towns, gas stations with convenience stores and convenience stores with gas stations, the inevitable "antiques" shops selling junk, a little manufacturing, a sprinkling of houses ranging from decrepit shacks to upscale dwellings, but everywhere pines, azaleas, dogwood trees – the essence of a southern spring.

Beaufort was a lovely, quiet old town on the water. Tori often promised herself to spend time there, but never found the opportunity and today wasn't any different. She stopped at a convenience store/gas station for directions. The attendant knew "ol' Doc Kostulos. "Doc Kostulos was my doctor ever since I was 'this high.'" The attendant indicated the height of a two year old. "After we moved here from Charleston, Doc Kostulos took care of me and my brothers. Yep, he's the sweetest ol' guy. I was heartbroken when he retired. I had to find me a new doctor." She shook her head. Then she directed Tori to the Kostulos house outside the sleepy downtown.

CHAPTER SEVENTY SIX

Spanish Moss Lane resembled streets in the old section of Savannah – lined with large Victorian houses displaying rocking chairs on wraparound verandas. The rocking chairs on Spanish Moss Lane were vacant, as the ones in Savannah typically were. Tori found the Kostulos home – a well-kept old Victorian house shaded by huge magnolia trees. The grass was sparse, perhaps it was too early in the spring, or perhaps the magnolias did not allow sufficient sunlight to encourage grass. Budding azaleas in various shades of crimson, pink and white hugged a large veranda with the ever-present rocking chairs. A sign, THE KOSTULOS FAMILY, hung on the front door above the street number.

After parking in the driveway, Tori walked to the porch, rehearsing what she'd say to Dr. Kostulos. She wasn't sure what she'd do if Grace Kostulos answered the door, but she was pretty certain Grace would not. She was right. An elderly black woman drying her hands on an apron opened the door. Tori gave her name and asked to speak with the doctor. The retired Dr. Kostulos was at home and the woman invited Tori to enter. If she knew the pain Tori would bring to the home's elderly occupant, she would have barred her entrance.

"The doctor don't get much company, now the girls is gone. I'll tell him you're here. Please wait on him in the sitting room," the woman said.

A well-worn room greeted Tori. It was comfortably furnished and decorated with family memorabilia: photographs, graduation tassels, diplomas, brass-plated children's shoes, and a slew of tennis trophies. She was examining a photograph of two young women when Dr. Kostulos came into the room. Time had not been kind to the doctor. The stooped man's hair was almost white and he walked hesitantly with a cane. He received Tori with warmth she didn't deserve. If her assumption was correct, she would cause him tremendous grief. Tori wished with all her heart she were anywhere other than in this home, but it was too late to go back.

"That's Diane and Grace," he said, nodding toward the photograph Tori held. "Aren't they the most beautiful young women you ever saw?"

Tori agreed. She replaced the photograph and introduced herself. Dr. Kostulos offered her a seat and moved to a reclining chair with an afghan over the arm. The table abutting the chair held his glasses, a lamp, some books, an ashtray with his pipe, and a few letters. His disabilities disappeared once he sat and smiled. He had a comforting voice, a gentleness that made Tori feel at ease in his presence. *He must have been a wonderful doctor*, she thought.

Tori told the doctor she was from the University of Florida, sending a cloud across the old man's face. Tori thought, *he hasn't recovered from the shock of his youngest daughter's suicide.* She asked, "Would you tell me about your daughters?"

Dr. Kostulos stared at the photographs of his daughters on the mantle. "My wife Suzanne was younger than me, beautiful and gentle. She had a rare blood disease, but blossomed after our marriage and the birth of Grace, our elder daughter. She wanted more children. I tried to dissuade her because of her health, but she insisted and I could never deny her anything. It took years and a couple of miscarriages before Diane was born. Her second pregnancy and childbirth were a drain on Suzanne. She never regained her health." Dr. Kostulos pulled out a crumpled handkerchief and patted his tearing eyes. "She caught pneumonia and died when Diane was a toddler.

"Diane was sickly. She inherited her mother's blood disease. Grace was an out-going and giving child and became Diane's surrogate mother. Grace breathed vitality into her little sister. She took her everywhere, even on dates." He chuckled as he reminisced.

"Maizi, would you please bring us some lemonade," Dr. Kostulos called. Turning to Tori he asked, "Would you like to see photographs of the girls?"

"Thank you, yes."

After Maizi placed a tray of lemonade and cookies on the table, the doctor asked her to get the family album from the bookcase. Maizi tut tutted. Turning to Tori she said, "Oh my. Dr. Kostulos loves looking at them old pictures. You best be ready for a long visit."

She was still laughing and shaking her head when she placed the album on the table in front of Tori. Dr. Kostulos laughed, too. Then with some difficulty, despite help from Maizi, he pulled himself out of his chair and joined Tori on the couch. He sipped his lemonade, while paging through the album and recounting his family history.

"That's Diane. She was dainty and fair with blond hair like her mother. Here's Grace. She's tall and dark like me. Both have their mother's violet eyes. Dr. Kostulos pointed to a photograph and said, "That's Grace serving a tennis ball."

"Are those her trophies on the mantle?" Tori asked.

"Sure are. I thought she'd be a professional tennis player. I didn't discourage her, but was glad she chose a science. You can work in science your whole life, but a tennis career ends in your thirties."

He pointed to a photograph of two young women, hamming it up in front of the camera. "That's Grace and Patricia. They've known each other most of their lives. I was Patricia's mamma's doctor and delivered Patricia. Grace and Patricia were roommates in the dorm their first year at the University of Chicago. Later they moved to an off-campus apartment together. Both majored in chemistry."

Tori admired the photograph and said, "They look alike."

"Yes," he said. "They wear their hair in the same style. But Patricia has brown eyes."

"Is this Diane?" Tori asked pointing to another photograph.

"Yes. Diane was like her mother – a poet, a dreamer. She wanted to go to the University of Florida like her mother."

Dr. Kostulos stared into space, his eyes full of pain. "She had periods of depression. They got worse if she was alone. But, the psychologist advised us to let her make her own decisions – it would give her strength and independence. I don't know what I could've done differently."

"I'm sure you did everything you could. Young people have to make their own mistakes." Tori pointed to a photograph of Diane with an attractive, intense looking young man, tall with dark hair and glasses. "Who's that with Diane?"

"That's Rob." Dr. Kostulos cocked his head and looked at the photograph. "He's a local boy. She dated him in high school. Rob idolized Diane and she seemed to love him."

"What happened to Rob?" Tori asked.

"He went to the University of South Carolina to study medicine. He tried to convince Diane to go there, too, but she refused. She told Rob they could write each other love letters and poems. She could read the letters when she was lonely." Dr. Kostulos retreated into his own world.

After a moment, Tori asked, "did she write to her boyfriend as she promised?"

"She did for awhile, most of the fall term. When she came home for Christmas, she told Rob she wanted 'space,' whatever that means."

Dr. Kostulos voice was bitter. "Grace tried to talk her out of it, but Diane wouldn't be swayed. She wasn't strong physically, but had a mind of her own, did our Diane. Diane thought she was in love with one of her professors – that Coleman character. I thought it was a passing fancy. What professor would be interested in a naive college freshman? He'd get bored and Diane would be back with Rob by summer. Grace disagreed. Grace was graduating that spring and planned to convince Diane over the summer to forget the professor."

Dr. Kostulos sighed. "It wasn't soon enough." He took a pressed handkerchief from the pocket of his cardigan sweater, shook it out, and blew his nose. He stuffed the handkerchief back in his pocket and sat forward with his hands resting on his knees.

Tori asked, "Did you know Dr. Coleman was murdered?"

"I'm embarrassed to say I was elated when I read about it in the paper. I don't like to wish anyone harm, but that uncaring, insensitive cad deserved what he got."

They sat in silence about two minutes, and then he patted her hand and sat back on the couch.

"Where's Grace now?" Tori asked.

"She's a chemist in a lab in Chicago. She'll set the world on fire, you wait and see."

"Do you see her much?"

"She's busy and I don't travel anymore. I had a stroke after Diane died. I'm doing okay, but can't handle the stress of flying – waiting in lines, delayed planes, searches, lost luggage, you know what I mean. Grace says she'll visit in about a week and we can go fishing. She calls every Sunday afternoon. We have a long talk, catching up on the week."

When Tori finished her lemonade and got ready to leave, Dr. Kostulos invited her to stay for dinner. She hadn't realized it was so late; she'd been there over two hours. She declined. Dr. Kostulos put his arm around her and gave her a hug.

"Do what you have to do," he said as he turned back to his seat. That comment seemed to come from nowhere.

CHAPTER SEVENTY SEVEN

When you track down a cold-blooded killer, you're supposed to feel like a hero, like the Terminator or something, not like an abuser. Tori faced a torturous drive to Gainesville thinking about how she would hurt Dr. Kostulos. She felt a horrible weight on her heart.

She inched out of Dr. Kostulos' driveway and turned the corner at the end of the street at a snails pace. Blue lights flashed in her rearview mirror and a S.C. State Trooper signaled her to pull over. She was so stunned she didn't move from the time he pulled in front of her, until he tapped on her window.

Tori rolled down the window. "What's wrong, officer?" Her voice quivered.

"Dr. Victoria Vincent?"

"Yes, sir."

"Please get out of your car," he said.

The cookies and lemonade Maizi had served rose to her throat and perspiration formed on her forehead, as Tori stepped out.

"Give him your keys and get in with me," Morrison said, approaching her car from behind.

"Morrison. What are you doing here?"

"Dottie and I want to know what you found out at the Kostulos house."

Dottie stepped out from behind her boss and waved at Tori.

"Did you tell him?" Tori accused.

"No, she didn't tell me. I'm a detective," Morrison said. "I knew DeMaio didn't kill his buddy over a woman, but I needed to arrest him to get the chief off my ass. I couldn't keep investigating after I'd arrested him, but I knew you two thick-headed women would. I figured you'd find the real murderer if I let you go and watched you."

"You were parked outside my house."

He nodded.

"You had us followed to Jacksonville."

"Yeah. But, after someone cut your brake lines and Jason told me about the fingerprints and Dottie almost being poisoned, I couldn't just stand by no longer."

"Jason told you?" Tori asked.

"Yeah. I told him I knew what you two were up to and threatened to fire his ass if he didn't."

"What did he find?" Tori asked.

"Exactly what you expected him to find. Now tell us what you got from Dr. Kostulos."F

When Morrison rang the doorbell, he, Tori and Dottie were accompanied by Jason Nolan and two other officers. Grace Kostulos opened the door and said, "I knew you were coming."

Morrison asked, "Can we come in?"

Without speaking, she opened the door and motioned them to the sitting area. Tori had trouble looking Grace in the eye. She understood why Grace hated the men who precipitated her sister's suicide. But why murder?

Grace said to Tori, "My Dad called and told me you went to see him."

"How could you cause that poor man any more grief?" Tori asked.

"I didn't mean to hurt him." She stuck her chin out. "Brad Coleman deserved to die, and so does Steve DeMaio. What they did to Diane was inhuman. I didn't expect to get caught and I wouldn't have it if hadn't been for you. That sorry excuse for a detective would never have figured it out."

Glaring, Morrison snapped, "Grace Kostulos, alias Trish Acosta, you are under arrest for the murder of Brad Coleman. Officer, read her her rights."

CHAPTER SEVENTY EIGHT

Morrison, Dottie, Jason, and Tori went to the Purple Porpoise while the other officers took Grace, "Trish," to jail. They sat around the table over wine and beer, discussing the case. Jason wanted to know how Tori figured it out.

"Steve DeMaio would not kill over a woman. He thought they were put on earth for his sexual pleasure and nothing else."

"That's a big jump to Trish Acosta, Coleman's mourning girlfriend," he said.

"It had to be someone who hated both Coleman and DeMaio," Tori explained. "Diane Kostulos was the only woman involved with them both. They'd avoided dating the same woman after Diane committed suicide. Diane couldn't have killed Coleman, so it had to be someone avenging her death. When I heard about the sister, everything fell into place." She turned to Jason, "You gave me the missing piece."

"Me?" Jason asked. "When? How?"

"I came across the name Kostulos on Dottie's list of women involved with Coleman. It sounded familiar. I tried to remember where I'd heard it. She was the pretty woman Junior stopped for speeding a month or so ago. You know, the one he tried to f... uh, sc... uh, seduce." Tori watched Morrison's face. He scowled at the mention of Junior's stopping pretty young speeders and almost choked when she said he seduced one. Junior was going to be in for it when Morrison told his father. Tori wished she could be a fly on the wall.

"Kostulos is an unusual name, there had to be a connection," Tori continued. "I called the brewing store in Jacksonville and sure enough the proprietor found a charge to Grace Kostulos from South Carolina. But how could Grace get to Brad Coleman's drink? I found a number of students from South Carolina, including Patricia Acosta, in the registrar's records. When I called Patricia 'Trish' Acosta's parents in Beaufort, they said she was working in Chicago at a chemical company. I learned from Dr. Kostulos that Trish was Grace's college roommate. Trish thought Dottie and I suspected her, so she cut my brake lines."

"How'd she know you and Dottie would be driving to Jacksonville?" Morrison asked.

"She called the night before and got Sean. She asked him where she could find me in the morning. When he told her about our planned trip to a capping store in Jacksonville, she thought we knew she poisoned Coleman. If she cut the brake lines she could get us both. The day before Dottie went to see Trish Acosta. Trish offered Dottie something to drink. When Dottie followed her into the kitchen and looked over her shoulder, she saw some Pepsi in the back of the refrigerator…"

"The bottle you gave me to check for fingerprints," Jason said.

"You got it!"

Morrison turned to Tori. "You gave evidence to Jason without my permission or knowledge?"

"You arrested Steve DeMaio. You wouldn't have given me permission to get fingerprints checked for someone else," she retorted.

Morrison winked at her. "Certainly not fingerprints you obtained without a warrant."

Tori added, "Jason identified Steve DeMaio's fingerprints on the Pepsi bottle."

"Why did she give you one of her Pepsis with his fingerprints on it?" Morrison asked Dottie.

"She didn't intend to. We'd been talking. I didn't ask for Pepsi, I said 'no' to Gatorade. I'm a lot taller than she is and was looking over her shoulder, so when I spotted the Pepsi she had to give it to me. I insisted on having the bottle and refused a glass. When she said she kept the Pepsi for Coleman, I realized she could have put the Pepsi in his cooler. She was stuck when I said I'd take the bottle with me. If she made too much fuss, I'd realize something was wrong. She offered me a cup, but I declined. Tori found the bottle still in my car and gave it to Jason to check for fingerprints."

Jason snapped his fingers. "That's why she tried to poison you."

"Yes, she thought I suspected her when I took the Pepsi bottle," Dottie said. "I told her I didn't think DeMaio killed Coleman and would continue looking for the murderer. I told her Tori agreed with me, so she tried to kill us both."

"I get how she got the poison in the Pepsi," Morrison said. "But how'd she get DeMaio's prints on the bottle?"

"Remember she was DeMaio's girlfriend before she took up with Coleman," Tori said. "She probably got DeMaio to help her unload some groceries, including a six pack of Pepsi bottles. She asked him to take them out of the plastic holder and put them in the refrigerator. He wouldn't remember such a trivial incident months later. Then she got a capping tool and practiced until she could get the cap off and back on without leaving evidence of tampering. She got the cyanide from DeMaio's laboratory. As DeMaio's lab assistant she had access to the chemicals and a key to the controlled substances in his lab. She doctored the books so it looked like no cyanide was missing.

"The morning Coleman was to play tennis with DeMaio, she put the Pepsi in his cooler. She timed it so it was the anniversary of her sister's death. She made it in the nick of time – another week or so and Coleman would have dropped Trish and been seducing someone else. Trish didn't realize Coleman was already on the prowl for a replacement. He didn't play tennis with DeMaio. He invited another woman. When I found the woman, I knew DeMaio was telling the truth."

"How did Trish/Grace get accepted to the University of Florida with a phony ID?" Jason asked.

"She used her college roommate's ID," Tori said. "They were both chemistry majors. She had Patricia Acosta's transcripts sent to the university, but she used her own driver's license. That's why Junior couldn't find her in the records at UF."

"So you went to Beaufort to meet the father?" Jason asked.

"That's the worst part; the dear old man has suffered so much. As soon as I saw the photo of Grace Kostulos I knew I was right. She had assumed Trish Acosta's identity and killed Brad Coleman as vengeance for her sister's death."

"Why didn't you leave?" Morrison asked.

"Dr. Kostulos walked in before I could. I didn't want to be impolite or have him warn his daughter." Tori asked Morrison, "What's going to happen to Trish? I mean Grace."

"She's up on first degree murder," Morrison said. Not likely she'll get indicted for less; there was obvious premeditation. This was a well thought out murder."

"And DeMaio?" Tori asked.

"We let him go when we went to arrest the Acosta woman," Morrison said. "He's probably out hitting on some naïve coed as we speak."

About the Author

Linda A. Foley is a psychologist who spent many years teaching psychology and the law at the University of North Florida. She interviewed inmates, conducted psychological autopsies for the police, consulted with attorneys on jury selection, and testified as an expert witness. She has written a psychology and law textbook, two books on offenders, and over 30 articles about legal, psychological, and criminal issues. She lives in Jacksonville, Florida with Roger Sharp, the wind beneath her wings. She now writes cozy mysteries.